The Secret Life of Rat Boy

Published by Rubber Tree Books
111 Calle Washington 4
San Juan, Puerto Rico 00907

Part 1

Maron Halvorsen snored. A few feet away her husband Johan lay in a recliner with his mouth open in an O and his thin pale lips, almost indistinguishable from the skin of his face, spread in a fine circle over his gums. His gray eyes were half-open. His right hand shook like a flickering flame that was trying to bring the rest of his body to life. The dust in the air glided down through the amber light filtered by the old blinds.

The lid of the mailbox fell with a bang. The sun was shining on few dirty patches of ice and snow. She reached for a knit shawl and navigated her bowed legs off the couch. She opened the screen door on the enclosed porch and got the mail. With the letter opener with the shells in the glass handle, she opened the bills first. She set aside the bank statement and a travel brochure. Pushing her glasses farther up the ridge of her nose, she inspected the postmark and the return address on the remaining letter and then jabbed the opener along the long edge. She held the tissue-like paper at arm's length. She read the first paragraph three times. Then she prayed.

The Tuesday before while reaching for another piece of coffee cake, she had told a neighbor that in nine or ten years she would be too crippled to take care of Johan, even if his Parkinson's didn't get worse. But she knew that God would be good to her. He had brought her and Johan together so that they could do God's work and now he would not forsake them. Here in front of her was the answer. Her sister Estelle wanted her to take care of her illegitimate grandson, of whose existence she had been unaware. Her connection to God and her prayers could change events and create people, if need be.

When she told of her great blessing to the other ladies in the neighborhood, one quietly pointed out that by the time she was crippled, the child would probably only be ten years old. Maron's face stiffened and her eyes locked on the space a few feet over the heads of the four women who sat before her. "It's a blessing," she repeated more forcefully.

In May, Maron gathered her friends in the living room to wait for the baby. Each time a car passed in the street, one of the women lifted the curtains and Maron stepped over to look out the window. A black Cadillac pulled up in front of the house, rubbing its white-walled tires against the curb. Maron peered out the window for a few seconds and then yanked the curtains out of hands of the woman who held them and let them fall.

When Estelle entered the room with the child in her bony arms, a spell was cast over the women Their bodies hardened and glowed like hot wax. Estelle's silk scarf exaggerated the nervous jerks of her thin head. Her mouth puckered and her cheeks rose to stem tears.

"Maron, this is just for a while, no longer," Estelle said. Her slim bony body waivered slightly on her black pointy-toed heels. In defiance of everyone present, she gave a toss to her shoulder-length, light-brown hair streaked with gray. But Estelle's ability to keep up this show of strength was short-lived.

Maron darted to the center of the room, placing herself between Estelle and the baby, who now lay in a basket on the orange horsehair chair. She stared at each woman in the room. Then Estelle moved to a corner where she hunched over sobbing. A few eyes had wandered off in her direction, but Maron was on her guard for pity.

"Nosiree!" The few wandering eyes shot back to Maron. "By God who loves us all's help, you won't be given another chance to sin. I always told you that you raised my niece wrong. You won't get a chance with this child. That won't be on my conscience."

Estelle had not tried to argue, instead she scampered into the bathroom, where she vocalized waves of anguish in long ascending screams. Maron gave a disgusted snort with the gasping break of each crescendo. Some of the women smiled wanly at Maron and shook their heads. The bathroom door swung open and crashed into the bedroom door, which was open, and then rebounded into Estelle's face. She was stunned, but held her own until almost a foot from Maron and then gingerly hurried by her, as if she were afraid of being hit. In the safety of the porch, she turned around.

"Mother was right. You are a devil."

Maron mouth fell open. After a few seconds, she had to curl her lips back around her dentures to pull them up. The other women were stunned.

"What do you think of that, sweetie?" Maron asked Johan. He awoke and began a rhythmic humming. The baby, which had been left lying in the chair next to him, began crying and Maron took the opportunity to escort the ladies out, wiping her hands on her apron.

"You know, I can't believe it. It always happens when you lose touch with the rat race. Johan and I were always so far from it."

A tall woman with deep wrinkles radiating out from her mouth turned back in the doorway and looked down at Maron's round flat face. She peered from one eye to the other behind the bifocals sliding down Maron's nose. "You know, you are a very very special person."

The porch door swung shut. The baby stopped crying for a second. Johan began to hum. She entered the beehive of noise, picked the baby up, put him in the middle of the table, and then flopped back into the orange horsehair chair. Dust rose from the chair and formed an aura around her, which glowed in the spring light coming through the yellowed curtains.

Later, as she bent down to pick the baby up from the table, she noticed the name pinned to his blanket. "Michael Durbin."

In June her friends began dying. One fell in front of her house and broke her hip, and then two months later died of pneumonia. Then the sisters who lived a block away went one right after the other. Another had a stroke and her daughter sent her to nursing home in another town and did not bother to inform Maron where she was.

Michael's thick brown hair started to curl around his ears and his long slow lashes blinked with her comings and goings. When he cried, she would lay him on Johan, whose body was soft as silk, and it calmed him. During daily devotions at nine in the evening, Maron's voice strained to capture the holiness of the words. Johan would chant, "Ya, ya, ya .. ." and Michael would babble. The light from the reading lamp over her chair formed a helmet around her wispy gray hair.

Just before she cropped his hair, a task she did before

sending out Polaroid photos to a few select former parishioners, she received word that her niece had died in a fire and that Estelle had suffered a nervous breakdown. She cried, twisting the cloth marker in her Bible around her finger. Nothing she had ever done deserved such kindness from God and she knew it. That day she mumbled to herself, "I never doubted you, Lord," as she dusted the floors and fed Michael and Johan. At devotion her voice was so high pitched and her thanks so emotional and confused that Michael began to scream and did not stop until he fell asleep in the crib.

When he began to crawl, she locked him in the bathroom so she could clean and feed Johan. Michael knew the sounds. First there was a long silence, then the blender would whir and then another long silence. Occasionally Johan would choke on the food and spew it over the kitchen walls. Finally if he lay still with his ear by the door, he could hear the slow swish of her slippers and he would sit up before she reached the door.

In the winter she wore a heavy flannel bathrobe over her pajamas all day, and he would breathe in the scent of mothballs and cedar from the bathrobe. He would hang on her bathrobe and bury his head in it to breathe its scent which would hang around him for a few moments after she had left. At night, in his dreams the scent would come and later her head would appear as it did under the reading lamp at devotions.

Michael was eighteen months old in June. The summer light did something miraculous. It dulled Maron's halo as she read devotions until by the middle of June, it disappeared. While she was reading, Michael would crawl to the window and pull himself up to look out, and Maron would stop, push herself up on her bowed legs, and grab him firmly by the hair and lead him gently back to Johan's chair. By the time she found her place again, Michael was out of the chair and at the window again. But Maron's resolve was stronger than Michael's. That first night it took her until ten o'clock to finish devotions and the next morning her legs ached from getting up so many times.

His walking became a crisis. One day she left him for only a minute to push Johan to the bathroom and when she returned, he had taken two of her favorite photographs from their cardboard frames and ripped them to pieces. She was later able to piece together the picture of her with the Custer, South Dakota Church Women, though it was no longer possible to recognize Melba Honnagurger or Frederikke Mons. But Michael had chewed the photograph of her and Johan standing next to the tombstone, which she had bought at the local cemetery. Her name and Johan's and their birth dates were engraved on the stone. At the sight of her, Michael had rolled up into a ball waiting for the blow and then had crawled off behind a chair.

"Papa, did you see what Michael did?" Johan's tongue poked out of his mouth several times, but he made no sound.. "Michael is bad. Bad, bad, bad." Michael cringed each time he heard the word 'bad.' "Lord, tell me what I am to do."

Michael hid behind the chair where she sat. Her house dress stuck to her back. The temperature had reached ninety-five. When Michael crawled from behind the chair almost an hour later, Maron woke from a trance and screamed, "Bad," and Michael scampered back behind the chair.

"Michael." Her voice was softer. He came around the chair and pulled himself up. Maron took the photograph from her hand which she had rolled into a ball. She smoothed it out and looked at it closely. There were small teeth marks in the tombstone and it was impossible to read the engraving. The rest was a marbled black and gray. "Bad," she said and held it up so he could see it.

That evening while she was changing his diapers, she tied one of her everyday handkerchiefs around his ankle and then tied laundry cord to that. She kept one eye on him as she read the devotions. She had an urge to yank the cord the moment he took off for the window, but took a deep breath and continued with the Bible verse. The moment he tried to pull himself up to look out, she yanked the cord and he fell. He was so startled that he did not cry immediately. Maron kept reading as if nothing had happened. He watched her until he thought that she was concentrating on the reading and again tried to pull himself up to the window. This time she yanked so hard that he fell face first and howled on the floor until he fell asleep. "Amen," she said. Michael and Johan were asleep.

The sound of the crickets swelled and subsided. A lightning bug flew across the room. She thought of the parishioners who once came to her for advice, wrote notes of appreciation, and claimed they remembered her in their prayers. She tried to remember one of Johan's sermons, but they were mixed together, and though her job as his wife had meant that she had also been his greatest public admirer, she knew that his sermons were short rambling anecdote without any fire. She imagined Johan moving to the pulpit in his black and white robes as the music from an old pump organ dyed away and a breeze from the Nebraska or South Dakota plains moved through half-opened windows and doors.

The pains in her legs disappeared and she dreamed of herself thirty years younger. She gazed around the church and faces set into smiles. She saw her own face that reflected kindness and inner spiritual joy which she had practiced in front of the mirror.

Michael was retarded. She was startled by the thought. It

broke into the pleasantness of her dream. His eyes were slow, that was certain. She mulled this over, looked at him asleep under the window, and hummed his name. His lips moved in his sleep, first slowly and then in a whispering gibberish. He straightened out for a second and then curled up again. She pushed Johan to the bathroom and then to bed. When she came back into the living room, she yanked the cord to wake Michael up.

"I didn't know you were retarded until today," she said as she untied the handkerchief around his ankle. He smiled at her, thinking he had been forgiven.

She had left it up to God. When the child couldn't say the first line of the Lord's Prayer by September, she no longer spoke to him. When she caught herself speaking to him, she would pray that the Lord would make her remember. Words could only be a source of pain. She had seen the way they had treated Mo Jones when he was young and Russell Johnson, who had lived with them at the parsonage in Custer until he was fifteen. Though it would mean a world of suffering, she was determined that it wouldn't happen to Michael. God was testing her.

After that day she let no one beyond the porch door unless Michael was hidden in the bathroom. When he could walk, she took him up to one of the upstairs bedrooms and locked the door, until the visitor had left. The mailman brought Johan's pension and her social security check. She had taught country school the first years of Johan's illness when he could still be by himself, so she would be eligible for social security. Once a month she walked the two blocks to the bank. She called for groceries and her orders were so predictable that the grocer delivered whether she called or not. The old grocery store still sold cloth, underclothing, and stockings. She bought pajamas for Johan, a few clothes for Michael, and perhaps a new pair of bedroom slippers for herself from the *Sears Catalog*. She began to send the checks to the bank and they sent her checkbooks. She stopped paying for the *Linder Signal*, but the paper came anyway. She took half the money she had out of the bank and bought aluminum siding guaranteed for twenty years. For a month the house shook and rumbled as the siding went on, and she moved Michael from one side of the house to the other, depending on where the workers were. When she was out in the yard cutting zinnia from the small garden on the side of the house, she noticed how the light reflected dully from the siding, changing as the afternoon wore on. It made her worry about its permanence. A few years after the siding was on, she noticed in the *Linder Signal* that the siding company had left town and the authorities were looking for them. She prayed that hers would last until she, Johan and Michael were gone.

Maron bathed Michael in the wide rectangular bathroom

sink since it was hard for her to bend over him in the tub. With her help, he climbed up into the sink. He watched their images in the mirror of the medicine chest and mimicked her movements and expressions. He tried to fool the mirror by moving quickly. When Maron opened the medicine cabinet, he saw how the figures in the mirror fit into the flat glass.

He realized that the image in the mirror was him. He lived in the mirror. He wondered if he was only another version of himself, caught in another mirror, and what he thought was thick and warm, only seemed to be.

He became aware of the differences between himself and Maron and Johan. He tried to give himself wrinkles like theirs, but his skin only reddened with his constant pinching and never stayed creased like the old newspapers.

One day when he was three, he snatched up Johan's glasses, which had fallen off as Maron was steering him to the bathroom. She laughed when Michael put them on. His nose was too small to support them and he had to hold his head back to keep them on. The world was twisted and blurred. He took the glasses off and put them on again. Was this the world that Johan saw? He tried to walk, but fell and felt sick to his stomach. He threw the glasses down.

The door to the front porch had a large oval window which

Maron had covered on the outside with a blanket hung from two nails. He felt that Maron, Johan and himself had other selves outside themselves, which were not identical, but more like the reflections from the door. He would sit in front of the door and wait for the images to come back, for them to appear on their own.

When he was alone, he chanted to himself "Oohan. Oohan. Dinne. Rrrr. Ouh fadeh who aht in heaven ollow be dy name. Bad. Bad. Rrrr. Rrrr. See. Michael. See. No see. No see. Ouh fadeh. Amen. . . ."

Maron laid him on Johan one day and covered them with a blanket. His hand slipped through the pajamas to the warm flaccid skin. At first he was startled to find a tuft of hair on Johan's lower abdomen and let out a gasp. He waited petrified to see if the sound would bring Maron. Then he heard the motor of the electric blender grinding up Johan's supper. He held Johan's penis in his hand and peered into his vacant eyes.

He waited until Maron took Johan to the kitchen for dinner and then crawled on all fours into the bathroom. The floor boards creaked under the rug, which was matted with dirt. The only way he could move through the house without making noise was by feeling for the sounds with his hands and then crawling over the loose boards. The board just before the bathroom pressed against an old heating vent that boomed when you stepped on the board. He carefully moved over it and then closed the door. He pulled down his pants and the plastic underpants. He was almost overcome by despair at the sight of his penis. He grabbed the foreskin and pulled until tears welled up in his eyes. Now it looked bigger. He went back into the living room where he found Johan once more in his recliner. He lay on top of him and pulled the blanket over them.

At first he did this several times a day, but soon the pain made him stop. A month later while he was in the bathroom, Maron barged in. His eyes shot to her face to read her reaction. One of her hands swung from her hip and caught him on the side of the face. He fell to the floor and curled up to protect himself from another blow. She grabbed him up by his suspenders and dragged him to his bed in the hallway and dropped him onto it. She made quick assaults at him in her fury, checking her hand just before it reached him. With each swing of her arm, he would go taut, bending back like a thin branch. He screamed until he was limp from exhaustion.

He sobbed for a few minutes unmolested. Feeling braver, he stared through the fog of tears, catching his breath in short rhythmic gasps. Maron was working the large belt of her housecoat through the loops. Her face shifted from fury to calm determination. Her small flaccid breasts shook with the pulls at the belt and Michael watched cautiously. By the time she got the belt off, she had lost interest in using it. She gave him a few half-hearted slaps and he reacted with high-pitched squeals to placate her.

Tape – 3 – Entry 1

What I know now is that you have to learn to know when you are passing from one dream to another and to always remember that the others exist, even if you are not there. Last night I was pulled out of the arms of Joe and without warning I was in another dream where I was being chased by a monster. I can't describe it because I remember the terror and not what it looked like, but I couldn't move and each time I seemed to be safe, it was there again. I thought of the other dreams, the one with Thomas running his hand from my forehead to my lips, Joe waiting for me in a room where only I was the right shape to enter, or the one where I fly over the home before it burned and put the flames out. I see the fire. I know the secret of flying, though it surprises me each time I rise into the sky. "Do not fear falling," I say to myself. Even as the monster is gaining on me and I strain to move my legs and arms and nothing happens, part of my mind knows that those other dreams exist, too. When I meet someone on the street who's in a bad dream, I say, "There are other dreams," and they understand.

Maron still spoke to Johan, but if Michael came in the room, she became silent. The only time she let him hear her voice was when she read devotions. If he mimicked her words during devotion, she stopped reading and raised her finger as if she were pressing it against his lips. She stared through the lenses of her glasses, which made her eyes look large and fluid, until he became quiet, and then she continued to read.

A woman ten years older than Maron, who came a few times a year when her son, when he had business in Linder, were her only visitors. She would display poor dear Johan in the recliner. She locked Michael in an upstairs bedroom, which had the windows boarded up after the branches of the maple tree had smashed the panes in a bad storm long before the siding was put on the house. He would lie on the floor and listen to "Oh my" and the "You don't say" over and over, looking for the sounds that were becoming familiar and repeating them. The minister's voice was strange, low and full of timber. He held onto his words when he spoke and his voice boomed as he prayed. Since he had not seen the minister, he wondered if it was a secret voice which Maron had. The words in the prayer sounded like the devotions. Their small-talk, which reached him through the floor boards and the heat vents, sounded like soft groaning.

Through the long winter evenings he spent hours curled up on the pink silky chest of Johan who never changed, never jerked or stood up, was always in the same recliner or in bed. The eyes in his gaunt sagging face never moved. Michael would listen for hours to Johan's heart.

What Michael saw of the larger world was from the upstairs windows covered in coal dust that had been streaked many times by rain. There were no windows in the front or back of the house on the second floor and the blinds, which Maron had nailed down to the windowsill on the two sides of the house, let through orange light. As years of sunlight made them brittle, they began to have tears. The coal dust partially blocked the light and what Michael could see, even at noon, was a shadow of the world outside.

Tape 10 – Entry 1

When Ernesto couldn't sleep, he would say, "Let's play this game. Remember everything you can from the very beginning of your life. It doesn't matter if someone told it to you or if you made it up and now can't remember if it happened or not. Tell me everything.

My memories of when I was young are all images and a mishmash of words. I see Maron reading from the Bible and Johan lying in his chair, pale and sunken. He seems to be covered in powder and with each weak cough a layer of it shakes from his body. I have talked to people who know about the thing he had, and they say that you don't lose your mind, just your body. You lose the part of your mind that takes care of your body. It doesn't make sense. I must have been in his mind, though he never said my name. When he died part of me went with him.

I made up stories for Ernesto where I had a dog and a cat and a brother and a sister and we lived in a white house made of wood. He liked these stories. They made him sleep. He never said, "That is not in the album. You are lying." Sometimes he asked questions. "What is your sister's name? What color was your dog? Did your mother plant flowers in the yard?" Sometimes I would invent. Or I would say, "I don't know," and he would say, "It's a long time ago." Some days my sister was named Vera and other days Roxanne.

Part 2

At age seven he had been to the doctor a few times in the town's only taxicab, but on those trips he had been well bundled up and one of the times he had been delirious and saw only the blurred interior of the car.

The first warm spring day of that year, he heard children screaming. Two little girls spotted him peeping out the window and came running up arm in arm. For a moment they whispered and giggled and then one of them yelled, "Retard!" They ran off pulling at each other and screaming. He tried to repeat the sound. The two girls came back with four other children smaller than themselves. The ringleader, a chubby girl with thick brown braids, called the others to a huddle. Then they formed a line and stuck out their tongues. Michael stuck his tongue out and the children doubled over laughing. A boy tried to get near the window but dripping rain from the rusty rain gutters had turned the ground below the window into brown syrupy mud.

The children huddled again and this time two of the children walked off to the side. The others pulled down their pants to their knees and wiggled back and forth like they were twirling a hoola-hoop.

Michael jumped up and down hitting the dusty blinds

with his head. He did not hear the swish-swish of Maron's slippers behind him. With one hand she grabbed him by the shoulder and with the other she opened the blinds. One of the children tried to run without pulling up his pants and fell, and rolled back into the mud. The others ran off too scared to scream.

He took the beating calmly. But he sensed that it would not stop until he cried. Maron took several steps back and caught her breath and then left, locking the door after her. The house was deathly silent. He heard a door in the kitchen open and minutes later, he heard it close. He heard tapping that came in short methodic bursts. It sounded like what he heard the summer Maron had locked him in the upstairs rooms, but fainter and with longer pauses. When he went to the window the next day, he tried to lift the blinds, but they stuck firmly to the windowsills.

An old doctor came every few months to look at Johan. Maron told him she was taking care of a relative's child and though she would never lie, she made it sound as if she were only baby-sitting. Nonetheless, she locked him in an upstairs bedroom and when her arthritis was bad, she put him on the stairs and locked the door. Those days Michael peaked through the cracks in the old door as the doctor put the stethoscope on Johan's chest, tapped his knees with a little hammer or looked into his vacant eyes with a small flashlight. The doctor's reactions were as passive as

Johan's and his face and neck sagged in the same way. The doctor's cement-gray eyes floated in the soft pink flesh of his face.

On a fall day when all the shades shone a bright burnt orange, another doctor came. This one was young and his face seemed startled and surprised by everything he saw. He did things to Johan that Michael had never seen the other doctor do. His movements were sharp and nervous and his smooth face had a doll-like glow. Maron talked to him at the door before she let him in, stood with her head raised and her arms crossed, so this young doctor would know that she wouldn't stop him from coming in, but it was not with her blessing.

Each time Maron raised her voice, he thought they might be heading for the door to the upstairs and he darted up three or four steps, where he waited to hear the key turn in the lock. Then he tiptoed back down.

Through the crack in the door he saw her coming, thought maybe she was on her way to the kitchen, and then the crack in the door became dark. He got up the stairs before he heard the key in the lock. She lifted one leg up onto the first step and swung the other after. The doctor patiently followed behind her as she made her way up the stairs. At the top she stood clumsily blocking the doctor's view of Michael, who was humming wildly in the corner of the bedroom with the boarded up window.

"I pray for him at least four or five times a day," she said.

He looked briefly up at the doctor, but Maron's eyes were on him and seemed to make audible screeches each time he ventured to look up. When the doctor stuck out his hand to stroke his hair, Michael jumped back and hit his head against the wall.

"Don't excite him." Maron's loud modulated voice startled Michael and the doctor.

The doctor whispered something to her and her fists knotted. Michael looked up at her but when he met her glare, he looked down again.

"Hopefully he won't be here the next time. It's too much for me. His grandmother said she was coming back soon and when she does, I'm going to tell her I can't have him anymore. You can go on first. It takes me a while to go down the steps." When Maron heard the doctor open the door at the bottom of the stairs, she quietly shut the door to the bedroom, and then slowly twisted down the stairs.

Michael chanted up in the upstairs bedroom, "I pway foh him Let us pway Foh times a day I pway Don esite Don esite He won be heuh On eauhth as it is in heaven He wose fwom the dead He won be heuh Johan Johan Amen."

Dearest Joshua,

I am in complete accordance with you that this boy at the home is an interesting case, but am not convinced that I am the one to write his story. As you requested, I did a bit of snooping and found out that he lived with his great aunt and her husband, who was severely afflicted with Parkinson's disease. Though I am promising nothing, I have begun a scrap book, or a file as we call it. As you mentioned, the first few weeks after he was discovered, there was a lot of news coverage.

I had hoped that you would be well enough to come with me to a restaurant the last time I visited. I know you always like to dress perfectly, but I think such worries are out of place in Linder. When you claimed that you now have the scent of the County Home about you, I was not convinced. I have seen you in the past scatter the infidels with a glance. If one of them dares to sniff, you are capable of turning them to stone.

If I do not pursue this story, it is not because my fondness for you has waned, or that I doubt that it could be a fascinating tale, but I must worry about survival and such a project would take many hours.

With true affection,

Bernice

Michael had seen Johan dead for a day, which was the time it took Maron to plan how to get the body out of the house without anyone seeing Michael. He had waited for the sound of the blender, went to the kitchen to see what was wrong, and found Maron at the small table pushing bread crumbs back and forth in front of her. Her face was red and tears dripped from her chin. Michael watched her scatter the bread crumbs and then cup her hands to gather them again. He went back to sit in the orange horse-hair chair. He picked up the Bible that Maron used for devotions and whispered to himself.

"Yours is the kingdom and glory. Yours is the kingdom and glory. Oh my. For goodness sakes. Yours is the kingdom and glory." He tiptoed up to Johan. "Forever and ever. Forever and ever."

He had not heard Maron come in. She looked at them without seeing them, and Michael for a moment wondered if he and Johan were their other selves, the ones in the door. Or perhaps Maron's other self was watching them from the reflection in the window of the door, and he turned from her to check.

As she approached, Michael dropped the Bible on Johan's lap. She took his hand and led him into the kitchen. He had seen Maron disappear down the basement door in the kitchen before, but had never been close enough to see what was down there. The door was always latched, and Maron had added another latch at the top, which she opened and closed by knocking it with a heavy cane. The door was painted a reddish brown and was worn in places so a lighter green showed. He recognized the smell of brown soap from his clothes.

Maron held the railing and tried to push Michael in front of her. She thought of the cellar as a grave, dark and damp, with weak yellowish light seeping through the dirty windows. He felt cobwebs on his face, but could not see them.

"He is up there in the light, and we are still bound to the darkness of the earth."

Michael stopped. He was frightened by this place. Maron's voice was disembodied. She never spoke to him any place other than in the living room, and usually from the orange horsehair chair. He wanted to turn and look at her. Her feet brushed across the steps. The floor was cold.

"You are in the light of heaven."

He looked up at her and she turned her face away.

"And we are in this cold damp filthy earth." She pulled the string switch for the light bulb over the wash basins. Beside it was a small enamel table with bars of brown soap, which mice had nibbled on. Maron usually did the wash in the kitchen sink and hung it on a line she tied from the back door to the cupboard next to the refrigerator, but when they first moved into the house, she had used the old wringer washer, which now covered in a thick layer of dust. She bumped it turning on the light and raised a cloud of dust. Michael sneezed, then coughed lifting more dust.

The door of the root cellar dragged against the floor and the hinges creaked. She pulled an old blanket from a box on a shelf. Moths fluttered toward the light. On the floor of the root cellar some dried potatoes lay next to two heavy cardboard boxes that had lost their shape from the dampness. A few ancient cans of Campbell's soup rusted on a shelf. She nodded her head in the direction of the cellar and Michael walked in.

The neighbor who answered her door to meet Maron thought she was from the Jehovah's Witness and only answered the door after Maron had stood and knocked for a long time. Maron tried to hide her anger at being made to wait so long behind a grim smile. Her head hung to one side and she did not speak at first.

"What is it? We don't need it, whatever it is." The woman was armed with a cigarette which pointed at Maron's forehead.

Maron tried to pull the veil back on her hat before she spoke, but got her fingers stuck in it, so it looked like she was trying to hide her face. "I'm your neighbor. Mrs. Halvorsen. My husband is dead. Call Dr. Mason. Please, could you do that?" There was a long moment of silence and then Maron shook with grief.

The woman's under-bite showed as she thought of what to do. "Okay, I can do that. Are you okay? Well, Dr. Mason's dead, you know. Let me call. Do you want me to go over to the house?" When the woman returned from calling, Maron was gone.

It was the young doctor who showed up at the house.

"He's gone," Maron said.

"He's better off where he is now," the doctor said perfunctorily.

"No," Maron said. "The boy. He's gone. I'm alone." She kept her eyes on Johan. The doctor could not tell if she was crying behind the thick glasses.

"Best for both of you," the doctor said.

Maron opened the door to the porch so she could watch the ambulance pull away from the curb. Neighbors whom she had never met or seen before stood in clusters in front of their houses to watch the ambulance. When she got back to the root cellar, Michael was still standing by the door with the blanket at his feet.

A minister, whom Maron had never met, performed the service. The church was almost empty and in the small reception afterwards, the few regulars from the retirement home left immediately when they saw that there was only coffee and a few boxes of stale cookies for fellowship after the service. Maron felt hot in her black wool coat and her feet were used to house slippers so the black low-heeled shoes dug into her feet. Her black hat looked like a pillow with a veil and she kept forgetting the veil was there and moved her hand before her face as if she were clearing out cobwebs.

"I don't know if I quite agree with your sermon. Times change, but God doesn't." Maron was determined not to like the minister, who had never visited her, and must have been told by someone that her husband had also been a man of the cloth.

"God is big enough to hold many opinions." The minister looked at his watch. He regretted having offered to drive Maron home.

"God is not opinions. My husband was a minister. He didn't have opinions. He had faith. And that altar was shameful. Doesn't your wife organize altar duty?" It had been ten years since Maron had been in the church.

"My wife does lots of things. I have to make a quick call before I take you home. You can wait here." Maron shifted from haunch to haunch on the metal folding chair to show how uncomfortable she was. Ten minutes later a young woman with a small child appeared.

"Pastor Schluter asked me if I could take you home. Are you ready?" the woman asked. Maron sat alone at the front of a small sea of folding chairs. "I don't think I have ever seen you."

"I don't go out. My husband is sick, was sick. We will miss him." Her voice sounded strange to her.

"I'm sure everyone who knew him will miss him." The woman's head tilted sweetly and she had large rosy cheeks and short pageboy haircut. Her child went to check out the cookies, munched on several and left them on the table.

"Those cookies stink. I'm hungry." The boy yanked at his mother's dark blue blazer..

Maron spoke loudly to drown out the boy. "My nephew and I, we'll miss him. He's retarded. He lived with me for a while." She tried to look even smaller and more crestfallen.

"You know, I don't think I have ever seen you." The woman took Maron's arm to lead her up the stairs. "Lark, come on. Lark."

"Are you from here?" Maron said as if she were trying to make conversation. Lark rushed by them at the top of the stairs and pushed a glass door open with both hands.

"All my life. Well, I went to college for a year before I got married. All my life." The woman held the door for Maron.

"That's wonderful. All your life."

Maron asked to stop by the cemetery. The hole had been dug and the woman, whose name was Fiona, tried to keep herself between the grave and Maron, fearing that she would lose her balance and fall in. She turned just in time to catch her son Lark as he slid down the loose dirt into the grave. He kicked at her, leaving brown marks on her navy slacks.

"Whew, that was a close one," Fiona said and caught herself before she started laughing.

"Can you see our names are on it?" Maron asked.

"Oh, yes. Johan and Maron Halvorsen." Fiona glanced perfunctorily at the grave and hummed in a way that she thought would show Maron that her patience had run out.

"When you're married in the Lord, it's forever. Let us pray." Maron commanded as if she were addressing the dead in the graveyard.

Lark tried to shake himself free. Fiona looked desperately at Maron. "You know the body isn't here yet. And Lark isn't behaving. Maybe we could say it in the car."

Maron moved her lips silently. When she finished, she looked around and saw that Fiona was already standing next to the car. She maneuvered between the tombstones to the car.

As Fiona was turning the ignition, Maron said, "They'll be another date now."

The woman didn't react and Maron repeated the phrase more dramatically.

"I don't know, I'm awfully busy," she said. "Don't you have relatives?"

"On the tombstone, there'll be another date," Maron said and turned away from the woman. She felt Lark kicking the back of her seat.

"Lark," Fiona said without turning back. Maron felt one last hard kick and then Lark slouched across the back seat.

"May you come to know the Lord as your savior, Fioga."

"Fiona. It's Fiona," Fiona said and Maron turned to walk up the sidewalk, leaving the car door wide open.

Maron stood with her back to the recliner and dropped back making a swoosh. Her black winter coat pushed up around her face and bunched up in the back so it made sitting uncomfortable. She thought that Johan's spirit encircled her. The scent of his hair pomade was on the pillow that lay across the headrest. It seemed like a weak presence, but that was what she expected from Johan. A loving spirit, true in the Lord, but weak. Like those pictures of Jesus with the lambs. She woke and it was already late afternoon. She had forgotten about Michael.

At the top of the stairs, she said to herself, "All her life and she doesn't know me. Imagine. All of that girl's life."

She stopped on the stairs to listen, but heard nothing. She wiped cobwebs off her face. When she turned on the light over the wash tubs, Michael sat up and hit his head on a shelf. An empty jar and several cans fell on the floor, the jar shattering.

"He's in a brighter place than we are." She made her voice low and loud. Michael whimpered and scratched at the door.

"He's in a brighter place than we are." Her voice became high and thin. She yanked open the door creating a cloud of dust.

He looked up from the cement floor to see Maron in a cloud of dust, silhouetted by the light bulb behind her. He could look at her for only a second before his eyes shut to keep out the dust, but he thought she was floating in the air, unattached.

"He's in a brighter place than we are," Michael chanted. He wept at the same time and Maron did not understand what he was saying. He was shaking from the cold and his pants and shirt were wet from piss and caked with dirt. His dark hair was sprinkled with the white fuzz from a moth-eaten blanket he had found on the floor. Snot and dirt streaked his face.

"And we are on this cold damp filthy dirt. . . earth, earth." She was shocked by the way Michael looked. "Filthy earth."

He had waited for her to return. When the wind had

rubbed a branch across the roof, he listened intently for the next sound, which would prove it was Maron coming to open the door. The timbers creaked and he crawled to the faint strip of light under the door, losing the blanket and stirring up the dust so he went into a sneezing fit. He had been even colder after leaving the blanket. He held himself perfectly still for a minute to listen, then tried to crawl back, but hit his head against the cinder block wall. The wind slammed a neighbor's door shut and he froze again. He crawled along the wall and found two damp cardboard boxes which he pushed in front of him. He found the blanket, but when he tried to move it and the boxes towards the door, his knee was on the blanket and he ripped it in two. Finally he reached the door and lay on the cardboard with the tatters of the blanket on top of him. He had twisted his legs together so he would not piss, but finally he couldn't control it. He thought he would let just a little out, but once he relaxed, he couldn't stop.

Tape 1 – Entry 9

People die. I know that. But I am not sure what it is to die. If I don't remember not being, how can I imagine it? Ernesto said death was a trip you take with your eyes closed. "Why go some place if you can't see anything?" I wanted to know. "It is good people don't have a choice about this trip or they would never go," Ernesto said.

For a week, Michael would leave the living room, then rush back expecting to catch Johan lying in the recliner. Maron sat down to pray with Michael every morning, her voice falling off before the end of her sentences, and then welling up again. When Michael would stand up to go, Maron's arm went out automatically to sit him down again. Once Michael rushed back to catch Johan, and found Maron whispering to the chair. She ignored him and Michael approached her cautiously.

"She didn't know me. All her life and she didn't know me. You are in a better place. Everyone knows you. Everyone. She didn't know me. My own town. Tell them about me."

A November cloud passed across the sun and the light coming through the blinds dimmed.

"You are in a brighter place," Maron whispered and Michael leaned farther forward. Maron gasped when she saw Michael. After a few quiet moments, she patted the back of the chair in the same way as she used to pat Johan as she walked by. She swung around and plopped into the chair and stared blankly at Michael. When he was about to retreat, she clasped her hands before her mouth and shook her head.

The chair was soon Maron's and she would lay in it all afternoon with an open box of chocolates in her lap. During the day, the downstairs had a sense of twilight. The brightest room in the house was the bathroom where light entered through the snowflake patterned glass, which showed the vague colors and shapes from outside. The house was a cave. Odors from the kitchen hung in the air all day.

Maron had begun to bring shoe boxes filled with photographs and cards with scented handkerchiefs out of her downstairs bedroom closet into the living room. She would find a card, read the message and the few lines written on the card, and then smell the handkerchief. She inserted photographs into some of the cards, and would peer at the picture as if she were looking for a telling detail.

"Oh, I was a solid rock in their lives," she mumbled, quoting a card that she had read an hour earlier. "A blessing to everyone. God sent." Michael wandered through the room and Maron straightened up in the chair. "I brought Jesus into their lives." She glared at him as if he dared to contradict her.

"Jesus. Jesus in their lives. Jesus lives." Michael parroted her, then opened the door and scampered up the stairs.

Maron no longer climbed the stairs and she wouldn't let anyone in to help her clean. Michael would come down from upstairs covered in dust and she would scrub him until he was red, but when he returned upstairs, he would wander from one dust-covered room to another. He used the dust for drawing, or on hot afternoons in the humid sluggish heat, he would lie down naked and leave the imprint of his sweaty body in the dust.

When he realized that Maron would no longer come upstairs, he pried the corner of one of the shades up, but the windows faced a tree that blocked the view. The soot from the cheap bituminous coal, used by most of the town to heat their houses, formed a dark gray filter which had been streaked into patterns by rain. He could still make out the shadow movements of the trees during the day and sat for hours watching them.

The upstairs not only became dirtier, it became darker as light bulbs burned out and weren't replaced. The last light to go was a closet light.

For the first weeks that Maron stopped coming upstairs, he stayed in the room she had locked him in before. Soon he had entered the other two rooms and within a year he had emptied all the drawers. He looked through picture albums and didn't realize that the pictures were of Maron and Johan when they were young. There were more recent pictures of them that he collected in a stack. He acted out scenes where Maron read devotions to them or where he locked her in the cellar and she had to wait for him to return. He used their pictures to represent their characters and part of a broken mirror for himself.

The other pictures from the albums he placed next to each other until they formed a trail from one dusty room to another. One day he discovered that he could take the pictures out of the shiny black frames in the albums. Soon the photos were strewn over the upstairs and grime and summer humidity bleared and curled them. Many of the ones that were face down stuck to the carpet runners and the wood floor.

There was an old pedal sewing machine with a small drawer that swung out . One day he pulled it out and watched it swing and then snap back. He did this again and again until he flung it open so hard that the needles flew across the floor. He had tried to pick one up that caught a gleam from the fall light coming in through a smoky window. He brought it up sticking from his finger and shook his hand until it finally came out. But in his jumping and shaking he had gotten a needle in his foot and couldn't control his screaming. Maron hit one of the heat grates with a broom handle, which was usually her signal for him to come down to eat. He held himself to keep from screaming and hopped away from the sewing machine. He pulled the needle out and threw it back with the others.

When he was angry with something, a picture that stuck to him or a dress that he was using as a pillow that had buttons which scratched his face, he would throw it into the sewing corner.

If Maron scrubbed him until his skin stung or slapped him for making too much noise, he would throw a picture of her into the needle corner.

All the surfaces were eventually covered with torn paper and a heavy gray dust. He slept in a nest made out of strips of paper and old sheets. At first he'd included photos in the nest, but when he felt them sticking to him, even in the coolest weather, he carefully picked them out.

In the summer he baked in the stuffy upper rooms and longed for the hours when he was let out downstairs to eat and bathe. On the worst days he whimpered at the bottom of the stairs where it was cooler.

He liked to play two games. One was to pick up a picture and try to think of it before he looked at it. He would play this until he could guess all of the pictures strewn across the floor. Then he would throw the paper and pictures in the air to scatter them. He usually ended in a spasm of coughing and would have to wait until the dust settled before he could start to play.

The other game he played was with the mirror on the closet door and on the one on the vanity. He had inch by inch dragged the flimsy pine vanity in front of the mirror and then pulled a chair between them. He looked at himself move, paying special attention to his back and his face. Often in August he took off all of his clothes and jumped and made faces and talked like Maron. Somehow Maron always knew when he had taken off his clothes. She put her hand over his mouth to stifle his screams and hit him with one of Johan's shoes that she kept in the kitchen.

Tape 8 – Entry 14

I meet two people, say, and they look alike to me. They look just alike for weeks when they come into the restaurant where I work. I stay quiet. Everyone could really be two people. Unless I know the person really well, that is what I am afraid of. I don't want them to know that they are the same person to me, that I can't see that they are different. It always takes me a while, but then I cannot imagine how I ever confused them.

This woman Bernice, Joshua's friend, came with pictures to show me. There were some of me that were not in the album and some of Johan and Maron that I remembered, but they weren't in the album either. She let me keep some of them.

I lie in bed some times and close my eyes. The house is huge. There is only one window in the upstairs bedroom, like the room I have now, but this window has branches over it. I can fall asleep imagining this room. I am staring into a mirror. I hear someone coming up the steps. For a second my heart is in my throat. Then I wait. It might be good or it might be bad.

There is a color picture of Maron and Johan standing in front of the house. Everything is weird. The colors are all turning light brown. And they are smeared. There's another inside the house. It's the house and the furniture I remember, but the colors are all wrong. The rooms look tiny. If I look at it long enough, I don't see Maron or Johan, but only the upstairs room and the branches moving across the dirty windows, leaving scratches of light. I seem to come so close to holding the center of myself. But then a feeling of emptiness comes in like when you hold your breath for a long time.

Part 3

One winter he put boxes on a chair and reached the upper shelf of a closet that until then had always been a few inches too far away. He found old clothes stuffed in hat boxes, including a black dress that he had seen in one of the pictures. When he put the dress on, seven or eight inches dragged on the floor. He stood in front of the mirror and made angry faces and snarled, "Michael bad. Johan descended into hell and the third day he rose from the dead. Forever and ever. Don esite him. Don esite him. Bad. Though I walk through the valley of death. Eetaad. Eetaad. All her life. All her life. He gave his only begotten son. Tell everyone about me. Oh my. Oh my."

There had also been a shoe in one of the boxes and he hit himself with it, at first softly and then hard enough to make himself scream. He heard the key turn. His heart leaped. He yanked the dress off over his head.

She wasn't angry, but had the weary look of despair. She stopped several times on her way to the downstairs bedroom and was gone for a long time. She came back with a heavy black shoe. Michael waited in the dark living room. There were only two blows and then she went into the kitchen.

He waited for her to come back and finish. Finally he walked into the kitchen and found her lying on the floor with sad eyes and an open mouth like Johan's. He crawled on top of her and put his head to her chest to listen for the beating, which he had heard in Johan's chest. He fell asleep trying to hear it.

Mrs. Woodcock became alarmed when the lights did not go off on the porch as they had for the past fifteen years, exactly at nine. She had not gone over immediately, but instead badgered her husband with questions about what she should do until he screamed, "Whatever the fuck you want to do," and turned up the television to screen her out. She tiptoed around Maron's house, pulling wild bushes and vines back from the windows and carefully cleaning a hole in the filthy glass with a tissue she found in her pocket.

Michael woke and listened. He knew the creaks and groans of the house, but these sounds were different. He remained motionless on top of Maron, his head raised slightly from her chest so he could listen better.

Mrs. Woodcock peered through the hole she had made in the soot and grime. She saw a bleary image of the living room and part of the dining room. She moved on to the back of the house, swearing as she stumbled through the weeds in the yard. The back porch was rotting and there were holes in the steps so she carefully tested her way up to the kitchen door, then cleaned a small hole in the dirty window and placed her right eye against the glass. In the pictures that the newspaper took of her later that evening, she had a dark half-circle around her eye.

Michael had heard her come up the steps. He stared at the door. When he saw the shadowy figure in the window and then the single eye, he froze. Mrs. Woodcock tapped on the glass and when Michael did not respond, she began to pound. She turned the handle and pushed the door with her shoulder, but it was warped so badly that she could not open it.

When Mrs. Woodcock left to call an ambulance and the police, he shot upstairs. He heard the front door open and several men talking. A few moments later three men came up the stairs with flashlights. He saw them from the corner of a closet where he had piled clothes on top of himself.

"Eetaad. Eetaad. Donesite. Donesite," he begged when they removed the covers. Then he began to hum and dig himself deeper into the clothes until a pair of hands took him under the arms and lifted him up. He went stiff with fear.

The neighbors gathered outside with heavy coats over their pajamas and nightgowns. He saw their red faces as the lights of the ambulance bounced across them. In the local hospital they examined him, scraped and pounded him and stuck needles into his buttocks, and gave him something so he would sleep.

Part 4

He woke up at Mrs. Woodcock's. She kept him in the guest room with the door locked, except when she brought him food or took him to the bathroom. Most of the furniture had been removed from the room. The dresser was pushed up against the window with the back facing the room.

He studied the wallpaper and looked out the window just over the dresser. It was fall and he watched the wind whip the red maple leaves. He could hear voices outside the door. He had never heard so much talking. Each night the same song was played when the talking stopped.

He did not know what to expect when the door opened. He did not recognize the woman as the same one from the first two days. She was all other women except for Maron, could have been any one of the faces that had flashed in the red ambulance light.

He looked out the window at the house he had lived in for nine years and did not recognize it. He saw his grandmother Estelle go in and come out with her arms full of boxes. The trees were suddenly quiet and leaves twisted as they fell to the ground.

The woman who brought him food was not like Johan or Maron. Her skin was full and red. She had a sweet smell and Michael sniffed at her to find where her smell came from. It lingered in the room long after she was gone. As she scrubbed him with a washcloth or watched him with her impatient eyes as he ate, he looked back as if she were a natural wonder. When she left, he stood at the door listening.

Mrs. Woodcock had been interviewed several times by big city newspapers and had been photographed pointing to the nest where the rat boy slept. There was another picture of the rubbish all swept into a pile and the physics teacher at the local high school had carefully weighed all of the dust taken out of the vacuum sweepers after the clean up. A Grand Heron radio station had held a contest and the person who came closest to guessing the exact weight of the dust won a Hoover from Earl's Appliance on Main Street.

For several days Linder was on the map. People gathered in their living rooms to see their town on the nightly news and to hear a member of the community defend the town or give some detail that until then had been overlooked. The town already knew, or thought they knew, what the person was going to say. People hung out at the barber shop, or took extra trips to the store so they could stay on top of the news.

Mrs. Woodcock gave her story about how she found him lying on top of Mrs. Halvorsen and that besides how filthy he was, the first thing she noticed was that his pants were on backwards and his shirt inside out. The rat boy hype went to her head and she described him as nibbling his food and crawling on all fours and sniffing the air as if he were looking for cheese. He wasn't the big eater her son was, who could down a triple-decker peanut butter and jelly sandwich in three bites and a Hostess Twinkie in one. She had begun leaving his food on a tray on the floor, but had never seen him eat off the floor.

Fiona Green came forward with the story about the time she took Maron Halvorsen home after Johan's funeral, and how Maron had tried to crawl into the grave. She claimed that she had seen a face in the upstairs window the day she had taken Mrs. Halvorsen home. She said they should talk to Pastor Ray and gave the Grand Rapids' newspaper his new address.

The local paper *Linder Signal* hadn't run a word about the rat boy until it made the national papers and the radio in Chicago and Grand Heron. Then they ran a short piece about the town making the news and Maron's obituary was on the front page. The last person to get an obituary on the front page was Franklin Roosevelt and the next one would be Marilyn Monroe. The lack of details was due to their editorial policy which was not to offend anyone, which they managed to do with only an occasional slip, when they forgot a name or two in the social column, which mentioned who had visited whom and who had entertained relatives from out of town.

My Dearest Jonathan,

Thanks for the note of encouragement. I cherish having a fan as discerning as you.

It's good to hear that you have fought your way out of your last depression, though your own description that you "seemed to slide out of it" is more appropriate. I am a great respecter of the mind, not so much its power, as its (I almost said its mind of its own) capriciousness. My own mind floats on a sea with small waves with a constancy that may be boring, but whose rhythms I fear losing nonetheless. When I was younger, I had more passion and more self-destruction. I do not think I could bear your wild storms with all their blinding lightning followed by clouded darkness.

I did look through the Linder Sentinel. It seems that at first there was no news at all concerning the boy, but a week after the death of Maron Halvorsen, there is an article on the front page about all of the reporters descending like locust on Linder in search of the rat boy. It is good that locust do not understand this insult.

Can you tell that I am succumbing to your suggestion? Yes, I have looked at the papers, local and statewide. I have driven past the house and hoped to see you, but at the time the administration at the hospital felt that you should not have visitors. The next time I visit, I will interview some of the characters in this drama. The paper mentions a Mrs. Woodcock. I have looked up her address in the phone book. She is only a few houses down from Maron Halvorsen's house.

When they give this to you to read, I suppose you will be better. Write me a quick note and I will make arrangements to see you.

From your loving friend,
Bernice

Tape -9 – Entry 3

Everything we do is because of something we remember. That's what Ernesto said once and then he said it wasn't so. Everything we do, we do so we can remember. I memorized it from the tape. Everything we forget was never done.

Sometimes I couldn't listen to him. He said one thing and then another.

It is important that you know how you got from here to there. The places where you are in between tell you who you are. How did you get to the home? I didn't know what to say. I couldn't remember it or couldn't remember it so I was sure. He read me one of the letters that Joshua's friend wrote and I remembered. I remembered the woman Mrs. Woodcock. She could make smoke

49

come out of her mouth in circles. I don't remember anything else.
Just that. But after he read the letter to me, I could remember things
about myself that I had never known before.

The day of the funeral Mrs. Woodcock stripped him again, scrubbed him and anointed him with her husband's cologne, but she still felt that she could smell his shit, which she had cleaned up for a week. Mrs. Johnson, who fixed Maron's hair for the funeral, cut Michael's hair while Mrs. Woodcock held his arms. When they took him out to the car, he ran back to the house and hit the door at full speed, like a bird trying to fly through a glass window. He had never been anywhere so huge before. Mrs. Woodcock grabbed him by the shirt collar and dragged him back to the car. Blood trickled down his face and the shirt was smudged with coal soot from hitting the door.

Mrs. Woodcock was shaking.

"You hold him, Marge, okay?"

"Sure. I never saw a dang thing like that before." Mrs. Johnson broke out in a hoot of laughter, which Mrs. Woodcock felt was out of place for the first second or two and then she joined in herself.

"Honey, that was nothing. This kid throws his food down so he can eat it off the floor."

When Michael came out of his daze, he began to sob.

"He doesn't bite, does he?" Mrs. Johnson asked. Mrs. Woodcock shook her head and laughed again, this time unnaturally high pitched. Mrs. Johnson took some tissues out of her purse and dabbed the blood on his forehead.

"That's some egg he's going to have."

People who hadn't been to church in years sat almost on top of each other for the service. When Mrs. Johnson arrived, people turned politely to look. A few stood up and some children were allowed to stand on the pews to get a better view. Later on, the general consensus was that Mrs. Maron Halvorsen must have been a saint to have made such a strong impression on this kid who was barely an animal.

Michael stopped sniffling and moaned to the sound of the organ. Mrs. Woodcock looked sternly ahead, afraid of catching sight of Mrs. Johnson, who was getting the giggles. A pained look crossed her face each time the groans got louder.

Michael thought he recognized several Johans and Marons and tried to get their attention. Estelle kept her eyes straight ahead. She believed that her grandson had really turned into a huge rat.

The regular church-goers stood up to sing on command and the visitors fumbled with hymnals. A man in a long flowing white robe swung out in front of them. Michael groaned along with the hymn and knelt on the pew and turned to the crowd behind him. An old woman gripped his hand and smiled at him. He sniffed the perfume in the air and the woman drew her hand back cautiously. The singing stopped as raggedly as it had begun. Michael turned around to face the altar where the minister's arms were raised in a benediction. At the word Jesus he shot up and screamed. Mrs. Woodcock continued to stare straight ahead but reached over and pinched him the way she would have her own son. He wailed and then sank down in the pew sobbing.

He looked through his tears at the liquid streams of colors in the strained glass windows. He moved his tear-filled eyes to make the shapes and colors change.

Mrs. Woodcock covered her mouth with a black gloved hand. Her eyes were riveted on the minister as if they were boring through him and the two of them were the only ones in the church.

Michael began to laugh and cry at the same time and Mrs. Woodcock slipped her hands under the black net of her hat and covered her ears for a moment, then hooked one hand around the back of her neck and returned the other to her mouth, without once moving her eyes from the minister.

Except for Mrs. Woodcock and Estelle, the whole congregation was now tittering and exchanging amused glances.

The minister's voice rose in desperation. "And Jesus raised Lazarus from the dead."

Michael gasped again. He didn't connect the man in front with the voice coming out of the loud speakers. Several people bent over hiding their faces in their hands. Women ushered small children out to keep themselves from laughing.

Mrs. Woodcock heard the woman behind her snorting softly with laughter. Michael screamed again when the minister left the pulpit. By the Lord's Prayer she had to leave. She snatched him up by his belt and carried him on her hip out of the church.

The minister's voice rattled out of a speaker that hung on the wall of the nursery. Michael, who was small for his age, sat on a chair for a five-year-old and rocked back and forth moaning. The windows looked out onto a row of old fir trees, huge dark green monsters. A strong gust of wind pulled them towards the window and Michael scurried under a table.

"Damn rat kid. You could make anyone look like a fool." She pulled a cigarette from a little pouch on the side of her purse. The end glowed as she lit it and sucked in deeply. She blew a white tunnel of smoke out of her mouth and caught Michael's look of wonder from under the table.

"You like that? Look at this." Mrs. Woodcock blew perfect smoke rings and as they stretched and floated, sent smaller ones gliding through them. When she heard that the service was about over, she went to get Michael. She squatted down and extended her black gloved hand. He took it with a look of awe and she yanked him along back into the church.

People shuffled past Maron's open coffin. Mrs. Woodcock swung him over the coffin. He felt as if he were falling and grabbed for the side. Maron floated among the shining satin. Her face was changed. Her lips were red and her gray eyebrows were now dark brown. The red broken capillaries of her button nose were powdered to a dull pink, but the wart on her lip stuck out even more against the lipstick, even though the hair on it had been carefully clipped.

Michael looked around for the Marons he had seen. Several people walked around them on their way out of the church. He reached out to grab Maron and Mrs. Woodcock pulled him away, knocking over a vase of mums that fell into the coffin. The water washed over Maron's face. Her hair became shiny and matted against her head. The black dress stuck to her bony shrunken body. Water seemed to spew out of her mouth.

Mrs. Woodcock couldn't move. All her strength left her and Michael slid down to the floor. Mrs. Johnson appeared out of nowhere and she and Mrs. Woodcock each took an arm and dragged him out of the church. The wind came up as they left church and sunlight polished their faces.

On the way back to the house, he stole short glances out the side window, otherwise he kept his head down. When he was back in the room, Mrs. Woodcock took off his clothes and left. He wrapped himself in the bed sheet and fell asleep.

Mrs. Woodcock's patience was worn thin and she lost her temper easily. When she washed him and he would not stay still or tipped the shampoo over, she grabbed and shook him, then whimpered in self-pity. After one of the more violent shakings, Michael had seen a small boy about his own size, peeking around the edge of the door. He controlled his crying to get a better look, but the boy disappeared.

The second day after the funeral Mrs. Woodcock's son, who was eight, opened the door to the bedroom. Michael was considerably smaller than James. He had been looking out the window when he heard the door open, and when he didn't hear the door shut again, he looked over his shoulder. The boy stared at Michael's white elf-like face, laughed and left.

Later that day he came back with another boy while Michael was sitting on the bed watching the trees, some of which were now bare. Even the rattling of the red-brown oak leaves no longer frightened him. He glanced at the boys and then back out the window. They walked slowly behind him and the one with brown hair, Slade, poked his finger into Michael's shoulder. He laughed from nervous fear and the boys jumped away. Slade reached over and grabbed him. James, who was hiding a rope behind his back, brought it out and twisted it clumsily around Michael, who gave a hollow spurt of laughter that scared the boys. They worked frenetically to finish tying him up and then ran out the door. Michael tried to get up and fell against the corner of the bed, scraping his head.

He lay on the floor for an hour before James came back. He pulled Michael up and sat him on the edge of the bed. Slade stood by the door with six children behind him. He took five cents from each one as they entered the room. A little girl with a green plastic head-band screamed as soon as she entered the room and ran back out. Michael threw himself on the bed and one of the boys pulled him up again. A chubby boy with a scar under his chin pinched Michael, who grunted, making the children giggle.

He looked at their smooth skin. The two girls had braids that seemed to Michael to be removable appendages.

"I want my money back. He looks almost normal. I don't see what's so great."

"Can't you make him do anything except scream and grunt?" a red-headed boy asked. Michael couldn't take his eyes off the reddish brown spots on the boy's arms and face.

"Why's his skin so white? You can almost see through it. He looks weird, but it's not worth no nickel. Let's get out of here, Suzy," the girl with braids and no bangs said to the girl with braids and bangs.

The two girls marched out with the three boys following them.

"We didn't want you to come anyway. Stupid cows," Slade said.

"You're the idiots. Idiots looking at an idiot. Idiots looking at an idiot," Suzy chanted.

James stumbled to find an answer, but before he could really think of anything to say, they were gone.

"Do you think he's maybe like Tarzan and maybe because of that he can't speak?" Slade's voice got louder as he became more excited about his own idea.

"Look how skinny his arms are. You never saw Tarzan's or boy's arms?"

"I heard my mom say he was just like a wild animal."

"Maybe a skunk." James laughed at Slade's joke.

"Let's untie him and take his clothes off. Let's see how he acts," James whispered, trying to make his plan sound interesting and daring. "I'm going to get some dog food."

James untied Michael and pulled off his clothes, which

came off easily since they were much too big for him. Michael lay motionless, arching only so the boy could pull his shirt from under him. He liked the brown-haired boy's buttons and reached over to touch one. Slade slapped his hand and jumped back.

"Does he bite?" Slade asked.

James was half-way down the hall with a half can of dog food. "I don't think so. He never bit my mom."

James put his hand into the can and pulled out a pale brown clump and placed it on the palm of his other hand. Michael backed up and Slade grabbed his shoulders. Michael began panting, then humming and rocking his head from side to side. Slade grabbed Michael's hair and pulled his head back and James mashed the dog food into his face.

When they let him go, he ran to the corner and curled up. James ran after him and kicked him, then suddenly became white as a sheet. "We got to get that diaper on him again. I can hear my mom's car."

Slade turned to look at James and then ran for the door. He tripped as he was going out and landed face down on the waxed wood floor. James could hear his mother set the groceries down on the kitchen counter. Slade howled.

"James? Is that you?"

She ran to the hall. "What happened, Slade? Where does it

hurt?"

"I fell and hurt my head."

She parted his hair to look more closely.

"Where's James?"

He hiccuped a "don't-know" between sobs. It was then she noticed the open door. She pushed Slade aside.

Her son had the diaper in his hand and was trying to force Michael's legs apart to get it on. They both were crying. When Mrs. Woodcock grabbed them and lifted them off the floor, they screamed so loud that Slade heard them as he ran home.

"The two of you think you've got something to cry about, well, when I finish with you, you'll really have a reason to cry." James knew what was coming and let out a blood-curdling scream.

"How many times have I told you not to play with that Marston kid?"

She threw both of the boys on the bed and started spanking Michael. He rolled up. Her son tried to get up. She grabbed him by his shirt and it ripped.

"You think we have money to buy you new clothes whenever you damn feel like it? It's not enough that I have this savage to take care of, my own kid is turning into a savage." She hit Michael until her rage calmed. Then she suddenly felt overwhelmed. His spine curved out from his back "like a long skinny maggot." Those were the words she used when she told Mrs. Johnson what happened.

That night Michael had a dream over and over again. Maron was floating in that black box among the white satin and she came to get him, but Mrs. Woodcock had lit a cigarette and had blown smoke at her and Maron had flown away in the box. The dream occurred over and over and Michael felt each time as if Maron might finally take him back to the house in the box. He had awakened and not been able to go back to sleep with the last dream. Everything had happened just as in the other dreams, but after Maron had flown away, he had heard laughter and had turned around to see Johan huddled over Maron in the casket.

My Dearest Joshua,

It was good to see you. You looked healthy. I suppose as you say a sunny porch makes all the difference. I am not sure that it is the panacea that you think it is, but you do look better in the summer, remnants of the boy I fell in love with twenty years ago before we went off to different colleges. I'm sure I told you the story of the retarded woman who showed up at my mother's house once with her children in tow. Her son had nearly put out the eye of a neighbor girl with a stone and she wanted my mother to give her the piano in our living room so she could play to them and "calm the savage soul." I doubt that she had read Alexander Pope, and she certainly could not play the piano. I think she put it, "So my kids don't blind someone." She probably wanted the piano to hawk. Before leaving, one of her brats urinated on my mother's sofa. We will call this. "The Stain and the Piano Story." This is not to say that I put the porch and the piano on the same level.

When I left you on that sunny porch in your recaptured youth, I headed in the direction of Michael's old neighborhood. The house was eventually sold and the trees cut back from the windows. The family who lived there were aware of the stories, though only vaguely and not especially interested. No doubt they are worried about the property value. They have covered the walls inside with the cheap plywood that imitates the wainscoting of the rich. The wooden floors have wall to wall carpeting which is stained and matted like an old dog. It was a challenge to get a feel for the old house.

One of the neighbors, an obese pregnant woman who lives in what used to be her parents' house, told me that everyone in the neighborhood "knew" that weird kid was there. Arlinda "had saw him just once before the funeral." After she and some of her little friends had mooned Michael, Maron appeared "just like a witch from nowhere" and the blinds of the house were never raised again. Some of the boys had tried to pry the windows up and claimed that they had seen wild orgies in the house between Maron and Michael. "But they were just trying to scare us or turn us on, going on about how big his thing was and what he did with it. God and it did make you think about it." Here she smiled revealing infected gums.

The woman thought we were best of friends. I felt a tinge of guilt having seduced her into revealing herself so completely and giving her nothing of myself. I am the journalist prostitute; I give them pleasure and only feign pleasure myself. But unlike prostitution, they do not know they are paying.

Arlinda led me to Mrs. Woodcock, literally. She grabbed my hand and pulled me along. And there she was, ensconced in a cheap folding lawn chair with some of the vinyl straps fraying under her weight, her hair curled and colored, her legs beginning in tiny pink feet and ending in the wide end of a cone. The only thing that moved was the smoke curling up from her cigarette. She talked to Arlinda out of the corner of her mouth, her eyes closed to the sun and beads of sweat on her brow popping through the calm sea of baby oil, which she had smeared over her body. She wasn't aware of me until Arlinda muttered something about the rat boy and this reporter.

Mrs. Woodcock had thought about the whole thing "more times than (she) wished to remember." She thinks of Maron as a saint and that Michael was sent directly from the devil. "I'm a strong believer in looks. That kid was like nothing you had ever saw." Her pimply faced son James stuck his head from the back door and whined that he needed five dollars and she pulled herself out of the chair, leaving me open-jawed that all of that gluteus maximus had fit into the frame of the chair, like the twenty rabbits hopping from the magician's hat. She lumbered to the screen door where James was letting the flies in to what looked like a kitchen.

I wondered how to gain her confidence. A little chat about sunning? I don't think I could be convincing. A few garden tips? Old tires and last year's lawn chairs were thrown in the corner of the yard. The lawn was cut, but weeds grew everywhere the mower couldn't reach.

As I was walking to my car, Arlinda told me of the trials and tribulations that Mrs. Woodcock had with rat boy, related to her when Mrs. Woodcock had a few too many beers on warm July *evenings. Boozy second-hand news was the best I could do.*

So you can see that I have begun to do something, but I'm afraid I have found more gaps than plaster, and the new information creates lacunae. I won't be able to visit for several months. I had some car trouble and will have to save money before I can make the vehicle safe for the longer trips. You are always in my thoughts.

Your loving friend,
Bernice

Tape 5 – Entry 1

Ernesto said one day, "Tell me the quickest way from the front porch of the County Home to the fire escape." We hadn't been talking about the fire or the home. He was like that. Things popped into his head. If you watched him, you could see an idea yank at his head. I tried to figure it out. But it had been a while since I thought of that place. Then I saw the porch, the big white doors that some times were left open in the summer to let air in. I walked down the carpet runner to the end of the hall where the linoleum started. I imagined people I hadn't thought about in a long time. I couldn't explain the way to the fire escape. Every hall was a hundred faces.

"Think about it," Ernesto said. I saw a new idea jerk his head back and he was gone into his mind. I have a dream where I am in the County Home and I wander the halls and find secret passages and places that I never knew existed. I find so many places that I never knew about that I wonder if it is the same place. And I wonder how I will get back. I forget where I came from as soon as I get to a new place. And I have a feeling that I am really not in a building at all, but falling in space. In the dream I meet Joe, Joshua, Harold, Thomas, Vera and others and they look like they can't see me. Other times they are so happy and I know that I always knew about the secret passages and they were not really secret. I just forgot about them.

Part 5

The ashen gray walls of the county farm sank under the soft yellows of May and the green of June. Later the colors blended into the baked dusty grass of late summer, the beige fall grass and the dirty winter snow. It didn't hide the buildings which stuck out over the walls for miles around, but it made the entering and leaving seem foreboding and mysterious.

The farm had its own dairy and barns and rented out some fields for part of the yield. Much of the food was prepared by the inmates under the supervision of a few poorer women from town. Many years later the same inmates would be called patients, and then clients.

The main residence towered over the flat farm land, and like most of the buildings, was the same ashen gray brick as the fence. The main barn was red brick and the laundry room was a small white wood-frame school house that had been moved to the farm when the country schools were consolidated. It still had blackboards on one wall. All the buildings and fields were behind the main building, which stood as a bulwark against peering eyes trying to see the mysteries of the farm. Only part of the orchard stretched out to the front fence, but the trees were old and barren and were only kept for their show of white blossoms in the spring.

A small river twisted along by the back of the farm and tangled barbed wire kept the patients safe from it. A western Michigan pine-root fence stood behind the tangle of barbed wire. Early mornings in the spring and fall, ground fog lumbered up the bank of the river and caught along the pines that surrounded the main residence. A new staff member once remarked that it looked like the place was floating on a cloud the first time she saw it. The other workers had smiled politely at what they thought was an attempt to amuse them.

Mrs. Woodcock had originally agreed to keep Michael for a month, or until he could be evaluated, but after she saw that he was going to corrupt her son, she called the county social worker to pick him up. His body had begun to disgust her and she couldn't sleep at night thinking of the stories people told her about the things which they had found in Maron's house.

The social worker arrived in a black Cadillac with its dome shaped top and curved hood and fenders. Michael had felt something ominous about the car and its glistening chrome bumpers made everything it reflected expand. Even the large woman in the A-shaped white brushed-wool cape seemed to be a mute signal.

An obviously shaken Mrs. Woodcock had led him to the door. She had dressed him in the clothes he had worn to the funeral, which her son had outgrown several years ago. She had tried to force a smile when she led him up to the black Cadillac, but the other woman had not seemed to be much concerned with either her or Michael.

Mrs. Mallick's husband was a lawyer in town and her job as a social worker had created a bit of resentment. It wasn't what she did, but that she was taking work away from someone who might really need it.

The hugeness of the sky, the trees and the buildings frightened Michael, but neither woman seemed to notice his humming. Mrs. Mallick held his hand with two fingers and placed him carefully in the car on a thick blanket that covered the entire back seat. Mrs. Woodcock sat in the front seat. During the trip, Mrs. Mallick glanced nervously back at him and twice stopped the car to glower; once when he grabbed the front seat and when he stood up to look out of the back window. Each time he froze as if under a trance, and Mrs. Mallick turned to Mrs. Woodcock without talking to her, pursed her lips and looked towards the road again.

The day was dead. The houses looked like cardboard cutouts in the clear autumn light. The world came alive when they hit the dirt road to the farm. A truck ahead of them sent frantic clouds of whirling dust into the air and Mrs. Mallick slowed down to give the dust time to settle in order to protect her newly waxed car.

The front gate of the farm was locked and Mrs. Mallick honked her horn impatiently. At the sound, Michael jolted and shot up. His head clunked against the glass and he fell back like a stunned bird. A bright red blotch on Mrs. Mallick's neck spread up along her face.

"Jesus Christ. Hold still, god damn it!" She reached over the seat and using her thumbs and index fingers took a shoulder in each hand. The whole mass of her body bore against him until he squealed in a thin metallic voice which seemed to frighten her, as if it confirmed her worst fears. She turned toward the front as suddenly as she had turned on him.

Sweat beaded on her upper lip and she dabbed it with a handkerchief.

"Jesus Christ," Michael tried to repeat. Mrs. Mallick ventured a glance into the rearview mirror. Mrs. Woodcock had stared straight ahead during the whole incident.

"They should have called you monkey." Mrs. Mallick said. She forced a smile for the attendant who let them in and a sigh of honest relief when she pulled up to the administrative building.

The air smelled of earth, trees, old buildings and dirty linen. The fan from the kitchen blew the smell of cabbage and sausage out into the yard. Michael sniffed at the air noticing the change from the perfume, stale smoke, car deodorizer and talc in the car to this heavier smell, which he couldn't categorize into elements, but felt was this place, divided from the rest of what he knew by the gate, as the upstairs had been with the door and as the car's black doors lined in gray felt had separated them from the world through which they had just passed. Mrs. Woodcock made a note of his sniffing. She would marvel to one of her friends how much he really did resemble a rat.

He was passing from mirror to mirror. Later when he thought about it, he sensed that these worlds were closed, since he found no one from the last world in this new one. They were like separate mirrors, which he only saw once, but he was sure that there was something in them when he wasn't around. He had never seen an empty mirror.

He looked at the mirror next to the hat stand in the administration office. He opened his mouth and peered into it, then closed it and opened it again. Mrs. Mallick strode up to the reception desk and tapped her fingernails on the counter. A small man came out wearing pleated pants and an open cardigan. Mrs. Mallick unbuttoned her coat and when the man turned away to make a phone call, she flapped the lapels to cool herself off.

Mrs. Mallick did not look up from the forms she was filling out when a woman came to take Michael away. He stopped at the window next to the entrance to study Mrs. Mallick's car, and the attendant, thinking that he wanted to go back to where he had come, as most of the patients did, jerked him along.

The main building was much larger than the church, but upon entering it, it shrank into small corridors and rooms. Michael could hear coughing, shuffling feet, screaming and the whine of old fans that were used to circulate the air both winter and summer. The woman leading Michael met another woman and while they were talking, he moved inconspicuously to one of the windows with wire meshed glass and looked into a room. There were eighteen beds, each with an open-mouthed old man staring up at the ceiling like Johan. He wondered if this was where they had taken Johan. His arms still hurt from Mrs. Mallick grabbing him and he rubbed his sore shoulders.

The woman caught him from behind and they were trotting down the hall at a clip that did not allow him to see anything. He breathed in deeply the smell of stale humanity. It bludgeoned, but didn't pierce the senses. They walked by two women mopping the floor. One of them was pouring ammonia into a pail. Michael leaped back as if he'd been bitten and fell on the wet floor. The attendant yanked him up to his feet and dragged him a foot or two and then stopped to wait impatiently. The two women laughed and the one who had poured the ammonia ruffled Michael's hair affectionately.

"Watch out. I'm taking him to be cleaned."

"He looks as clean as a whistle," one of the women said.

"Do you know who this is?" She didn't wait for an answer. "This is the rat boy." She waited for a reaction, then gave a condescending smile and turned to walk away with Michael in tow.

The woman who had touched him looked nervously at her hand. The other one poked her and laughed.

He was led into a white room which was cool. The smell of the room made him think of the medicine cabinets at Maron's house. He had tasted one of the bottles and his mouth had filled with a flat smell and foamed with tiny white bubbles. After that, he had never done anything but smell them. The man stood in the room was dressed in a white coat.

He jumped back at the touch of the cold stethoscope. Then the doctor did something that Michael never forgot and that he dreamed about for weeks to come. He pulled out a long needle. Michael did not react until it went into his arm. Then he twisted and tried to run. The doctor caught him and stuck the needle in again, next to the first attempt where blood formed a small ball and then trickled down his arm. He was aware of the pain and these hard strong determined hands on him. He was so exhausted from struggling that when the doctor let go of his arm to get another needle, he went limp. At the sight of the needle, he mustered all of his strength and shot for the door which he hit at full speed, bounced back and headed for a window. He had swung a leg up on the sill when he was grabbed from behind.

The doctor picked him up several times and slammed him down against the cold metal table. When his breath was knocked out of him, he sat blue-faced and trembling.

He was led into another room where the assistant was pouring a bath. Maron had always given him sponge baths with a plastic basin full of water. The water in the tub glistened in the light from a window high up the wall. At first it was too hot and he tried to fight getting in, but he was no match for the angry strength of the assistant. He could feel his small heaving chest moving the water and the assistant rubbing him with a soaped sponge. When she had finished washing him, she stood him up dripping wet in front of a mirror. His body was glowing red and steam floated from his back and arms. She lowered him to the floor and he howled so she raised him again. And then she smiled.

"It's good for you that you don't know how weird you look,"

she said and the doctor yelled from the other room to ask what she had said.

Tape – 6 Entry 2

Ernesto said on one of the tapes that we were both born in the County Home and had the same mother but our mother had many husbands. The husbands made us different. Our mother made us the same. But on one tape he talked about his mother in Texas and sang sad songs in Spanish. He always said, "Dwindie, I'll teach you Spanish." I could say the words of songs and I knew what the songs were about but I didn't know what the words meant. What said what in the song, I didn't know. It was like one long word and I knew the meaning.

I didn't meet Ernesto until I worked with the semi-independent. Before I met Joshua, him and Joe, I knew people. I thought the people were made by the building and were unmade at night. At night I watched people sleep. Their life went out of them and was pulled into the building and in the morning the building gave it back to them. I can't remember how long I believed this. There was never a moment when I thought that now I would stop believing that. I told Ernesto about this and he told me it was opposite. The building went into the people when they slept, but it stayed. When the fire came, the building was already in them. It was in us, too.

At first he was kept in a beige room with high ceilings where cobwebs swayed when the door opened. There was a window with black steel mesh that cast a shadow on the floor. Michael slept during the day, lying next to the mesh shadow and waking regularly to move farther along the floor as the shadow moved, until by the late afternoon it was on the wall. Then he would stand up and look at how his body was cut into checks by the light, and then how the light turned reddish and liquid.

Occasionally a nurse peeked through the small rectangular window and came in to pick him up and put him in bed. He woke as soon as he was touched, sniffed frantically to capture the scents of hairspray, sweat, and clothes starch. At times there were other smells: rubbing alcohol, bleach, menthol, and tobacco. The nurse would feel if he needed to be changed. He did not open his eyes until he sensed they were walking away. They thought that his sniffing was a reaction to being awakened, an attempt to hold onto a dream or escape from a nightmare.

During the day he heard nothing from Maron. But at night he would climb into the bed and lie waiting for her. He first knew she was coming when the room began to hum with particles of light, like dust hit by light. He looked around the room and Maron appeared on the large window ledge before the blinds. If he felt the light and stared at the window ledge, she would not come until he looked away. Then when he looked back, she would be there, larger than she was in life. He would slip out of bed to see if she would notice, but her eyes, small and bleary without her glasses, stayed fixed as her head moved reading a text written on the air. She wore the same gingham dress every night. The tiny blue and pinks flowers had faded and the large lapels were tattered. He remembered the dress. One night she wore the black dress that she had worn the last time he saw her. She brought with her the smells of the house; old furniture wax, yellowed paper, brown soap, stale air, geraniums with brown-edged leaves. These odors were layered over the smell of steam escaping from the radiators, the heavy scents of human squalor that pervaded the home, and the disinfectants. When Maron left, the scent from the house hung in the air and the light faded slowly until all he saw were the pale green walls, the door and the blinds, like huge brown boxes about to fall on him.

He repeated the devotions word for word, his voice rising in the places where her voice had risen. If he walked to the windowsill, the scent of Maron was so strong that tears came to his eyes. But he was afraid of the huge yellowed blinds that rustled from the heat rising from the steam radiators.

One night she came in a dress he had put on in front of the mirror upstairs. He knew she was wearing the dress as soon as he sensed the particles of air begin to sparkle. His chest tightened and he moved his face up to look at her with his eyes closed. Her body swelled with his breathing and finally her tongue and eyes bulged from her head. Her skin was the color of the floor upstairs in the house where it was worn through to the varnish.

He watched without looking her directly in the eyes for as long as he could and then scurried to a corner under the bed and prayed.

For a moment the next day the nurse thought that he had escaped, but just before she was about to hurry from the room, she checked under the bed. He looked like a puzzle forced together. His neck pushed into the corner, his legs sprawled and his arms bent in like the wings of plucked hen. His mouth was open and there was a small puddle of saliva or clear vomit on the floor.

She clapped her hands and he straightened out so fast that he banged his head. He had never heard anything like the long rolling laugh of the nurse. The scream quivered on his lips. Then he felt the sound go into him and he began to sound like the nurse, the same high gasping laughter.

He stood in the middle of the room, not quite out of his dream where he had tossed between the branches of trees that caught him with such gentle care that it was as if he were falling asleep each time they took hold of him. Gradually the room replaced the dream and his head hurt from hitting the springs of the bed.

"Come along. Now!" she ordered and he followed her to a small square room with a toilet. She flipped on the light and pushed him in. He stood up to turn off the lights and sat back down. There was a thin line of light under the door. He stretched out his toes so he could see them in the light. He hugged himself in the luxury of darkness and felt himself swelling.

"Hurry up. I'm opening in two minutes."

He searched for the toilet paper in the dark and unwound several feet. He dropped it into the toilet and flushed. The sound of water filled him and his back tightened and he stretched his arms and fingers out.

The light shocked him and he grabbed to pull the hospital pajamas on.

"Bulb burn out?" the nurse asked and switched the lights on again.

"You one of those that plays with water?"

She moved out of the way so he could come into the room. Then she shut the bathroom door and locked it.

"I told them you weren't so hopeless. Always making work for themselves. Ninety percent of the time."

He faced her looking seriously, as if he were paying special attention to what she was saying. As she spoke he felt the branches of the trees gently release him. The floor was hard and cold.

The janitors at the Home never painted for more than a few days at a time and painted with whatever was available. Three days it was battleship gray, then four of beige, then one chalk. Michael stopped where the colors changed and tried to feel the difference between the spaces. The young pregnant girl who was assigned to walk with him yanked him from the part of the hallway painted battleship gray to the part painted yellow, but he struggled back to gray.

"I ain't in no hurry. We can spend your time right here. No hurry." She pulled her hair away from her face and wiped the spit from the sides of her mouth with her thumb and index finger. Her legs were long, skinny and milk white. She walked stiff-legged with her back curved so her buttocks stuck up.

"I got ten more to do and my feet don't care."

Michael stepped into the pale yellow part of the hall and then back to the gray, peering up to the ceiling so that he lost his balance and stumbled back a few steps. Bare light bulbs hung from long twisted asbestos covered cords and their filaments twitched like live insects.

The girl placed her hand in the small of her back and

arched her back so her stomach stuck out. "Jesus Christ."

". . . and ascended into heaven and sat on the right side of God to judge the quick and the dead." The words came out automatically as he walked back and forth. He felt a cool hand on his face as he moved into the yellow and the hand pulled away when he crossed over to the gray part of the hall. He took a deep breath as the hand moved down his neck and he pulled himself back before it went under his shirt.

"They ain't your feet swelling with liquids. I should have married a goddam rich farmer or something. Your time's about used up." She gave him a nudge into the gray and he walked with his chin up in the air as if he were wading in a pool and trying to keep his mouth above water.

"God, I hope this ain't catchy," she whispered and passed a hand over her stomach.

Michael stopped when people passed in the hall. He noticed that the woman smiled at some people and was not aware of other people.

"You ain't going to drown, you imbecile," she hissed when she noticed his head was tilted back and he was sucking air into his lungs in gasps. She cautiously took his head in her hands and moved it down. "Put your head right. You know what your head is. And these are my swelling feet." She whimpered and her face tightened as she fought back tears.

A man shuffled toward them in a long open bathrobe with a dirty hospital gown underneath. His lips were puckered in disgust and his cheeks rose so his eyes became two small cuts in his face. He walked down the middle of the hall, seemingly oblivious to them.

Michael halted and the woman pulled him along.

"You don't want to get them crazy people riled up, buster." She bent over as if to itch her knee and whispered, "Buster, get going."

"Sometimes them old senile ones stick to you and you got to find someone to take them. We want no problems."

The man was within a few feet of them and the woman jerked Michael so his feet flew up and he fell in front of the man.

"Shit. Goddamn," the woman hissed and slapped her hand to her mouth as if she were going to vomit.

"You don't want to get them crazy people riled up, buster," Michael said imitating her voice.

The man pulled his robe around him, looked down at Michael lying at his feet, and shot a few bullets of laughter down the hall. "Pulling filth through these sordid mental tunnels and engendering more in your entrails."

The woman dragged Michael to the side of the hall. The

man threw his robes open and shuffled on. Michael pulled himself up. He sniffed the scent of the man. The air was thicker. He moved his head back and forth to feel it on his face.

"I can't take you out anymore in my condition. You understand that? Not like you are."

The next day the woman came to his room, but lay down on the bed, looking occasionally at her watch. Michael sat on the floor.

"Come over here." She yawned.

He moved closer, balancing on each leg like a heron, then taking a small step.

"You do that real good." She contorted to scratch her calf. The skirt of her uniform came up to her mid-thigh.

"We're not going no wheres today, understand?" She acted out each part, flapping her wrist back and forth.

"We're not going no wheres today, understand?" Michael said. He stuck his stomach out, exaggerated her gestures, and imitated her Midwestern clipped speech that had a slight twang.

"Oh Jesus," she said.

"Jesus, loves me, this I know, because the Bible told me so."

"If the nurse comes, understand, you act like you won't leave the room. Understand." She repeated herself several times. She had to sit up on the bed to act out nurse, and took off the pillow case to make a nurse's hat. She spoke louder so he would understand.

"If the nurse comes, understand, you act like you won't leave the room. Understand."

She looked wearily at him, pulled all of her hair down over her face, and then gathered it in her hand and pulled it back. "Are you foreign, or something?"

"Are you foreign or something?"

"No," she said drawing the 'o' out into a long u.

"What you say. . ." she pointed at her mouth and moved her lips, "is. . ." she pointed to him, "'I won't leave this room, I won't leave this room.' You shake your head and grab onto the bed and kick your feet." She climbed down from the bed, groaning and sighing. "Like this." She held onto the bedpost, and lowered herself to her knees. She grimaced and twisted her head and was able to lift her feet a little to show him how to kick.

She pointed to him and then the bedpost. Her head dropped to the level of her shoulders. "Well, show me."

He did his heron walk again.

"Don't do that. That is so dumb. It's faggoty," she whined.

"No?" he asked.

"Do you know what I'm talking about?"

"No."

"Come here and practice." She sat down on the bed again.

Michael lay down on the floor and kicked. "I won't leave this room. I won't leave this room."

"Good," she said disinterested. "Scream some. You know." She went through the options: long drawn out howls, breathless weeping, growling, whimpering, sniffling. She laughed.

Michael laughed.

"If I get one like this, I'll goddam kill myself." She dropped back onto the bed with her legs hanging over the edge.

"I'll goddam kill myself," he said.

"Say that and they'll put you in the locked ward." She lay on the bed for another ten minutes, then jostled to get up. "Not every day. But some days I got to stay here. At least part of the time. Or I'll be swolled up."

"If that Billy goat don't pull, Daddy's going to buy you a. . ." She stopped singing and leaned back on the bed.

"Put your head here," she said and moved his head onto her stomach. He smelled her sweat and Clorox and a detergent and the bacon fat that had spattered on her uniform when she made breakfast.

"Hear it? Do you?" She moved his small fine head around her stomach like a stethoscope.

She twisted back and forth until she had managed to sit

up and reach the edge of the bed. "I got to go. Tomorrow I'll find some way to show you the locked ward. You better know."

He followed her to the door.

"Tomorrow. Stay here. Tomorrow. Stay here," she said trying to act out the words with her hands.

He stood for almost an hour at the door trying to make her come back by repeating everything she said and imagining her face, the brush of her uniform against his ear, her hard round stomach, her hands moving his head around, her smells, the sound of her weary breathing, her shoes shuffling.

A face pressed against the small rectangular window and the eyes scanned the room. It looked like the man in the hall from the other day but he wasn't sure. The eyes narrowed and moved slowly from side to side. The face began to pull back.

"Pulling filth through these sordid mental tunnels and engendering more in your entrails," Michael shouted with the same voice that the man had used the other day. He frightened himself and stood stiff under the door waiting.

Perhaps two minutes later the same face pressed against the glass and the eyes stared down at him. He felt protected and looked calmly up at the face.

"A world built purely of memory and gibberish. Interesting specimen of human variety," His voice through the door sounded like he was speaking in a cave. Then he yanked his face away from the window.

The next day the pregnant girl came. She bit her bottom lip and arched her eyebrows. "I got a chair hid so you can see the locked ward. We got to hurry."

She ruffled his pajamas and passed her hand over his hair with motherly efficiency.

"Okay, follow me and don't go fucking weird on me."

She pulled him along, waddling and grimacing. When he tried to stop between the colors, she yanked him forward and he felt the same hands as before moving up and down his body. He shivered and groaned. They took two left turns and he sensed that they were closer to the center of the building and perhaps had been moving down also to the basement, though they hadn't gone down any steps. Before a door larger than all the others, she stopped and put both hands on his shoulders to set him in place. Then she put her finger to her lips.

She pulled a folding chair from the closet and brought it next to the door. She cautiously glanced through the window and then set the chair before the door. She nudged him up on the chair and he peered in.

A man was lying on the floor with his arms bound around him. Several others were tied to chairs. Michael saw an orange hot light throbbing in the room. It got brighter and brighter and gathered to a point and then spilled out into the room. A heavy set man dumbly inspected the room.

The woman yanked at the back of his pajamas and he lost his balance and tumbled from the chair. She caught him by the arm and pulled him up before he hit the floor. She folded the chair and returned it to the closet. Then she knocked on the window and waved.

Before they could move on, the man with the robe appeared at the end of the hall.

"Showing your young ward the sights of Bedlam," he called and his words echoed.

The woman turned her back on him and pulled Michael along, but soon the man was close behind them.

"A world built purely of memory and gibberish. Interesting specimen of human variety," Michael said as the man whisked by them opening his robe so that it fluttered.

"You don't want to get them crazy people pulling filth through mental tunnels riled up, buster," Michael said and the man slowed down so that they would catch up with him.

"Amazing idiot," he said and then he sped away down the hall.

"Oh shit," the woman said and she stopped completely. She

panted and used a wall to lower herself to the floor. She pointed to Michael.

"Get help. Run. Help. Help. I got contractions." She wagged her arm to show him that she wanted him to go down the hall.

They were standing next to where the wall colors changed from a dull peach to pale green. Michael moved past the peach and heat moved up his legs to his head.

"Help, help. I got contractions," she repeated and acted as if she were pulling the words out of her mouth with her hand and then she pointed to Michael.

He moved farther down the hall but the heat in his body became intense and he looked to see what the next colors were. "Help, help. Jesus loves me. Michael bad. Engendering more in your entrails." He put one foot down and balanced on it and stretched his arms out and opened his hands and then closed them finger by finger. The heat left his body.

"Hurry up. Damn it."

"Don't be faggoty. Help. Help. I got contractions." He mimicked the panic in her voice. He now had passed to where one side of the wall was still green and other was chalk colored. "Help, help. Hurry up. Damn it. Help, help. Hurry up. Damn it. I got contractions." He took a short leap with each step and soon was coming up on the man in the robe who was resting with his hand on a door knob and his back leaning against the wall.

"Help, help. Hurry up. Damn it. I got contractions."

The man turned wide-eyed towards him.

"Where's Louella? Does she have contractions? She has contractions?"

"Don't be faggoty. Help, help. Damn it. She has contractions?" Michael stopped in front of the man and balanced on his tiptoes.

He grabbed Michael by the arm. "You behave. Come with me." Then he pounded firmly on the door.

A nurse came out.

"What is it, Joshua?" her voice was unfriendly.

"I found Louella's ward running down the hall screaming, 'Help, help. I have contractions.' I assume that it is Louella who is having contractions. He came that way."

The nurse called for someone else and Joshua followed them down the hall, pulling Michael after him. Michael screamed when he got to the green walls again and Joshua looked down at him.

When they got to Louella, she was wailing, "I don't want to have my baby here. Please Jesus, I don't want to have my baby here. Get me to the hospital. Oh Jesus."

Michael cried along with her, repeating the words she said

and mixing them in with the Nicene Creed. The two nurses helped her up and one of them took her arm and walked away with her.

"Joshua, Mr. Mandment made a mistake letting you loose in the halls," the other nurse said and put her hands on Michael's shoulders and moved him away from Joshua.

"Another minute and Louella would have lost the pea-brain mind she has. Not even an educator of my standing and credentials could have taught her anything."

The nurse looked very tired and walked away with Michael. "I know your story, Joshua."

"Don't be faggoty. Help, help. I got contractions. She has contractions?" Michael said.

The nurse turned slowly back as if she were making a mental picture of the scene.

Tape 12 – Entry 16

Ernesto and I had a neighbor once with many children and she was pregnant. Ernesto told me that it was the most beautiful thing in the world. Babies came out of women and for a while they were connected by lights that you couldn't see and the lights became weaker and weaker, but they were always there. Even when people died, they were there. I told him that when I was at the home I saw women who were pregnant and their bellies grew and grew and then they disappeared for a while. I always thought that what was inside them was eating them and that when they came back they weren't the same. They were less. They were never completely there. He told me that that was true, too. Then he said that everything was true for a while. He said our neighbor could never be just herself again. It was impossible. It was impossible for anyone to just be themselves.

Part 6

The home was going through a reform and had divided the young from the old. The very young were sent to special schools and many of the others of Michael's age went to foster homes or the state mental institution.

There was a problem getting Michael's birth certificate and by the time all of the papers were shuffled around and requests were sent and answers received claiming no information, Michael had gained three years on paper. When the number of patients in the boy's ward didn't really warrant having a separate ward, an administrative memo was sent from the state that children from twelve to sixteen were to be kept in the adult ward, but separate from the other patients. By now Michael age had been inflated again and his small stature was blamed on malnutrition and lack of sunlight for what was estimated to be the first sixteen years of his life.

For the first month he ran to a corner every time one of the others approached him. If he saw a man in a white or light blue coat, he hid under a heavy couch with lion feet legs and when he was dragged out from underneath the couch, he was covered in the couch's seemingly endless dust balls and cobwebs. Several of the other children began following him under the couch, until the couch was removed and replaced with a bench that had been next to the chain link fence along the river.

The ward supervisor was Vera, an older woman who wore pale pastel prints like Maron's and was slightly bow-legged. Her hair was pulled back at the top and the sides with large barrettes and it made her slightly curly hair bunch like a short mop at the back of her head. Her receding chin, small smooth forehead, and her fine pointed nose created the impression that her head was in rapid movement away from her body.

When Michael was hiding in the corner, Vera would come to coax him out, reaching down and taking his hand to lead him back to the others. He watched beads of sweat on her neck run down to her cleavage, making lines in the talcum powder. Her odor was sweat, a lilac-scented cologne, and talcum. She had a sweater that she draped over the back of a chair and Michael would go there to smell it when he wanted to think about her.

Her talking frightened him. Steams of words flowed from her dry deep-lined lips. She talked about what she was doing as she did it. To Michael it was as if her words filled the room and left no space for any other noise. When patients screamed, Vera's drone would hypnotize them.

She was a big woman and it seemed as if she was

performing a circus tight rope act when she walked. It was as if her body went one speed and her face another. But when Michael dreamed one night that there was a room where all his selves existed together, he recognized his self now because it had the odor of Vera and when he touched it, it felt like her sweater.

Michael was only four feet tall when he entered the country hospital. Vera, who was five-ten, would not see him if he was standing next to her. He would disappear among other bodies, louder voices. She had also been accused of having favorites, an accusation to which she had replied in a long rambling and disconnected letter to the superintendent of the hospital, in which she both admitted and denied having favorites and finally found a mantra, which was "I have no favorites because they are all my favorites."

The days she was gone, the male attendants made all the patients sit or lie down while they listened to a baseball game on the radio, or played checkers. There were more incidents. An inmate would be sitting for an hour like a time bomb, ticking and ticking, and then would stand up swearing, trying to rip off his clothes, or throw himself on someone else. Michael could hear the ticking and knew when the bomb was about to go off. He would move to the corner and face the wall, and inevitably a minute or two later an inmate would have a fit, as the attendants called it.

"God dammit. Did you see that? That little guy gets up and it sends the others off." The one who had been winning the checker's match screamed to the other attendant as they pulled a short stocky man with fleshy lips away. "How many times have I told you? Let one up and it's like a nuthouse."

"Wow, like a nuthouse." The man who had been losing at checkers said and laughed.

Fans were on during the day and Michael thought they were the sound of the world. He imagined that he had heard it at the house with Maron and Johan, but hadn't noticed until now. Now he knew where it came from.

Michael gave Vera presents, a piece of cake he had saved from lunch or a page from an old magazine that he had torn out. She would clap her hands and become silent for a second, put whatever he gave her down and move on.

Usually when he saw her, she was moving between the inmates, calling out their names and asking if they had taken their medicine. "Tom, take your medicine? Take your medicine, Tom. Jake, take your medicine? You took your medicine."

Inmates were not responsible for taking their own medicine, but there were paranoid patients who hid it under their tongue, fearing that it might be poisoning their brains. Vera's voice coming harsh and matter-of-fact was like a truth serum. Inmates who were retarded did not receive medication, unless they also had emotional problems, and Michael wondered if the ones who took medication were from another mirror. Perhaps he had a self in another mirror that took medicine.

The man from the hall took lots of pills. Joshua was subject to long depressions where he would have to be forced to wash and would lie in bed in his own urine. The attendants heaved his white flabby body out of bed, sat him in a corner chair where he would weep at times for hours until he slumped over in exhaustion, his chest resting on his soft stomach. When he was deep into his depression, his eyelids became bright red and puffy. When he was coming out of his depressions, he would shout out lines of poetry, which he had written and Michael would repeat them.

"The brain is the factory of time," he shouted sporadically for several hours one morning. Michael went up to inspect Joshua. His skin was chalk with scarlet blotches blooming on it. He was a thin man thrashing around in a swollen formless body.

Michael shouted it back, "The brain is the factory of time." He whispered it to Vera who looked perplexed and worried for several moments.

"Memory is the machine that makes the moment."

"Parrot boy." Joshua said with a smile of discovery.

Michael shook his head gravely, "Rat boy."

"Hmm," Joshua said and his mind seemed to fade away.

"Parrot boy," Michael said. Joshua moved his eyes but not his head to look at Michael, then shut them.

The next day Joshua was leafing through *Life* magazine, which the mother of one of the inmates brought for the ward when she visited. He noticed someone behind him looking over his shoulder and was about to shut the magazine and turn around when he saw that it was Michael.

"Look, Michael. This is a Kenmore dishwasher. Here are Marlboros." Joshua flipped through the magazine, stopping at the ads. "Polaroid," Joshua said in an exaggerated teacher voice. Michael held Joshua's hand to look closer. "North Polar Roads," Joshua beamed at his own cleverness. The ad showed a scene from a party and then the people from the party still in their New Year's Eve hats looking at themselves a few minutes earlier.

"Making memories. Saving memories. Keep your memories on six by fours. Stack them in boxes. Snap, snap, snap, snap." Joshua wanted to go to the next ad. He pushed Michael's hand away.

He held up an ad of a red and white car with a smiling, almost laughing woman waving, and her handsome husband beaming with ownership. "See the U.S.A. in a Chevrolet," Joshua said in his most dramatic voice.

"See the U.S.A.," Michael repeated and pointed to the woman.

Joshua smiled for the first time in weeks. "That's right," he nodded.

"In a Chevrolet," he said and pointed to the man.

Joshua gave a spurt of laughter.

"See the U.S.A.," Michael said again and pointed to the woman. "In a Chevrolet," and he pointed to the man.

Michael pointed to Vera. "See the U.S.A." He pointed to Joshua. "In a Chevrolet."

"Michael, no. Michael, don't bother Joshua. Don't bother Joshua. Come. Come." Vera was making her rounds. Her voice was soothing and she repeated everything she said twice, a habit she had started recently. She raised her voice so that Michael could hear her from the other side of the room. The room became quiet.

Joshua pointed to himself.

"In a Chevrolet," Michael said.

"No, no. In a nuthouse. Joshua in a nuthouse."

Joshua smiled again.

"Vera, see the U.S.A." He pointed to Vera. "Joshua in a nuthouse. Joshua in a nuthouse."

"That is who I am now. Joshua in a nuthouse. Charles the

Great. Ivan the Terrible. Joshua in a nuthouse." Joshua slumped in the chair.

Michael babbled on without getting a response. He walked up to Vera. "Vera, see the U.S.A. Memory is the machine that makes the moments. See the U.S.A."

Vera's husband was ten years older than she was, wanted to buy an *Air Stream* and wander the country. He was angry at her because she refused to give up her job and go with him. She had smirked at the stories about Michael when they brought him into the county hospital, but she had begun to think of him as other worldly, perhaps psychic, maybe possessed by a spirit. Despite her vacant smile, her nostrils were flared and when her smile faded her lips formed a fleshy trembling opening.

"Polaroid," Michael said and giggled, as if he were trying to unsay something. "Save memories. Snap! Snap!"

"Oh my," she said mixing ingratiating praise with high-school-drama alarm.

One of the guards on the ward was a bachelor farmer named Lester Pantry, who was large with arms that seemed to hang from his neck and not his shoulders. He was more a presence than a force and Vera had complained that Lester was not active enough. When she told him to do something, he nodded, never asked just how to do it. "He doesn't like taking orders from me," she complained to Mr. Mandment, the superintendent of the home. It was some consolation to her that he treated the director the same way.

"That's just Lester," Mr. Mandment said.

Lester didn't always use his false teeth, so some days his lips bunched together as if he were in constant consternation. "What is wrong with you," Vera would hiss, turning on him after watching him out of the corner of her eye.

She had come in the day after she had complained about him to Mr. Mandment and seen Lester actually talking to Joshua.

"Why do you show him ads? Why don't you show him real pictures?" Lester had to repeat himself several times.

"Because there are no real pictures. A picture tells a thousand lies. An ad tells only one; that you have to buy what they are selling you," Joshua snapped. He was intrigued that Lester was speaking to him. "You're not the nurse."

Lester nodded as if he was pondering the fact that he wasn't the nurse and walked away with the concerned look that he had when he wasn't wearing his dentures.

Lester had noticed it first. Michael sat with an old *Life* magazine and turned the pages as Joshua had done. "See the

U.S.A. in a Chevrolet. Save your memories." On the pages without ads, Michael chanted, "Jesus, save us from our sins. On the third day he rose from the dead. Not by deed alone. Forever and ever. For his is the power and the kingdom." Then he would turn the page to an ad. "Builds bodies eight ways. Wonder bread."

Vera was not used to Lester coming to her. He did his work and left. She had to invent things for him to do, such as move furniture, or repeat instructions she had told him a hundred times, to remind him that she was in charge. She looked up from her desk in the little office she had in the hall, and stood up immediately, thinking that something must be seriously wrong.

"It's a miracle," Lester said. He had his dentures in and his words were clear, but he spoke each word separately.

"Michael," he said, "He's speaking in tongues. It's English and all. All English. But tongue-like. Holy Ghost stuff. It's a miracle," Lester repeated. Vera was already at the door to the day room and Lester loped behind her.

She surveyed the room. Lester had caught up to her. He pointed at Michael and Vera moved between the chairs and tables as if she were doing what she did every day, stopping to talk to patients as she crossed the room. When she reached Michael, he smiled, but it was barely an acknowledgment.

He finished parroting the Phillip Morris ad and turned the

page to an article on an accident at the Indianapolis 500. "Roll the stone away. They have stolen our Lord. The women were weeping. Forgive them, for they know not what they do. Forgive those who trespass against us."

Michael flipped the page. "It melts in your mouth, not in your hands."

"Michael, you are reading. You are reading." Vera said a little startled.

"See the U.S.A. See the U.S.A. It melts in your mouth. It melts in your mouth." Michael laughed and hid his head in the magazine.

"He's the parrot boy. Amazing talent. If you gave him one of Senator Dirksen's speeches, the rest of us would be asleep after five minutes and he could repeat every word." Joshua liked his pronouncements to have plenty of room. He waited for their effect to sink in.

"Perfect example of an idiot savant. Put him on a stage and we'll be rich." Joshua turned to walk away.

"But he mixes it up. Yes, he mixes it up. And where did he get that religious . . ." She paused looking for the right word. " . . get that religious stuff," she said.

"He listens to God," Lester muttered. "It's a miracle," he said more clearly.

"Don't you remember that he lived with an old woman who had been a minister's wife. Crazy as a loon. It was in the papers. They called Parrot Boy Rat Boy." Joshua had not left, but stood awkwardly with his head turned over his shoulder. He looked down at Michael, who had turned the magazine into a game and turned the pages faster and faster and chattered in a purling stream of phrases.

"Bye, Michael the Parrot," Joshua said.

"Bye, Joshua in the Nuthouse," Michael shouted in the middle of his chatter and furious page turning.

"Well, well," Vera sighed.

"See the U.S.A. See the U.S.A.," Michael blurted out in the middle of his chatter.

"Maybe it's a demon." Lester had kept his eyes on the boy.

"Maybe is, maybe is." Vera was someplace else and didn't really register what Lester had said.

During the fall Michael became Joshua's pupil. For a month they played the naming game. Joshua pointed at an object or a person and Michael had to give the name. After one night when Joshua had pointed at the moon through the wire mesh of the windows and told Michael its name, everything that shone was "moon." Michael seemed to take a perverse delight in calling the lights in the hall moons. Joshua had gone along at first, even calling the light switches "moon switches," but he soon became furious that Michael refused to distinguish lights from the moon. He had stayed in bed for a day, which did not bother the attendants. When he came back, Michael had pointed to the hall light and called it "light" and the lamp in the day room "lamp," but after Joshua seemed to be basking in his success, Michael said, "No, moon, moon," and laughed. Joshua had spun around so fast on his heels that he ran into a chair, knocking his shin. He limped to the door by the time Michael yelled, "Light, light. It's light."

Joshua halted by the door but did not walk back to the couch where they usually began their lesson.

"It is most definitely not the moon. It is a simple contraption called a light. An electrical light to be more exact." Michael had captured even the tone of Joshua's voice.

"Is mockery the greatest form of flattery." Joshua addressed this to Lance, a young man who had extreme compulsive behavior. He stared suspiciously at Joshua.

"Oh, that's right, Lance. Imitation is the greatest form of flattery. So sorry." Lance moved away as Joshua spoke.

"Very well, Michael Parrot. I accept your apology." Joshua bowed.

"Oh, that's right. So sorry." Michael bowed back.

"This is uncanny, Poe-esque." Joshua rolled his eyes.

On one of the walks around the yard, Joshua pointed and explained in an unbroken stream of words. Only Michael seemed to be able to tell which objects Joshua was talking about. After the walk, he flipped though the pages of *Life* magazine with Michael at his side. He usually became angry when Michael looked at *National Geographic* since it was a waste of time to show Michael places that he would never see. He would shake his finger at Michael, "Too exotic. Stick to *Life*. It is our world." He flung his arms out as if presenting the contents of a prize on *Let's Make a Deal*. "These halls and walls and white coated masters and baby blue robed peons are our own little *Metropolis*."

Joshua frantically ripped pages out of old magazines which he had gone through with Michael. He had filled two groceries bags in two days.

"What are we going to do with all these ripped magazines? Think of the pleasure the others would have received." Vera looked like she was floating in a sea of trouble. She gazed around the room as if searching for help. In the summer the county hospital hired students to take patients for walks around the yard and they were always off schedule. Her mind stretched paper thin until the tardy summer attendants brought their wards back.

"It's a test. Very important pedagogical experiment." Joshua clipped his words and made it clear that he had no time to pay attention to Vera.

"What are we going to do with. . ."

"I don't care," Joshua said.

Vera ambled through the almost empty room. ". . . all these ripped magazines. And the others?" she said to herself.

She came back to the table a few minutes later. "Make sure you clean this mess up. Don't leave it for the attendants." Her voice was stern.

Joshua waited for her to repeat herself, but she marched to the door with her body tilted forward.

"And here I sit waiting for the other shoe to drop," Joshua said and laughed theatrically until an attendant ordered him to lower his voice.

He removed the chairs from one of the large tables and covered it with the pictures from the magazine. Michael came into the day room with a group of patients who had gone on a walk to look at the river which was running full because of a storm the night before. Many other day room patients were still outside on a walk.

"Michael, come here. Today we will prove that you are not a parrot boy, but mind boy." Joshua swelled with pride.

Another member of the group had misunderstood Joshua and screamed, "Mine, it's mine. Mine."

"Shut up, you imbecile," Joshua's voice reverberated through the room. Michael jumped back.

"Michael, here is the world, life, so to speak. I want you to pick up the papers as I call them." Joshua held up his index finger, which Michael knew was the sign to wait. "I say the word. For example, 'beehive,' and you find the object." He picked up an illustrated ad for a bank which featured a beehive. "Beehive."

"Let's start. Volkswagen." Joshua wore an old suit coat with roughly patched elbows to give the proceedings the air of a game show.

Michael scanned the table. He could hear other inmates talking all at once to the young red-headed man who had taken them for a walk.

"Pay attention. This is extremely important. I cannot tell you how important this is. Look to that corner." Joshua waved his hand toward one corner of the table. "Perhaps I put too many images, but it will become easier as you remove them."

"Excellent, excellent," Joshua said before Michael had even picked up the page from the magazine.

"Bon Ami," Joshua said and Michael picked up another page near where he stood.   "Excellent. Maytag washer. You have to concentrate. This is a test."

From a far corner of the room came a burst of laughter and Michael stepped back from the table and looked vacantly towards it.

"What you do now will determine whether you win or not. It is vital." Joshua's face was red and his limpid cheeks trembled. "How do you expect to go out into the world and earn a living?"

Michael stopped for a moment and turned to look at Joshua, who was turning red and swelling. But the redder he turned and the more his eyes pleaded and his loose neck trembled, the more he looked like he would disappear.

Joshua began to walk towards Michael, but restrained himself. "I can't tell you how important this is."

A new inmate Michael's age, but almost a foot taller, came up to the table without Joshua noticing. In a second handfuls of paper were falling from the air. Joshua was speechless. Then he began to weep.

Michael slid his arm across the table pushing the rest of the paper on the floor. The other boy kicked it up in the air. Joshua reached for Michael first, but missed him, then he thrust himself at the boy, but fell over one of the chairs which he had placed near the wall. One of the young summer replacements ran up to Joshua and knelt down by him.

"You okay?"

"No," Joshua groaned. "I am in a nuthouse."

"What happened?" Joshua looked up at the young man who was speaking. For a second he thought he recognized him as a student he had years ago.

"Are you Stephen?" he asked.

"What happened?" the young man repeated.

Joshua pulled away from the young man and got to his feet. He dropped into a chair and buried his head into his folded arms. "I can't tell you."

"In a Chevrolet," Michael yelled as he ran after the boy around the room.

Part 7

For the next several months, Joshua's only pleasure was to ignore Michael. By October, Joshua had returned to his bed. The first day the guards had forced him out of bed, they had to tie him to a chair. He had refused to eat for three days. Michael had not missed him, but was surprised to see Joshua tied to his seat. "It's Michael Parrot. In a Chevrolet. I am talking to Joshua in the Nuthouse."

Joshua turned his head away.

It was six o'clock and already dark. A large harvest moon shone on the edge of the horizon. Michael pointed out the window. "It's a lamp, not the moon."

"Phyllis's eyes are the lamps of heaven, with what sad step, Sir Philip Sidney, I think." Joshua's head fell onto his chest and he sobbed.

Vera disappeared for six months. When she returned, she had changed. Now when she walked through the day room, she still stopped to talk, but was not able to listen. Walking between the clusters of tables and chairs, she stopped and gazed at the ceiling and her lips moved as if she were about to talk. Harold, with whom Michael usually played, became afraid of her. When

Vera walked into the room, he crawled under the sofa. Michael would follow him and spy on Vera, but Harold kept his head to the wall, putting his nose up against the floor board. When he came out, his nose was black from the dirt that was mopped against the walls.

Harold seldom said more than "don't" or "I want it." So Michael did most of the talking. Harold paid little attention, his green eyes with their huge irises wandered about the room and his wide fleshy mouth set into the neutral expression. His hair was blond and straight and one of the younger female attendants loved to comb it. Except for infrequent fits of rage and frequent escapes from the day room, which never lasted longer than a few hours, Harold was little trouble to the attendants.

One day Harold's nose was running and he took a deep breath and snorted like a horse. The sound lifted Joshua's depression for a few moments and he turned to Michael and said, "Rat boy, how can you stand to be with that animal? Oh, yes, yes. The name should have told me."

Harold was terrified of the boy who had ruined Joshua's intelligent test. The boy didn't speak, but howled at and hit the other inmates. He had a thin axe-like head, copper eyes and red hair which would have seemed less metallic if his skin had been freckled, instead of a transparent white. Dirt filled in the crevices of his cracked skin. Occasionally when the boy entered the day room, Harold began to hyperventilate, and only stopped when his nose was pushed into the dirty crevice under the sofa. A few minutes later he would begin to snort and cough violently, then for a few minutes would be silent again. Michael would crawl after him and watch the boy from under the couch. The boy would kick under the couch and Michael would grab for his legs.

It had come as a shock to everyone the day that Vera had grabbed the boy and shook him. He was almost as tall as she was, but was thin as a rail. One of his hands got free, and he hit her on the nose and suddenly her dress and the floor around her were covered with blood. She tried to slap him back, but missed and whimpered. Lester came to lead Vera off and two other men grabbed the boy.

For a week both Vera and the boy were gone.

Lester was especially talkative that week and wore his dentures every day except on Sunday. "Mr. Mandment says she has to stop being a mother. These inmates don't need mothers. Mothers are why they're here. That's what all the big brains say." He talked to everyone, but mostly to Joshua who seemed to ponder all of this in his depression.

When Vera showed up on Monday, her eyes were red

and puffy. "Vera, are you okay, honey?" Michael had heard one of the women who worked in the lunch room ask Vera this same question and raised the pitch of his voice, affecting the woman's accent. She silently peered at him through her swollen eyes. Lester, who had been sticking close to her most of the day, whispered to her, "He's possessed."

Vera made a short strange sound, almost like laughter, and walked on.

Lester caught up to her and whispered again, but when Vera did not react, he said loud enough for others to here, "Maybe it's your husband."

The day the boy came back, he avoided Vera most of the day. Harold was out walking with some of the other inmates. When he came in, he saw the boy and noticed that the sofa had been removed from the day room. Vera hurried towards Harold, but when she reached him, she turned and surveyed the room. Harold wanted to get away from her, but saw that he would be between her and the boy if he moved. He lay down on the floor and stuck his nose against the door jam. His coughing and hyperventilating was so loud that everyone in the room turned to look at him. Vera bent down, but the closer her head got to him, the louder he coughed. She was straightening up when she felt the boy pissing on the back of her leg. She screamed.

Michael laughed as the boy pissed on Harold, who had been hyperventilating so long that his legs and arms began to curl up, and he was in a fetal position. One of the aids came to help Vera, but slipped in the urine and fell next to her. Several inmates screamed when they saw the aid go down. Vera had taken off her sweater and was trying to wipe up the urine with it. She glanced at Harold. The aid tried to get up, but she had broken something. The boy, Michael, and two other inmates ran in circles around the day room, knocking over chairs and throwing magazines and newspapers. Vera stood up. She seemed to be oblivious to what was happening. It suddenly occurred to her that the sweater in her hand was soaked with urine, and she dropped it onto the floor. When she reached the small lounge for employees, her message was short and matter-of-fact. "Beth fell in the day room. Can someone help?"

The two men who got up to go to the day room did not notice that the skirt of her dress had large wet stains, nor did he smell anything strange since the hospital always smelled of urine. So they were completely unprepared for what they saw.

Vera and the boy never came back. Michael waited for several weeks to see them. When he asked about her, the assistant told him, "She's gone." He thought he saw her several times when he was on a walk with one of the attendants. For a while they tightened the rules so when Michael tried to see if the woman was Vera, someone was there to stop him. One day the woman turned, and he saw that it wasn't Vera, but a woman who looked like Maron.

"Where is Vera?" he asked Lester constantly.

Joshua would call across the room, "On Jupiter or Mars."

One day Lester mumbled, "Where you'll go if you don't behave and find Jesus."

Suddenly Joshua had perked up, "What? Speak clearly you imbecile."

"Where you will all go if you don't behave." Lester held his mouth. His dentures had made his gums swell, but now that Vera was gone, he felt it was important that he wore them.

"Oh no," Joshua said in his most school-marmish voice. "We are there already. He must be in hell." His laughter frightened Lester.

"He descended into hell and on the third day he rose again from the dead and ascended into heaven," Michael chanted.

"Hallelujah, Parrot," Joshua laughed.

Part 8

When he reached thirteen, he became fascinated with a retarded boy named Peter. He helped him put on his clothes, sat up nights to watch him toss and turn, sat on the sofa for hours observing him. During meals, he sat next to him and scolded him if he ate with his hands or spilled his milk.

Peter at first enjoyed the attention. He was now the one following Michael around.

"Oh, the degeneration of the species," Joshua moaned. "A confederacy of dunces."

"And when I am formulated and sprawling on a pin," Michael muttered as he passed with Peter in tow.

"Uncanny bits and pieces. It has taken me a long time to realize this, but you will never, never be a person. You will always be bits and pieces." Joshua stood as if he were going to continue his sermon, then collapsed into his chair.

Michael yanked Peter's arm and they spun back towards Joshua. "Parrot Boy, uncanny bits and pieces. You will always be bits and pieces of Joshua in the Nuthouse," Michael taunted and sped past Joshua with Peter faltering behind him. He turned to Joshua and did an imitation of Peter eating supper, mimicking uncannily the way Peter shrugged with his left shoulder and then swept his hair out of his face with his left hand.

"Mock me. Then mock him. A mirror reflects diamonds and dirt. You will never be a person. Never original." Joshua attempted to stand up, but each time he fell back in the chair.

Michael led Peter in a large circle around Joshua.

"Have you noticed that Peter tries to walk like you? That bounce where your heels never touch the ground. Engendering idiots." Joshua clasped his arms around himself. "Bits and pieces," he said in a loud clipped voice.

"Memory is the maker of moments. Memory is our maker. Bits and pieces." Michael ran so that when he turned, Peter tripped along on the outer edge of his circle.

Thomas, the supervisor of semi-independent men, appeared in the doorway. Lester, who had been sitting at a corner table reading the newspaper, adjusted his dentures and rose to walk over to Thomas. Michael stopped in his tracks so that Peter stumbled on ahead and Michael yanked him back. Joshua glanced over at Thomas, whom he disliked for usually ignoring him completely.

"Our words go out as words and come back as truth," Joshua said. Thomas turned in Joshua's direction and Joshua bent over in his chair and sobbed.

Lester folded his hands and tilted his head in stern reverence. He nodded in servile agreement. Thomas did not look directly at Lester, but surveyed the room as he spoke. Michael let go of Peter's hand and approached Thomas and Lester. Thomas stopped talking and sternly inspected Michael who froze. People at tables farther from the door began to talk again.

"Michael," Thomas said and Michael took a step towards him.

"Do you have a problem?" Thomas spoke again.

"No," Michael said confused by the question.

"Then mind your own business," Thomas said.

Michael wasn't sure what he meant. Peter grabbed his hand and pulled him away from the door. Michael shook free and pushed Peter to the ground. Thomas grabbed Michael by the back of the neck and marched him over to a chair.

"You have too much energy," he said as he pushed Michael into a chair. "Stay there."

"That's right. I'm sorry," Michael said. Joshua raised his red tear covered face to peer towards Michael.

Thomas turned his head and seemed to be listening to a sound far off, then slowly moved back to where Lester stood, glancing back at Michael a few times, who sat as straight as a pin in the chair.

That evening when he was by himself for a moment in the bathroom, he mimicked Joshua, Peter, Lester, and Thomas in the stainless steel mirror. "Bits and pieces," he said, imagining how each of them would say it. When he imagined Thomas saying it, he snapped himself into attention. Then he mimicked Lester saying it, first with his dentures and then without them.

When he first began to follow Peter, Harold stopped playing with him. If Michael and Peter walked past Harold, Harold would poke Peter without seeming to notice that he was there. Peter would give a high pitched squeal. Michael would purposely pass by Harold and when he saw Harold turn his head away in preparation for jabbing Peter, he would yank Peter at the last moment so Harold would miss him.

Harold began escaping from the day room. He waited nonchalantly by the door and darted out when an attendant or Lester entered. Lester insisted on finding him, though some of the new workers, who were looking for a break, would offer to go after him. It usually took Lester at least an hour to find him and while Harold was gone, Michael felt that the room was incomplete. He would pull Peter behind him and set a chair in a corner or carefully turn it over with the back pointing towards the wall. Joshua was also gone, but no one ever used the chair that he sat in when he was not in the day room.

"Say hello to Harold," he would say. "See the USA."

Peter shook his head and Michael grabbed him by the back of the neck the way Thomas had done to him. "Hello, Harold," he coached Peter.

One day Michael marched Peter to a chair and sat him down, "Stay there." Peter squirmed and tried to escape. Lester ambled towards them. He had one eye on Harold who stood a few feet from the locked door. The door opened and Harold took a step towards it. Lester glanced from Harold to Peter and Michael, as if he hadn't seen Harold at all. But Harold made no attempt to escape. The door shut.

"Harold, stay away from the door. Do you hear?" an attendant said who had just come in.

"Okay, okay." Harold closed his eyes. His breathing was low and rhythmic.

"Did he try to get out when you came in?" Lester questioned, turning away from Michael and Peter.

"I can't get in his mind. He escapes once a day at least. He must have known I was watching him." The attendant snipped at Lester.

"Gets a little exercise." The words came out jumbled and Lester rubbed his jaw before he tried to speak again. "He gets exercise."

"You get the exercise," the attendant said and Lester blushed.

"I know how to handle him," Lester found it hard to give his voice the right authority.

Harold moved over to Michael and Peter. The door opened again and Harold pushed Michael to the door and ran through it himself. Then when the startled nurse swung around to grab at Michael, Harold flew past her.

"Everyone stay here. Stay here." Lester lisped and held his hands up to make it clear that no one was to leave the room. He squeezed by the nurse and closed the door behind him.

Harold pulled Michael up a back stairway that Michael hadn't known existed and through a hallway to a small compartment that was the entrance to the fire escape, which was a tubular aluminum slide.

They heard Lester's footsteps coming up the stairs. "Harold, Harold, meet me. Meet me the other place." Lester's voice was just audible and seemed not to be directed anywhere. There was no sound for a minute, and then they heard him going down the stairs.

Michael listened to the echo of Lester's footsteps. The fire escape was completely dark. Harold opened the door a crack so there was some light and Michael noticed that he was naked.

"Don't tell," Harold said and lay on his back and moved his hips from side to side. "Oh, so good, so good."

He pulled Michael over on top of him. "Ah, ah, ah, ah," Harold grunted and Michael became afraid and moved for the door.

"Oh, baby, baby, baby." Harold writhed on the aluminum floor. He turned himself around and his head hung over the edge of the fire-escape chute.

Michael ran down the stairs and back to the day room. Lester was coming in the back door from outside and saw Michael.

"Go back to the day room. Right now." Lester was on his way up the stairs before Michael got to the main hallway.

Harold ignored Michael again and Michael teased him by dragging Peter in front of him, but when Harold tried to jab Peter, Michael would thrust Peter into him. The attendants wanted to put Michael in isolation for a few hours, but Lester claimed that these were only boyish pranks, and he was in charge.

Michael dreamed of Harold in the fire escape. Several times a year they practiced going down the fire escape and he saw himself walking to the chute and finding Harold there with his legs open and his back arched. He lay naked next to Harold and

Thomas was the next person in line. He was afraid that Thomas would find them and closed his eyes to wait for him, but he couldn't make himself slide down the chute naked until Thomas had seen him. He didn't know why, but he knew that it was that way.

Part 9

At fourteen, ten months after going to the fire escape with Harold, he moved to the ward for the men who did some of the work on the farm. He was the youngest. The man closest to him was a thirty-year-old alcoholic named Gus who had suffered a severe head injury in a car accident. Michael was given the bed closest to the window and farthest from the heater, the bed Gus had until one of the old men died.

His body began to change. Hair was growing in places where it had not been before. He vaguely remembered Johan. Some of the old men slept in the nude and would sit hunched over on the edge of the bed in the morning, as if they were trying to gather the strength for another day. Michael stared at everyone.

"God dammit. Keep your fucking eyes to yourself. You give me the willies," Walter, the oldest man among the semi-independents, screamed.

"You act like you never seen nothing," another snapped and jumped up from the edge of the bed. He had his hands around Michael's neck. A Chippewa Indian named Joe pulled the old man off.

"He's been in the nuthouse. He never seen no one who

wasn't crazy before," Joe explained to the old man.

The old man shook his head and made another move toward Michael who curled up into a ball.

For a time when he lived with Maron and Johan, he had stared at his fingers and watched them move. He spent hours moving them through the air in front of the mirror, twisting his fingers and twirling his arms. He would move a leg up slowly until he lost his balance and fell off the chair.

Now he was aware of his body when someone touched him. At times he felt their hand on his shoulder or hip or leg long after they had taken it away. When Peter tackled him in the yard, Michael had held on, rubbing himself furiously against him, like he was trying to wear away his skin, then without knowing why, he would hit him. An attendant would rush up to comfort Peter, who would be crying too hard to explain what had happened.

During meals some of the inmates were assigned seats and others were assigned sections. Michael had only been assigned a seat for the first six months and then had been able to choose whom he sat with in the ward. Now he had moved to the section for the semi-independent inmates who either worked on the farm or in town. There was a small table for the men and women who went into town every day to work, which was behind the table where the staff ate.

Lester brought in a group of inmates from the day room and when Michael looked up at him, he turned abruptly away. Peter waved. During lunch Harold rose from the table and without speaking began to rub his hands up and down the sides of his body and gyrate. Lester did not notice at first. Some of the men from the semi-independent table shouted, "Give us a show Harold. Give us a show."

Walter, who had gravy dripping from a corner of his mouth, jerked his head from side to side. "You're a bunch of fucking faggots, just like he is."

"Sour grapes because you never got to fuck him," Gus spit mash potatoes as he spoke and wiped his mouth with his shirt sleeve.

Walter made a show of getting up, but two older men about Walter's age put their hands on his shoulders as if to restrain him, and he settled back in his chair.

On the other side of the room two attendants had wrestled Harold to the floor after chasing him over the chairs, which he had pulled out to put an obstacle between himself and them. One of them put a full Nelson on him, but he pushed himself with his feet so that his head was under a table and his nose pushed against the floor board. Then he went limp.

"God, Jesus. It was never that hard to fuck him. God,

Jesus." Joe spoke in a monotone, breaking his words up into short phrases. "We should tell them attendants for him that he don't like it rough. And God, gives it up in a second." Joe was missing his left hand and he rested his elbow on the table. "It goes from this." His arm lay flat on the table. "To this." He snapped his forearm with the stub up. "In a second." Then he moved the end rhythmically back and forth. "Bong, bong, bong, bong." He had trouble keeping the rhythm of his speech up since he laughed in between the words.

"Not getting started he don't like it rough," Gus said, and about three other men chuckled.

Walter was unaware of the food dripping from his mouth and there was a large gravy stain on his shirt. "That fucking Injun's sick," Walter said and Joe bugged his eyes out like he was shocked.

"I would have scalped you by now but you been fucking bald so damn long." Joe patted his mouth the way Indians in Hollywood westerns did when they were on the war path.

"You been in the same ward as Harold. You learn anything, *duende*," Ernesto, who was called Ernie, asked Michael.

Michael stared at Ernesto and then his plate.

"What's this d*uende* shit?" Joe asked. "Speak fucking English."

"He looks like a *duende*. A spirit. He's got that skin white as soap, almost you can see through it. And he's little. Spooky. Curly black hair. And them big frog eyes that never seem to look at anything, but see everything. And he laughs like a bell. Maybe got wings." Ernesto chuckled.

"Sounds like a fairy to me," Gus said. Even Walter laughed.

Harold was hyperventilating and one of the attendants ran to the kitchen to get a paper bag to put over his head. The two attendants pulled Harold's stiff body away from the wall and one of them lifted his head and put the paper bag over it.

"Hey kid," Walter yelled. He raised his head back to look at Michael. The gaps in his teeth were filled with bits of chuck steak. Michael turned his eyes slightly away from Harold, but didn't look at Walter. "Kid, you a fairy?"

"Maybe." Michael nodded seriously, but didn't look at anyone in particular.

"He doesn't know what words mean. He just says them. He was rat boy, then parrot boy, now duende boy," Ernesto said. "He's faking like he gets it. That's what you do before you really get it. You fake like you get it, and if it works you keep doing it."

"And now Jesus Christ, he's a fairy boy." Joe said and the others laughed. "Maybe." He drawled the word out and chuckled.

"That's Harold. I know him," Michael said and turned back to where Harold still lay on the floor. Most of the other inmates were fascinated by the way Harold had escaped from the rules for a moment and now was lying on the floor curled up in a ball. As some carbon dioxide in the bag began to replace the excess oxygen in Harold's muscles, his arms and legs uncurled and his neck straightened out. One by one the heads turned back to their plates of peas, chuck steak, and mashed potatoes and gravy.

"Oh, oh, oh, I bet you fucking know him or know fucking him." It had been a while since Michael had spoken, so it took a while for the others to understand Joe's comment. He bobbed his head and laughed, and the other's joined him, though only half-heartedly.

"One day I have to get you on your stomach so I can see if you have wings." Joe said.

Part 10

Michael was too busy working with the men in the yard to see the people he knew from the day room. In the summer, they were on a different schedule from the others and had their meals at different times. He noticed the respect in people's voices when he told them that he was working with the semi-independents. "Yup, working with the men," he would say self-importantly, often as a greeting.

Joshua had spent a day on Indians once, choosing carefully the issues of *National Geographic* and *Life*. Michael seemed incapable of telling the difference between the archaeologists and the natives, or the missionaries and the Indians. Finally he had found an article on the painting and sculpture of the Old West with Indians in flowing headdresses mounted on spotted horses, or riding before a backdrop of bluffs with bloodthirsty looks in their eyes. Michael never understood. He identified anyone wearing colorful clothing as Indians, or any scene that was exotic and melodramatic. Joshua was baffled.

Michael struggled to find the common element that made Joe and the pictures from National Geographic and the Old West paintings all Indian. Perhaps Joe had another self that Michael couldn't see, an image in a mirror that lived behind russet, yellow and blue backgrounds and dressed in red and blue feathers, and rode horses with his teeth bared and his body thrust forward. Everything about Joe seemed slow and measured, even his swearing and his jokes.

Michael couldn't keep his eyes off Joe's arm. When they called him Indian, he tried to fit Joe into those romanticized pictures with their reddish brown and sandstone colored backgrounds. In his dreams Joe had eagle wings instead of ears and could fly.

"Feel it. Go on feel it. It's real, Jesus Christ." Joe stuck his arm out so fast that Michael jumped back. They were alone in the cattle stalls and Michael had stopped sweeping and stared at Joe's arm.

"Ain't fire and it ain't no weirder than you. Fucking bug-eyed rat boy. Dwindie-boy," he said mispronouncing the name Ernesto had given Michael.

Michael took the broom and ran out of the barn.

"Dwindie, come back here. I ain't going to do all the work."

In the glare of the sunlight, he could barely see the figure of Joe in the dusty darkness of the barn. "Come on."

"Come over here now." Joe extended his arm and rubbed Michael along the side with the stub. "Touch it."

Michael's white hand rested on the stub.

"Feel it. Go on. It ain't going to bite you." Joe's voice had changed and it was soft and deep.

Michael hadn't expected the uneven skin to be so soft and smooth. He could tell where the scar ended without looking at it since the skin became dryer and coarser.

"It's a nice arm," Michael said.

"Fucking right, it is," Joe said and laughed.

Michael pulled his hand away and moved back.

Joe had words that made people laugh, but when other people used them, no one laughed. If Joe said, "fuck, damn, Jesus, shit," people laughed. But when other people said them, it seemed no one laughed. Almost anything could happen, Joe could look at his food and say, "Damn," and people laughed, or Lester could walk up to them with his mouth already twitching like he was going to scold them, and Joe would say, "Holy shit," and a few of the men would snicker, sometimes break into real laughter.

Michael recognized some of the words. Maron used them. She had laughed some times. If she found an old card with a kitten on it playing with string, she would laugh and then begin to talk to the card, "Missie, missie. Kitty, kitty." But when Maron had said, "Jesus," or "Holy God," or "Christ," a heavy dark buzz had surrounded her that Michael could see. It was like the air around her had turned thick and brown.

Joe swore even when he was talking to himself. Usually he would mumble something, swear, and then chuckle a little.

"I like working with you," Joe said to Michael the first week that they had been paired up. "Know why?" Joe seemed to be talking to himself and Michael went on shoveling a dusty mix of grain and hay into the feed trough. "Because you don't talk. Hey Michael, hear that. You don't talk."

Michael stopped shoveling for a moment. "I can talk."

"You can, but you don't. Fuck that's great. Jesus, this loony bin is full of talkers. I feel like my goddam ears have been crapped in all day." By Joe's laugh, Michael could tell that he wasn't talking to him anymore. "Hey man, I could hear what you was saying if you fucking stopped yapping or crapping."

The next week Joe was sick, so he missed two days. When he came back, he didn't seem to notice Michael. By now Michael knew more or less what to do. He followed Joe around, not too close, and if Joe was throwing hay down on one side of the barn, Michael would throw it down to the stalls on the other side. It was hot and the sunlight that came through some of the cracks in the roof made the dust visible. Michael began to sneeze and wipe his face with his sleeve.

Joe walked behind a stack of bales. "Dwindie, come here."

To Michael it sounded like Joe was mumbling to himself. He continued to move the hay to the edge of the loft with the pitchfork and then push it over.

"Dwindie. You fucking deaf? Come here."

Michael lay the pitchfork down and walked to the edge of the bail. He didn't see Joe right away and when he did see him, because it was dark where he was, he could barely tell it was Joe. He was motioning with his hand for Michael to come closer, then he patted the hay next to him as if he were offering Michael a seat. Joe unzipped his pants and pulled his underwear down without pulling his pants down. He shook his head in a way that Michael had learned meant, "Come on, get with it." If Joe had started to feed the cattle, and Michael was still dawdling, he gave him that sign. It meant do what I'm doing.

Michael unzipped his pants and pushed his underwear down, but Joe reached over with both arms and managed to pull Michael's pants down to the knees. The hay was scratchy and Michael tried to pull them up again, but Joe stopped him. He reached over with his hand and grabbed Michael's left hand and placed it on his penis.

Michael watched himself get an erection. Joe laughed. "Hey, Dwindie, help me get this hay moved. The dust is killing me." Michael moved to get up, but Joe stopped him and pointed to his ear and then to below. "Just in case," he whispered and Michael understood that what Joe said wasn't for him, but the others if they were around.

When Joe touched his cock, Michael froze and then went limp and froze and went limp. His breathing followed the movements of Joe's arm. He thought maybe he should think about what he was doing. He saw Maron's face for a second on the stairs. She was coming up and he was naked and couldn't find his clothes. Then in a second his mind was blank, or what he saw was white light. He opened his eyes. Joe was biting his bottom lip in intense concentration.

Turning and seeing Michael, he asked, "Like it, huh?"

Joe stretched out in the hay and stroked himself. His handless arm moved between Michael's legs and across his cock. Now the arm moved with the same rapid motion he was using to stroke himself. Joe grabbed Michael's right hand and placed it on his cock. "I'm coming, I'm coming, I'm coming. Squeeze it. Jesus. Jesus. Jesus."

Michael touched it hesitantly. Joe was shaking and moving his head back and forth like some of the inmates who had fits. "Tighter. Shit." Then he threw his head back against the hay and grunted in spasms.

That night Michael awoke from a dream. His underwear

was wet and sticky. He had been with Joe in the hayloft and the sky had been the green of the walls of the day room. They had gone through a door that he had never seen before and on the other side was the upstairs of Maron's house, and as soon as they crossed the threshold they were naked. Maron was on her way up the stairs, but Joe made the stairs get narrow at the top and Maron had been stuck. Michael had wanted to go to the stairs to look at her. Joe held on to him, grabbing and pressing his body against him. Then he fell asleep and Michael lay on top of him, moving his hand over Joe's stomach and down to his pubic hair. Joe had turned to stone so he got up to look at the stairwell. Maron had grown two more arms and two more legs. She was in the middle of a web which she was still spinning. "Jesus Christ," she said and when he started to laugh, she spit at him and blinded him. That was when he awoke and for a few seconds, he couldn't move or see.

The curtains glowed dull yellow from the moonlight. The window was open and sporadically a breeze rushed across his bed. From the far end of the room he heard an incessant creaking. He lifted himself cautiously on an elbow and saw Walter's hand moving under the sheets. Walter's hand stopped and Michael heard him release a tight sigh in short gasps. Outside he heard crickets. Walter's snoring grew louder, and Michael got up to look out the window. He could see the cows standing in the pasture, like they were blocks you could move and stack. There was a breeze, but the trees were still. He was the only thing moving in the world.

After breakfast he met Joe standing by the barn door smiling. He approached with his eyes down, but looked up when he was next to the door. Joe pushed playfully against his shoulder and nodded. He signaled for Michael to follow him. They walked down behind the barn to a small creek that cut across the pasture and walked behind the willows that lined it until they came to the fence again. Michael stopped to pull off some burrs from his pant legs.

"Hey, we ain't done yet, Dwindie. Do that when we get back to the barn." Joe held up the bottom line of barbed wire fence and motioned for Michael to crawl under. Then Michael did the same for Joe. They were behind a large clump of spirea bushes and Joe held him back with his arm while he looked to see if anyone was around. Then he ran to another clump of bushes next to a small wooden building which served as the storage room for unwashed laundry. He followed Joe into the building. Michael caught his breath at the stench, but Joe pulled him along.

"This room ain't bad and it got a window. We keep the blinds down and let a little air in, see." He pushed Michael into the room and stood just outside the door for a second as if to listen.

Michael had sat up against the wall, like in the hayloft and pulled his pants down to his knees and began to masturbate. Joe grabbed his hand, "Wait, Dwindie. Not yet."

He watched Joe as he undressed in the light that came through the blinds. He seemed to no longer to be flesh and blood, but a moving image, and he looked bigger in the dark. He flexed his muscles and ran his hand over his chest and broad stomach to his penis.

"Don't tell shit to no one, Dwindie. Don't tell shit," Joe whispered. He pulled Michael up and bent down to lick his face and shoulders. "Jesus, to no one. And only do this with me. Understand. Only with me."

When they were getting dressed, Joe said, "Dwindie, you don't know shit and you ain't no natural like Harold."

"Yes," Michael said, not knowing what Joe was talking about.

"Fucking ain't."

For a moment among the darkness and the stench, he wanted to pound on Joe to see if he really was there, if anything had happened.

"We're going out separate. Wait and then come." Joe held up his hand like a policeman stopping traffic and then folded his fingers in to show Michael to come. He made the signal for stopping again and closed the door.

Michael listened to his footsteps, could hear the outer door creak shut. He closed his eyes and wanted to open them and see the upstairs of Maron's house, like it was in his dream. He felt powerful at times. By closing his eyes, he could make things disappear. They were still there when he opened his eyes, but it was in his power to make them disappear.

It was the first time he had been completely alone for several years. It had its own sound, a slight whirring, and the darkness of being alone was different. He felt himself spread out through the room. He could smell Joe on his hand. He put his hands over his mouth and nose and breathed in deeply.

Someone knocked at the outer door and Michael swept his clothes together with his arm and scrambled to the corner. The person turned the door knob, but did not open the door. Michael lifted himself up to the curtain and peered through one of the cracks. It was Lester. As soon as Lester turned onto the sidewalk to the main building, Michael ran for the door. He had his shoes and pants on, but carried his socks and shirt in his hands, and they fell as he ran. He picked them up and stumbled on to the fence. When he rolled under the fence, he noticed that he was missing a sock. It was by the spirea bushes. As he was putting it on behind the bush, he saw Harold run for the laundry building, and about twenty feet behind him came Lester.

Joe was up in the loft throwing hay into the stalls when he reached the barn. Thomas was looking up at him and shading his eyes from the fine dust that cascaded from the loft.

"You know he's new. Sometimes the new ones wander off. He told me he was going to take a leak. He don't even talk. One of them." Joe balanced the pitchfork and hay in the air. He seemed too intent on work to look at Thomas.

"Here he comes. Must of got lost looking for a place to pee." Joe didn't swear in front of Thomas.

Thomas inspected Michael. "You know, maybe you need more supervision."

"He works okay," Joe said and stomped across the loft under his burden to the other side to toss the hay.

"You can't wander off. Something might happen."

Michael fidgeted under Thomas's gaze.

"Ain't nothing to worry about. I'll show him where to pee next time, and how to if he don't know." Joe held the empty pitchfork in his hand and caught the bottom of his shirt with the stub of his arm and brought it up to wipe his forehead.

"That won't be necessary." Thomas smiled at Michael, deep furrows forming between his eyes and along the wide lines of his cheeks which had been dimples twenty years before. He reached out and placed a hand on Michael's shoulder. "You'll learn, won't you?"

Michael moved his arm up to place it on Thomas's waist, but before he could, Thomas had wheeled around and was walking towards the pasture.

"Shit, Dwindie, that was a fucking close one." Joe wiped his brow with his stub and scrunched up his face in mock terror. "Fuck."

"Get your ass going or you'll be fucking pulling weeds in the damn bean field." Joe barked.

As Michael was coming up the ladder to the loft, Joe stood right above it. "You'll learn won't you." Joe mocked Thomas's seriousness. Michael wondered if Thomas might have known.

"You liked it in the laundry room?" Joe asked and when Michael didn't answer, he said, "Where you got it wasn't no laundry room. Harold's got a fucking laundry room. Fucking day room." Joe laughed and slapped Michael playfully.

They had finished feeding the cattle, which was light work in the summer when they were grazing. Joe leaned against the barn door chewing on a strand of straw. He was covered with hay dust and had taken his shirt off to wipe himself off with a handkerchief. Joe handed him the handkerchief. "Take off your shirt and clean up."

"It hurt me," Michael said. It took Joe a second to catch on.

"Fucking hurt you. Your fucking damn eyes went white and I had to put a towel in your mouth to keep you from screaming when you was coming."

Michael handed the handkerchief back to Joe.

He was quiet and withdrawn all evening, but no one noticed since he only spoke in bursts and usually it made little sense. There was a bustle in the hall. Ralph, one of the psychotic patients who thought he was Raphael the arch-angel, had tried to fly from a window on the second floor and had broken a leg. Other patients were crowding at the window and a fight broke out on the women's ward between two women trying to get a better view. Michael stayed in his seat. He watched Joe shoulder and elbow his way to the front of one of the windows in the day room. Michael turned away when he felt that Joe was going to turn to look at him. For a minute he could feel his eyes on him, but when he looked up, Joe was pulling himself up on the mesh wires that covered the windows to get a better view.

"Fuck," Joe winced and a couple men behind him craned to look over his shoulder. "No fucking wings."

The men were still at the window when the eerie lights of the ambulance spun across the walls of the day room. To Michael it was miraculous.

The next day after breakfast, Joe was waiting for him by the barn door. Michael nodded as he walked past him. Several times during the morning, Joe called Michael over to help move bails or to clean up a stall. When Michael got there, Joe grabbed him, and Michael pulled away. The tension grew all day. Joe swore to himself and kicked a bale so that it fell down and almost broke the railings in one of the stalls. Thomas appeared as they were cleaning up the mess.

"I don't know why you stuck this kid to work with me. Look what happened." Joe kept his eyes on his work.

"What happened?" Thomas kicked a bunch of hay out of his way and moved over to Michael.

"Don't ask him. He don't talk. Don't make sense. It's all words." Joe spit in between phrases and Thomas frowned hopelessly.

"What happened?" Thomas planted himself next to Michael, who stopped working, but didn't look up.

"Fell," Michael said.

"He thinks you're dumb like you don't see nothing. It's all words," Joe said.

Tape 12 – Entry 7

Sometime I think that if I didn't have a body, I wouldn't be alone. Your body is what keeps you separate from everyone else. Before Joe, I was alone, but I didn't know it. After Joe, I knew it. Before I got old, I thought I would meet Joe again. We would be together, and then we would go off, but this invisible stretching stuff would keep us connected. People could walk through it and not know it. When I met someone at the bus station, I would think it would be like Joe. But a lot of times they never said a word to me and a moment later, they looked at me like I wasn't there. But the part I like most about sex is when my mind shuts down and I don't seem to have a body anymore. I have been swallowed by a huge monster and everyone in that stomach is part of the monster. Ernesto said that the universe was like an animal and not like an animal. For a while when we are human, we believe that we are looking at the stars and moon and sun. He said that we are just a pair of the universe's eyes and when we look at the stars, it is like looking at our toes. I asked him what universe meant and he said it meant everything.

The next day Michael was in the soy bean field pulling weeds. It was cool the first day and having to wear a hat, gloves and long-sleeve shirt didn't bother him. Some of the men yelled back and forth to each other, and the supervisor, a skinny blond man with metallic sunglasses and several gold teeth walked across the rows and screamed orders and insults. "Come on you fucking faggots, we ain't got all day. Gus, you can wait until you get to the end of the row to drink water."

The second day was in the upper eighties and Michael took off his hat as he was working and couldn't find it. He was afraid Mr. Winston, the foreman, would be angry, so at lunch time he stayed out in the field and Gus came looking for him.

"Where's your hat, kid? Mr. Winston, you asshole, is going to go ape shit if you ain't got it."

Michael went on pulling weeds.

"Hat, dummy, hat. Where is it? I'm hungry. Can't wait for ever. Dammit." Gus began walking across the rows, stopping to look as far as he could in both directions. Then he lost his look of attentiveness when he saw it and trudged to the right.

"It's a damn sorry hat they gave you, Dwindie." Gus yelled waving the hat over his head. It was the first time in a while that Michael had stood up. The fields went on for ever, flat and bleached dull green in the noon sun. He became dizzy and felt that the sky was pushing him down, and that the earth was moving slightly in waves. He turned slowly around. Wherever he looked, everything was the same. He could move ten feet and it would be as if he hadn't moved at all.

"Dwindie, the truck is this way." Gus waved for him to follow. When he caught up with Gus, he stopped again to look around. "Yeah," Gus said, "It's a damn big field and we got to do the whole fucking thing."

"What happened with you and Joe?" Gus asked.

"Don't know," Michael said. He had been thinking about Joe and him and the laundry room all morning. Every time he ran it through his mind, he got an erection and would try to work harder, keeping himself bent over the weeds so the others couldn't see it. Nonetheless, he had fallen behind the others and had heard their chatter slowly fade.

"He said he fucked you in the laundry room." Gus spoke matter-of-factly.

Michael stopped and turned slowly to look at the field. He could see a clump of stunted mulberry trees near the truck. The trees looked like they could be swallowed by the ground at any moment.

"No," Michael said.

"Wanted me to be the first one to cornhaul you, huh?" Gus laughed. Michael didn't answer. "I understand," he said and grabbed Michael's ass so hard that he screamed and ran two rows over.

"No." The tears in his eyes made the field twist and jump.

"Cut it out. They going to put you in the locked ward and fry your fucking brains." Gus had picked up the pace as they got near the truck.

"Where you two faggots been?" Winston asked.

"He lost his damn hat, Mr. Winston. Then he does this weird stuff like stopping to twirl around. Like he never seen a bean field in his life." Gus sat next to Walter, who handed him his plate.

"I thought you old *peterassed* was fucking him up the row." Winston took a long drag on his cigarette and moved his tongue around between his lips and teeth to clean his mouth. He laughed to himself in short spurts, as if he got the humor of his own comment little by little.

"No, Mr. Winston. Sure didn't do that. That scrawny little thing with the monkey hair on his lip." Gus was the only one still eating.

Walter had his hand in his mouth fishing for salami that was stuck between his remaining molars. Michael sat in the shade with his head in his hands. Ernesto fidgeted with his hands, then shot up as if someone had screamed at him, paced in front of the truck and then sat down again. His eyebrows seemed to become confused with the black frames of his glasses.

"Thanks, Gus, for getting him. He looks like a weird puppy." Winston turned on the truck radio. Some of the men who had been talking stopped so they could listen.

At breakfast Michael saw Joe, who was the same as always,

but didn't speak to Michael. There was some tension between the men who worked in the fields and the few who worked in the barn or on the grounds during the summer. When there was field work, the two groups sat at different ends of the table. Michael sat in the same place the first day he was in the field since he didn't know the rules, but the next morning when he got down for breakfast, the men who worked on the grounds and the barn clustered their chairs together at opposite ends so Michael had pushed a chair up so that he was sitting between the two groups.

He thought of Joe all the time. When he closed his eyes at night, he could follow every move Joe made the day they went to the laundry room, and in the fields he thought about what Joe had said or done at breakfast. He closed his eyes and imagined that Joe would be standing in front of him when he opened them. If he did it enough times, it would work.

"I think, Dwindie is stuck on you, Joe," Ernesto said while everyone was lined up for dinner. "When he don't seem to be watching you, he is. He sticks to you like fly paper."

"That's 'cause I'm the only one can understand him. It's just words. He don't mean to make no fucking sense," Joe explained.

Two weeks later they were at breakfast. It hadn't rained a drop since Michael started and the men who worked the fields were praying for a day off. "I'm going to beat the shit out of you if

it don't rain tonight, Dwindie. I mean really rain so we don't work."
Gus threatened Michael with his spoon. "I gave you lots of chances
to make it fucking rain. My patience is thin, Dwindie."

"I make it rain." This game had been going on for a week.
At first Michael was confused, but now he played along.

"Dwindie, the rain fairy. He going to go up to heaven and
piss on you, Gus." Ernesto no longer called Michael *duende*, but
the mispronounced version of the nickname he had given him.

"I don't give a damn about how he make it rain, just get me
out of them damn fields." A piece of a roll that Gus was stuffing in
his mouth flopped up and down when he talked.

"I don't see why they send you out there. You don't do no
damn work. Try the barn. That's hot. No days off. Rain don't help."
Joe glared at the others, then dropped his head over his bowl of
cereal.

There was silence. A couple of the men exchanged smirks.
Michael kept his eyes glued to Joe.

Joe looked up to see Gus twirling his finger next to his
head to show that Joe was crazy.

"Don't believe? Ask Dwindie. He couldn't take it." Joe faced
Michael who had been staring at him. Michael imagined that the
others were not really there, that Joe had moved the two of them
into a separate world, into a mirror or one of his dreams.

"It wasn't the work he couldn't take," Gus mumbled as he got up from the table. When Gus was safely by the door, he said it again much louder, "Wasn't the work he couldn't take. That old Indian dick of yours." Joe acted like he was going to get up and Gus burst open the double swinging door, and shot into the hall.

That night there were tornado warnings. When the lights went out in the yard, the room where they all slept became pitch dark. Some inmates in the other wards became frightened. A man escaped into the hall during the confusion, screaming, "We're damned. We have been cast into darkness. The flood has come. Close your eyes or prepare to turn to salt. Jesus hates all of us. Hail and brimstone. Hot and cold. Cold and hot."

Michael heard Joshua's voice, "I am in a nuthouse. My God, my God, look not so fierce on me! Adders and serpents, let me breathe a while! Ugly hell, gape not! Come not, Lucifer! I'll burn my books! Ah, Mephistopheles!"

The attendants who were moving patients from the wooden structure on the east side of the grounds to the cafeteria, which was brick and cement, passed the room of the semi-independent men. Several times the light of a flashlight shot under the inch-wide space below the door.

"Everyone away from the windows," a man's voice called and his footsteps were heard shuffling quickly up the hall.

He didn't know why he began to cry. He sobbed into the pillow which he clasped in his arms. He was aware of the moldy sweaty acrid smell of the pillow. The thunder shook him and he peered up in the lightning to see the bleary figures of the others sitting on benches at the other end of the room. Joe was still in his bed.

"Dwindie, get up." Ernesto's voice cracked as he spoke. Thunderstorms made him even more hyperactive and tense. He ran to Michael's bed and shook him by the shoulders. Michael twisted angrily loose.

"Close that door," the man with the flashlight barked as he ran up the hall again. "Away from the windows."

Ernesto hopped back to the other end of the room. "He's too scared to move," Ernesto said.

He heard Joshua scream again and Michael began to repeat like a mantra lines from one of Joshua's own poems which he had forced Michael to learn.

"*As we thread the needle's hole,*
we wade in memory's soul.
Its waters rush into the second's slot.
Sew a moment. It is and not.
It becomes us. Remake remake.
 We its threaded vessels break."

"Is he praying or something?" one of the ground workers asked.

"No, he ain't fucking praying. It's words." Joe turned his back to the men and pulled the covers over his shoulders. "It's a chant. He's fucking making it rain. And it hurts." He added the last sentence after a pause. For a while no one spoke and then Joe laughed.

The wind became more violent. Ernesto darted several times to Michael's bed to plead with him to get away from the window, then hopped back to the others. The last time he tripped on someone's shoes and fell. Everyone in the room laughed and Michael sat up in bed to see what had happened.

There was no field work the next day. The field workers were supposed to clean up the grounds. Several trees had fallen down during the storm and branches were scattered across the grounds.

"Why didn't you get out of bed?" Walter asked Joe the next morning.

He usually ignored Walter's questions, which were for the benefit of Thomas.

When Thomas had walked into the kitchen to get some coffee and talk to his cousin, who had just started working as a cook's helper, Joe turned to Walter. "Cause I had a fucking boner. I didn't want to make no one jealous."

Michael noticed Thomas's face in the small rectangular window of the swinging door. He was talking to someone, but watching all of them. He waved to Michael without stopping his conversation.

"We got to work in groups today. Dwindie, you go with Joe." Thomas usually didn't use nicknames.

Michael was at the barn before Joe. He thought that Joe was barely moving as he approached him, that he got slower and slower the closer he came. Joe walked past him. An hour before lunch, Joe left the barn and headed for the creek. He didn't look back until he got to the fence and when he saw Michael about thirty feet behind him, he smiled, but otherwise continued as if he didn't know Michael was there. When Michael reached the laundry storage room, Joe had already undressed and was lying on the floor.

Michael hesitated at the door. "Can I come in?"

"Shut the door." Joe's voice was strained.

In the dark Michael couldn't see anything. The blinds glowed a dull yellow. "Can I come in?" Joe said. "What a fucking question!" He laughed and Michael turned his head in Joe's direction.

Michael was balancing on one leg to get his pants off in the dark, when Joe swung his arm out and toppled him. He grabbed Michael as he fell and pulled him into him.

"You going to like it this time, Dwindie?" Joe said and pushed Michael's hands back. "Huh, Dwindie?"

Being restrained made Michael nervous. Words shot out of his mouth. "Jesus Christ. Hallow be thy name. Fucking damn."

Joe freed Michael's arms. Then he embraced him. "They don't understand you. They just words." Joe spoke absent-mindedly.

Michael felt like he had moved to where his body was at the point of capturing a ball of fire that moved just beyond his skin. It began to bathe him inwardly, but stopped. He seemed only partly conscious of what he was doing. What he had done only a minute ago was gone from his mind and that search to bring the fire under his skin, not even conscious, consumed him.

"Take it easy. Easy," Joe said and reached out to pin Michael's arms down.

The fire was inside him. He held his breath and streams of yellow light rushed through his mind. He closed his eyes and still saw the dark outline of Joe's face. Sweat dripped from Joe's chin, and Michael felt that the drops of Joe's sweat were passing through his own skin.

Then the fire was gone. As soon as it got inside him and flared up, it vanished, leaving his body in spasms. Joe was still rocking against him, now contorting and gritting his teeth. He looked like a stranger. Then he slumped over and Michael squirmed to breathe.

"You don't tell no one and you don't do this with no one. Understand?" Joe whispered.

"I understand," Michael said. He felt cold the moment that Joe rolled off of him.

Joe pulled a sheet out of a laundry bag and wiped himself off, then threw the sheet to Michael. He went through the hand gestures of the first day. Michael caught a glimpse of him along the creek. Joe had taken his boots and pants off and walked in the creek in his underwear. Michael wondered if Joe was going to follow the creek to the river and he lay in the tall grass to watch him. Michael saw Thomas at the back of the main building directing some men who were sawing branches into smaller pieces. Thomas suddenly broke off his instructions and headed for the barn. Michael had lost sight of Joe, so he hurried across the open field to make it to the barn before Thomas.

When he arrived to the side of the barn, he heard Joe and Thomas talking. "Field work done him good," Joe said.

"I don't know about that, Joe. They're some pretty foul-mouthed codgers. Winston let's them do what they want as long as he gets to yell at them once in a while." Thomas knit his brow and caught his lower lip with his teeth as if he were mulling something over. "Well, you know Gus."

Michael came around the edge of the barn as if he didn't know that Thomas was there. He walked by him.

"Dwindie, you want to work here? Get out of the field?" Joe said. Thomas looked sternly from Joe to Michael.

"Okay," Michael said.

Michael was back in the barn and he and Joe went to the laundry room three times a week. By now he couldn't imagine not going and yet while in the room, every branch that scraped against the window, or squirrel that leaped from a branch to the roof paralyzed him.

Joe got moody. He skipped days or stayed in bed sick, though Michael couldn't see anything wrong with him. "Joe," he would say and imagine that the word would materialize him before him. He closed his eyes, but when he opened them he couldn't see Joe, but he felt that Joe was there. "Just words. He don't mean nothing," he said and pictured Joe speaking.

Part 12

Joshua was sitting on the balcony of the main building with other inmates. It was a hot July day and when trucks passed beyond the wall they lifted a cloud of dust from the gravel road that floated over the wall and settled on the grass.

"Smoke signals from the other world," Joshua said pointing to the last dust cloud coming over the wall. "So hard to read and such filthy communication. Repeat after me, Mind Boy, 'Trucks sent clouds of dust, smoke signals to the walled city.'"

"Joe's my friend," Michael said. Joe had stayed in bed and Michael had done the morning chores already. He was thinking of going upstairs to see how Joe was, though he knew it was against rules to be upstairs during the day without permission.

"Oh, Parrot Boy, I have something for you to look at. I've been making a scrapbook of your life. You went national, you know." Joshua looked around self-importantly at the other people on the porch until he saw Lester. He leaned into Michael as if they were fellow conspirators. "Your name shared people's lips with stamps, wind, food, fine wine and genitalia. Stay here." Joshua shook himself when he stood up, as if he were shaking the dust off. He whispered briefly to Lester before shuffling nervously into the building.

"I hear they're sending you to town." Lester wasn't wearing his dentures. Michael thought he caught the scent of the laundry room and sniffed the air intently.

"I don't know," Michael said.

Joshua came back with a large album embossed with a cowboy on a horse. "Oh, I found out such interesting things. My favorite is the obituary. American gothic completely."

He had the sections indexed with labels attached with paper clips. "Here she is."

Maron Halvorsen, a minister's widow, who died in her home last Thursday, was born Maron Pikerup in Middelfart, Denmark in 1875.

"Oh, the obscenity of the foreign," Joshua interjected.

She came to this community in 1880, married Johan Halvorsen, a Danish missionary minister in 1907.

"Rather old for those days, I think."

They moved to parishes in Nebraska, South Dakota, North Dakota, and Saskatchewan where they ministered to the new settlers and to all in need of spiritual guidance. They were childless, but took Indian orphans into their home.

"A string of thankless Indian reservation brats. A euphemism for kitchen help."

Her beloved husband became ill in 1942 and had to

relinquish his duties as a minister. During this trying time, Mrs. Halvorson worked as a school teacher in Greensted, not far from Linder to support her and her husband. When he needed constant care in 1945, she quit her job and dedicated herself to his care. Pastor Halvorson died in 1948 in the loving company of his wife.

"You were already in the picture." Joshua's finger moved down the article and stopped when he read a line. "**For the last twelve years, she cared for her niece's child.**"

Michael was not paying attention. He thought he saw Joe pass behind the pines that formed a windbreak on the north side of the grounds.

But Joshua was oblivious to Michael, too. "That, that. . ." He slammed the album for effect. "A crow was your mother, so to speak. Parrot boy was raised by a crow and got his Bible babble from that same crow, the minister's holy widow."

Michael had jumped a little when Joshua slammed the book. Joshua's face was tight and his soft white cheeks bunched under his eyes.

"Is Joe upstairs?" Michael asked Lester.

"He's sick," Lester answered. "Must be."

Joshua opened the album to the page with Maron and Johan's wedding picture, which had taken up half of the second page of the local newspaper. Michael had seen it thousands of times over the kitchen table. There had been several copies upstairs which Maron had sent to relatives and then accumulated as she inherited the personal belongings no one else would take.

"Recognize her?" Joshua said and inspected Michael's face as he stuck the album in his face. "Your wicked stepmother."

At first Michael didn't look, still trying to catch sight of what he thought was Joe between the pine trees.

"Take it. Look at it. I have a friend of mine working on an article about you. Imagine. I will be in the article. All kinds of interviews. Mostly with people who should have known you were alive and didn't. Won't that be fascinating! How you didn't exist! Of course, I want her to interview you. Not ask you questions really, but listen to your marvelous abilities. Rat Boy, Parrot Boy, Mind Boy, and Duende." Joshua twitched with excitement. The soft folds of his neck trembled. He tapped his finger on the album to bring Michael's attention to it.

Joshua had expected Michael to gasp or to reel in confusion, but instead he looked at the picture without apparent emotion.

"Do you know who that is?" Joshua barked.

"It's a picture," Michael said. He moved to the edge of the porch. The kitchen had been in his dream that morning. He and

Joe had managed to trap Maron upstairs. Joe had made the stairs narrow and she couldn't get down. They had begun to make love on the kitchen rug. Joe had pushed the table in front of the door to the basement, so they wouldn't fall down the stairs. But Maron had begun to talk from the wedding picture on the wall and Joe had simply turned it around.

"Do you want to look at the rest?" Joshua asked.

"Not now," Michael said. He was concentrating on something else. Suddenly he walked back to Joshua. "Joshua in the Nuthouse, shut that book." He took the album out of Joshua's hands and shut it. "She's gone. Now Joe will come."

"And if you want to keep him away, open the book." Joshua was pleased. "The boy of the golden bough and his sympathetic magic. I will let you know when the woman is coming to observe you. And if you ever want to look at the book, you know I have it."

Many times during the day he had been sure that he had seen Joe. He followed Harold to the laundry room and thought he saw Joe coming along the creek. When he met Lester, who also seemed to be on his way to the laundry room, Lester turned and walked back. Then he called to Michael, "Dwindie, come here. Why aren't you at the barn? You're supposed to be at the barn."

When he reached the barn, he heard noises in the loft and hurried up to look for Joe, but what he found were two pigeons that flew away as soon as he poked his head above the floor of the loft. When Michael was younger and still spent his days in the day room, a volunteer came to read to the inmates and one of the books she had read was a collection of folk tales. He remembered one where the man could change himself into a coyote, an eagle, or look like another person. The pigeons flew to an electrical wire and perched there. The one puffed up its throat and sidled up to the other.

"Joe, Joe, turn back to a man. Joe," Michael called in the kind of voice that Thomas used when he was angry. The two pigeons flew off.

Michael didn't find Joe until supper. He looked sick. His eyes were red and he seemed dizzy.

"You look like you sick alright. Sick of partying," Gus yelled from the other end of the table.

"I hope you go to this same party," Joe said and slumped over the table.

"I hope I do too. Good ass and booze. Looks like Harold went to the same party." Walter shook trying to control his laughter and spit out the food in his mouth.

All the color left Joe's face, and he covered his mouth and flew out of his chair.

Thomas had been watching from the kitchen. "I don't

know who it was who helped Joe get that stuff. He's not telling. But if I find out."

Except for a few titters from Walter, the rest of the table was silent.

It was a week before Joe came back to work. He looked like his old self and acted like he enjoyed working again. After a few hours he told Michael he had to take a break, but that Michael should stay there because Thomas was coming to talk to them.

Joe got back a long time later and Thomas hadn't shown up. Joe smelled like he had been in the laundry room and every time their paths crossed in the barn, Michael sniffed the air.

"Hey Rat Boy, stop that, goddam it. I ain't no rat bait. That nose shit. Sniff, sniff. And you even got whiskers like a rat now." Joe pushed Michael against a bail of hay and his knees buckled and he fell back.

"God fucking dammit." Joe stepped past him without looking down.

The next day, Joe was friendlier at breakfast. Michael was at the barn first and waited at the door until he saw Joe coming down the driveway. He ducked inside and scrambled up to the loft.

"You fucking trying to do all the work yourself, Dwindie?" Joe called from below.

"No," Michael said. He stopped working to listen to what

Joe would do.

"You did it for those fucking days I was gone. We can all be replaced. I'm an Indian. I fucking know about being replaced and placed," Joe laughed. Michael's laughter went on for another minute before he realized that Joe had stopped.

"You don't know shit, Dwindie. To you it's all words. You're the fucking Parrot Boy like that asshole Joshua says. What a mouth he got."

Michael waited at the ladder up to the loft as Joe came up. "All words," Joe said and shook his head as he went by him.

When they began to clean stalls, Michael worked in the stall next to Joe. "Hey, Dwindie All Words, I'm still the boss here. You work on the other end. No reason for me to breathe the fucking dust you stir up and mine, too."

At break time, Joe said, "Thomas ain't coming today so you can follow me. But not close."

The pasture along the creek wasn't mowed. Mallow, ragweed, milkweed, thistles, wild bushes, and tall grass grew next to the willows. Michael was wearing a tank top and the grass and bushes scratched the skin on his arms and chest.

Joe had hung a sheet over the window so it was completely dark. Michael saw him when he opened the door, but as soon as he closed it, Joe disappeared. He stumbled to get his shoes and pants off, found the door with his hands and moved in the opposite direction to find Joe. He whispered his name. Joe's leg swung out and Michael fell hard on the floor. He moved his hands out to find Joe, and Joe grabbed one of them and brought Michael flat onto the floor.

It was not like the other times. He tried to move in towards Joe, but Joe forced his head down.

"Joe? Joe?" He wanted him to say something.

As Joe was coming, he spoke. "Dwindie, don't ever look for me. You fucking got me in a lot of trouble. Don't ever fucking look for me." Michael's pelvis and head hurt with every thrust. He lay for a while after Joe left. Michael's legs felt wobbly. He yanked the sheet from the window, so there was a little light. As he was pulling up his pants, he was startled by two raps on the window. He looked through the blinds and saw Joe walking to meet Harold. Then he saw Lester turn onto the path, but Lester stopped and rushed away when he saw Joe. Harold walked back towards Lester and Joe took off down the path to the creek. Michael picked up his boots and socks and ran out the door and down to the fence. He caught up with Joe at the creek.

"Dwindie, was that close or what? We better not go there for a while. Too fucking busy." Joe walked in front of him without turning back. When they reached the barn, Thomas was standing outside.

"You seen Lester. Harold was out for a walk and ran off and Lester went looking for him. Joshua and Peter got into a fight, and we can't find Lester. The new girl says she's leaving. She's not used to working here and they leave her alone." Thomas walked through the barn and Joe and Michael followed him a few feet behind.

"No, we wouldn't have seen him. We went down to the creek to cool our feet for our break. When it's hot and sticky, the dust seem to glue to my lungs."

Thomas nodded.

"It might be time to get Peter out of the ward. I think you could teach him to do chores. Michael's going to work in town next week." Thomas looked at Michael who was working on another stall.

"I knew that," Joe said. "But Peter ain't too smart."

"He might be more talkative," Thomas said.

"I ain't afraid of anyone talking." Joe's face became stony.

"But it might be nice to have someone to talk to." Thomas was unaware that Joe was being defensive.

Part 13

He had wondered when he first lived at the county home if there was anything beyond the fence, if it ended in a wall like the one at the front entrance or in endless bean fields. Joshua had made a point when they came across Chicago or New York or Los Angeles in *Life* to bring Michael to a window and point to the picture and then point in the direction of the city, waving his hand many times to show the distance. If Michael saw a picture of the Empire State Building or the Statue of Liberty, he would say New York, but Michael never understood why Joshua pointed from the porch. The world beyond the walls did not exist. The pictures were in the magazines in the day room. It was like his dreams. They were huge, but existed in his mind. Like mirrors they held people and things but stopped existing when he wasn't there.

With Joe he felt like his mind was failing him. If Joe was in his mind, he should have been able to make Joe do what he wanted. But in his dreams things happened that he didn't want to happen. He would be lying on Joe's chest in Johan's easy chair and his arm without a hand would begin to tremble and fingers would spring from it, and then when he looked away from the hand, Maron began to come out of Joe's body. Sometimes in his dreams he was with Joe in the laundry room and when they were going to leave, they looked out of the window and they were in the main building on the third floor. They would fall and get hurt if they left and Joe couldn't leave. He didn't want this dream to end. He would wake up exhausted and happy and look at Joe asleep several beds away.

At six in the morning Thomas came to pick Michael up. Gus and Walter were already down at breakfast. Michael sat silently with them until Thomas came to get him. He was supposed to eat breakfast at work.

Michael barely knew the other four men in the truck. They worked in town and two of them visited relatives on their days off. The other two were twin brothers who never talked to anyone other than themselves and were called Trotsky and Stalin, names they received from a fellow inmate, a farmer's wife who was paranoid schizophrenic whose fears focused on the Soviet Union of the thirties and forties. Few people knew who was supposed to be Trotsky and who was supposed to be Stalin, but since they were always together, it didn't seem important to know. Their real names were Hank and William.

Since it was his first day, he sat next to Thomas in the cab of the truck. He trusted Thomas. He looked through the small window in the back. Hank and William huddled together and whispered to each other. Once they both looked up at the same time and their heads knocked and they bowed their heads as if they had been chastised. Herman and Peterson, who was always called by his last name, sat in two different corners of the truck and only exchanged words when they got in the truck.

Thomas drove to a side entrance and got down to unlock the gate. Michael tried to follow him, but couldn't find a knob to turn. He pushed against the door, then saw Thomas turn towards the truck again. He recognized the bean field as they drove by and the clump of mulberry trees which were full of birds eating the dark blue fruit.

"Roll down your window," Thomas said.

Michael looked at him, then straight ahead, then in the back window at the others.

"Roll down your window," Thomas repeated.

Michael shrugged his shoulders. "I don't know." He took a deep breath. A couple hundred feet in front of them, a truck was creating a cloud of white dust as it rumbled down the crushed limestone road.

"Turn the handle." Thomas pointed to the crank for the window. You've never been in a car before? Course, you have. Maybe I got you all wrong, Dwindie."

Thomas glanced from the road for a second. "Not that one. That's for the door. Michael, don't touch that." Michael latched his hands under the edge of the seat and stared ahead at the whirling dust that they were approaching.

"This one. See? Okay good. Now turn it. Turn it some more. Good. Look at the window go down." Thomas sighed. A few minutes later they were in a thin cloud of white dust. "Close the window. Other way. Good."

They were in the thick of the cloud until Thomas passed the truck. Michael saw what he thought were the bean fields again. Were they really going anywhere?

Thomas said the same thing to each man that left the truck, "Work hard. Be ready at four."

"This is it, Dwindie. The All Day Bakery." Thomas climbed down from the truck and shut his door. "Come on, Michael." Michael pushed at the door and looked for a door knob. "Michael, hurry up."

"I don't know," Michael said. "I don't know this." He pushed at the door and shook his head.

"Okay, take it easy." Thomas opened his own door. "Take it easy. Watch. Push this one down and the door opens. Push it out with your shoulder."

He forgot how high off the ground the truck was and fell sideways when he pushed out. He sprung up and dusted himself off. "I don't know," he said.

"Now the parrot thing. Maybe this isn't a good idea." Thomas said under his breath as he brought Michael to the back door of the bakery and knocked twice.

A tall thin man in a white apron opened the door and nodded to Thomas. Michael nodded, too, but the man peered over him at Thomas. "Anything I should know about this one?"

"Try him, Les. I think he'll be okay. I don't know, though. He did okay in the barn. Not great in the field. He's the one I told you about last week." Thomas was apologetic, almost like some of the inmates when they talked to Mr. Mandment or Lester.

"We got some late summer weddings. I can't spend a lot of time with him. It would have been better if you had brought him next week. I'm not paying until he can do some work. You understand." The baker and Thomas had moved into the bakery with its shiny metal counters. A fan whined on low. Two women wearing hairnets and sleeveless dresses looked Michael over and then smirked to each other. One of them was sweating and she had pasty flour dust on her forehead.

Thomas waved and then was off. Michael was left standing by the entrance. The stainless steel oven formed a wall to his left. One of the women was cutting out rolls and the other had a large squirt bottle and was dripping icing on pastry. Her hips were huge and when she walked the two steps to the other counter so she could fill the bottle again with icing, her massive legs seemed to get into each other's way.

No one in the bakery bothered to look over at him. He knew this was supposed to be a big step out into the world, though he wasn't sure what that meant. His clothes had been carefully picked by Thomas from the basement where clothing donations were kept. Whoever had donated the shoes, which were a size too big for Michael, left small blobs of polish which had cracked into deep veins. The toe on the left shoe was dented.

"Maureen, could you take a minute and ask that guy what his name is." Les came to the back again after attending to a customer. Maureen scrunched her lips up in a show of annoyance and put the pastry knife down which she was using. Roxanne, the woman with the squirt bottle, rolled her eyes. Les seemed oblivious to all of this and darted back into the shop where the temperature was ten degrees cooler.

"Your name? What's your name?" Maureen opened her mouth wide and repeated the question, nodding her head to mark the separation between words. Her voice seemed weighted by the heat from the bakery.

Michael was confused at first. What name was he supposed to use here?

"You got a name?" Roxanne pointed her squirt bottle at

him.

Maureen shook her head and walked back to the counter where she was working.

"He's just another body making heat in the kitchen," Roxanne said and wiped her forehead with the skirt of her apron, clearing a path through the whitened sweat.

"Les thinks he's going to get some cheap work. God, he bugs me standing there like a road sign." Roxanne navigated her body around the counter. She picked up a large measuring cup. "Get me some flour, No Name." She thrust the measuring cup out to Michael who grabbed it. "Over there."

"Roxy, he don't know what you want. Show him. He looks like a deer in headlights. This is the spookiest one we ever got from them." Maureen had moved to a metal folding chair next to the door to the shop and was taking a cigarette break.

Roxanne moved to a large tin that held the flour and took off the lid. "Scoop. Fill that." She pointed to the cup and the tin and to Michael and pointed again. Michael put the measuring cup into the tin and filled the cup.

"Bring it to my table, No Name." Roxanne rocked her way back to the table. "Bring it here."

Michael followed her cautiously. He was dwarfed by her and in the narrow confines of the kitchen, she blocked his passage.

When she reached the counter and turned back to her work, he set the cup down.

"Mix the icing so it don't get crusty on top," she said and pointed to the bucket of icing behind her. Her hands twirled in the air to demonstrate what she wanted.

"Better tell him to use the spoon and not his hands," Maureen said from where she sat. Michael had already grabbed the spoon and was stirring carefully.

"You speak? No name, you speak?" Roxanne barked over her shoulder at Michael.

He seemed not to understand.

"No," Roxanne said answering her own question.

"Just words. Only words," Michael said.

Roxanne cackled and Maureen, who was snubbing out her cigarette in a glass ashtray, asked, "What he say?"

"I asked him if he spoke and he said, 'Only words.' What else would you speak?" Roxanne handed Michael the squirt bottle to fill up.

"I don't mean nothing," Michael said to explain.

"Guess not," Roxanne said. "Put that pan back on the rack and get that one for me," Roxanne pointed to a tall cart with ten racks of pastry pans.

Maureen opened the oven and put the pastry she had cut

inside. Michael felt the wave of heat ripple through the room. The sweat dripped more quickly from Roxanne's billowing upper arms.

Maureen waved Michael over to one of the three mixers. "Fill this mixer with flour up to here." She dipped her finger into a large bucket of lard that stood open on the counter and marked a spot on the inside of the huge mixer bowl.

"I'm done," Michael said a few minutes later and Maureen came over to inspect.

"Okay," she said. "No Name, what's your name?" Roxanne looked up and smiled at Maureen.

"No Name. My name is No Name," Michael said.

Both women chuckled. "But do you have another name, No Name. What do we call you for short, No? And how do you know if I'm saying no or talking to you? Tell me that." Maureen swung the oven open again and whisked the pastry pans onto a rack of the cart.

"Call him Known or Gnome for short." Roxanne suggested.

"No Name, also known as Known."

"I have lots of names," Michael said in his own defense.

"To play it safe," Maureen said, "what does Thomas call you?"

"He calls me Michael sometimes and he calls me Dwindie sometimes."

"Is Dwindie your last name?" Roxanne asked.

"I think so," Michael said.

The women forgot him again as they chatted. He sat on the chair where Maureen had smoked her cigarette.

Maureen poured water, salt, sugar and yeast into the mixer. Michael stepped cautiously on the tips of his big shoes until he was a few feet behind her.

"Make him stand back." Roxanne called.

Maureen stuck out her arm and pushed Michael back about a foot. The dough twisted into the blades of the mixer and wrapped and unwrapped. He tried to look beyond Maureen, but when she whirled around to face him and pointed her face and her bony shoulders toward him, he backed up. She flipped a switch without turning completely around and the machine stopped.

During a break Maureen and Roxanne huddled together on two folding chairs and made a list of what Michael could do. Les came back and looked at his watch.

"Forget the time?" Maureen asked.

"There's a reason they call them breaks," Les said.

"Is there a reason they call you Les?" Maureen chuckled and glanced over to Roxanne.

"Oh you know, Les, his name is Michael." Roxanne attempted to stop the bickering between Maureen and Les since she wanted to leave early and if Les was in a bad mood he would dock her.

"And his last name might be Dwindie. He ain't sure," Maureen said.

The bell over the door in the shop rang and Les wiped his sweaty hands on a towel that hung from a nail on the wall and rushed off.

When he returned to the Home, he followed Thomas around, stopping three or four feet behind him if Thomas stopped to talk to someone.

"You can go and do whatever you want, Michael. You're done for the day," Thomas said.

"Oh, okay," Michael said, but did not move.

He heard Thomas and Mr. Mandment discussing whether he should be moved to the rooms where the men who worked in town lived. Thomas glanced uncomfortably at Michael several times and nodded for him to move on. It was common for Mr. Mandment to discuss inmates' cases in front of them as if they were deaf or spoke another language.

"One change at a time," Thomas said.

"If it's going to upset them, it's my opinion that it should be done all at once." Mr. Mandment had been caught on his way into the office and opened the door to show Thomas that he was in a hurry.

Well, I think we should test Peter first," Thomas knew that to be too assertive was the only thing that could make Mr. Mandment make a decision.

"I'm in a hurry. You decide." Mr. Mandment closed the door and Thomas waited until he heard the lock turn.

"You heard." Thomas told Michael.

That night he saw Roxanne and Maureen captured in a white light that twisted like dough in the blades of the mixer. Roxanne's own light was pink but he couldn't see it in the dream, but he knew it was pink. Maureen's was green. He and Joe lay in the cellar. Maron opened the door and Michael tried to hide Joe behind the tatters of the blanket. Maron seemed to have seen him until Roxanne and Maureen spun in front of her in the twisting white light. She no longer noticed him and Joe, but was fascinated by the light. He and Joe laughed. He thought he woke up and saw Joe laughing in his bed. For a long time he wondered if he were dreaming or really awake or if he and Joe dreamed together.

Maureen hadn't arrived yet and Roxanne was sitting on a bench that seemed to fit her build better than the metal folding chairs. She tapped the place next to her on the bench and Michael sat next to her. She reached forward straining until she could grab the list on the counter.

"The first thing you do when you get here is sweep. You know how to sweep?" Roxanne studied the list.

"That means you sweep and you don't get in the way. You sweep in the morning and before you go home."

"I swept the barn," Michael interjected and Roxanne mulled this over as if it were an unexpected problem.

He looked at her and noticed the fine red lines on her cheeks, her scalp below the thin smooth helmet of red hair sprayed into place. She raised a hand to scratch her neck and the folds of flesh hanging from her upper arm swayed. Her hair had been covered the previous morning by the paper hat that formed a bubble over her hair. He was looking through her layers. She was revealing herself. He could see the pink light around her clearly. It did not shine, but clung to her wooly and tingling.

"Maureen and me can't be running around all day. I told Les what my doctor said. He knows. You have to be my legs. We tried to write it down yesterday, but it got too messy and we thought we would just put it like you were our legs for the time being. If it works out, then you'll know." Roxanne shifted her weight on the bench before she pulled herself up.

"Just be my legs," Roxanne said again and seemed almost

winded by the time she got to the counter where Les had left rolls to be frosted. She circled around to look at Michael. "You know what I mean. If I need something, run and get it. That's what I mean about be my legs."

She showed Michael how to mix the powdered sugar, vanilla and water, then had him put flour in the mixers. Les ran to the back a few times and Michael noticed how Roxanne heaved when he came in, but acted too busy to pay any attention to him. Michael acted the same way towards Les.

Maureen arrived with a bandage around her head, talking as she walked in. "It's nothing. I asked the doctor to make the bandage big so I could use it to stuff in Les's trap if he says something."

"I told Mickie he could be our legs," Roxanne said. Her pink light had disappeared as beads of sweat formed on her upper lip.

Maureen's head jerked like a pigeon's as she took in the room. "Mixers ready?" No one answered and she walked over to inspect them. She showed Michael how much water to put in, using sign language as if he were deaf.

"What did Doc Lader say?" Roxanne took a deep breath and the squirt bottle fell off the counter onto the floor shooting a line of frosting on impact.

"He said it was a growth and not a tumor."

"Huh?" Roxanne said suspiciously. "Mickie, come clean this up and pick the squirter up for me."

He handed her the squirt bottle and knelt down next to her legs with a damp rag which Maureen had tossed on the floor.

"I ain't moving until you get it cleaned up. All I need is to stick to the floor."

The skin on Roxanne's legs was bumpy and blue jagged lines bulged around the bumps. Next to her skirt, he could smell talc and cologne. Her tennis shoes were scuffed and her ankles hung over the edges of the tops of them. He felt a large drop of sweat land on the back of his neck. Another one hit the floor and it exploded in a small pink light.

Maureen switched on the mixers and Michael sprung up to watch the mixer blades.

It'll break your arm like a twig." Maureen mimed breaking a twig, then tapped Michael on the arm and pointed to the mixer blades. She nodded seriously.

During the morning, he heard Vera repeat the instructions that Maureen gave him. He felt Vera's everywhere. Roxanne hardly spoke, but dropped the squirt bottle again, this time when it was full and it shot over her shoes.

"If Abe saw that you had some kid up your skirt." Maureen

was taking a cigarette break. "You have to wash them tennis shoes. Let him try to wipe them."

Maureen had the green light around her when she sat down to smoke a cigarette. The bandaged part of her face had no light. Looking at her made Michael nervous and he kept his eyes on his work or the mixers.

"How many cakes I got to ice?" Roxanne asked as Les rushed into the kitchen.

"Where's the kid?" Les shouted as if the mixers were still on.

Between Roxanne's legs," Maureen said.

"Did they leave any of your face?" Les showed his teeth and pulled his shoulders in and his head back as if he were a bad actor in a horror movie.

"Doctor told me not to come in to work, but you know me. Work is work."

"The kid?" Les asked again.

"Like I told you, between Roxy's legs."

He didn't answer, but was about to run back to the front.

"Some icing fell on the floor. He's cleaning it up," Maureen took a long drag on her cigarette.

Les leaned over the counter and peered down at Michael.

"Make sure he washes his hands," Les said and was gone

again.

The women left and Les was locking up the front, covering trays and putting them into the refrigerator in the back. Michael swept carefully around the legs of the counters, pushing the pile of dust and flour around as if it were alive and fragile.

"No, sweep everything to the center. To the center." Les confusingly mimed the word center. "It's not a game. Sweep everything to here. Understand? Here."

He ran off again and Michael followed his instructions. He came back to lead Michael into the front of the shop. He outlined the area behind the counter with his hand, "This area, sweep everything here. Then pick it up with the dust pan." He strode dramatically to the area in front of the counter and repeated himself. "Until you get some decent clothes and learn how to shave, I don't want you out here until closing. Okay. Got that?"

Michael nodded with his head down the way Roxanne did when Les talked to her.

"Say, yes, sir. When I tell you to do something, say, yes, sir." He spoke as if Michael were hard of hearing.

Michael nodded again.

"I just told you to do something. Tell me, what are you supposed to say?"

Michael looked up into the air as if he were thinking.

"Can you figure it out?" Les had consolidated several trays and was stacking the empty ones. He stopped briefly and looked in exasperation at Michael.

"Yes, sir," Michael said.

Les shot to the back room with the trays. "Tomorrow you can wash these before you go."

"Yes, sir."

Les stood looking at his watch as Michael put the broom and dust pan away. "I got to go. You can wait out here for Thomas," Les said.

The back of the bakery faced an alley with a creek on the other side that had been straightened into a gully. A building with a butcher and a meat locker stood twenty yards away and flies swarmed up and down the alley. Michael didn't recognize the smell of rotting meat and was afraid of the two stray dogs that barked at him when he came out the back door.

"Don't go nowhere. Thomas will be here in half an hour." Les locked the door without even glancing at Michael.

"Yes, sir."

Les got into a shiny red car with large fenders and pulled slowly into the alley from the parking spot next to the bakery and drove off.

The smell of the meat locker offal made him sick to his

stomach and he sat on the cement step behind the bakery and put his head between his knees. One of the dogs scurried lightly by with a bone in its mouth, and then took off running as soon as it was past him. Michael looked up when he heard the dog scattering gravel as it darted past. The other dog barked as it turned back to the weeded lot.

He put his head back down. When he looked up again, two small boys were frozen in their tracks ten feet away from him. They ran back past the meat locker. The dog, which had been sniffing through the lot, barked and chased them to the end of the alley.

Michael stood up. His pants were sweaty. He felt nauseous and his head hurt from sitting in the sun. He knocked at the door to the bakery. He went to the side where the car had been parked. A dark green picket fence prevented him from going around to the front of the building. At that moment Thomas drove up.

When he went to the door of the passenger's seat, Thomas yelled through the window, "I got some stuff up here. Get in the back with the rest, Michael."

He bent over so he lay with his torso on the bed of the truck and grabbed onto Peterson's pant leg to leverage himself and swing the rest of his body into the back.

"That ain't how you do it," Peterson said and kicked at him.

Hank and William communicated like two bugs. Their miniature close-cropped heads had a stone-like passivity, as if they had been shocked by lighting and captured for eternity in the second before surprise. Herman snored in the far corner.

Thomas glanced back through the back window and slammed his fist against the back wall of the cab just as Michael was swinging his legs up into the bed of the truck.

The heat made him feel dizzy. Peterson scooted over almost next to Herman.

"Shut up," Herman said without opening his eyes.

Michael saw Thomas's head in the window again. He stretched out his arm to steady himself against the bench as the truck took off. His clothes were drenched with sweat and the breeze that shot through the back of the truck gave him chills. He put his head between his knees and felt that the truck was spinning down the road. He looked at the road behind them. The dust billowed like clouds in a dream. Luckily he was facing the back of the truck when he threw up.

"Goddam," Peterson said and acted as if he would kick Michael again.

When they got out, Thomas asked what happened. Michael vaguely heard Peterson explain. The twins shrugged their shoulders in alternate tempo so they looked like a two piston engine.

"The kid was sitting out in the sun when we got there, wasn't used to the back, so he pukes." Herman walked past everyone.

"He don't know nothing about nothing," Peterson said. "He was asleep like always and then he thinks he knows."

The halls flickered with their florescent lights. As he walked by the fans, the whiz and clatter filled his mind and he forgot his nausea. He imagined himself on a large ball. When he reached the top he was next to a fan and then the ball would turn so he was at the bottom between the fans and climb again until it reached the next fan. The hall was not a straight line, but made of circles. It had no glow other than the nervous light on the ceiling. He stood outside the day room to listen, but all he heard was mumbling interrupted by brief moments of silence.

The fans had all been moved to one side of the day room. The curtains had been drawn against the sun. Michael closed the door behind him, but no one turned to look at him. They were all gathered around a television which stood against the farthest wall.

Joshua placed a magazine on his chair and peered around to threaten anyone who might think of taking it. He shuffled in Michael's direction and then made several sharp movements with his hand towards his chest. "Look at what the Rotary gave us. Finally the outside world. The real world. In movement. Isn't Loretta Young beautiful?" He stretched his arm out in the direction of the television and let his hand hang at the wrist.

"Faggot," Walter said, spitting near Joshua.

Michael wandered toward the box.

"Sit down. Sit down. Sit down." Voices shouted over each other.

"On the floor in front of me." Joshua tripped over to his seat and picked the magazine up and held it to his chest.

Michael sat a few feet from the set, looking up at it. He raised his hand and could vaguely see it reflected in the set.

"Put your hand down. Hey."

The images spoke. It must mean something. Everyone was looking at the box. Maybe it would give them a message. He expected to see people he knew, like in his dreams, but everyone he saw was new and looked like no one he had ever seen before. The men dressed like Mr. Mandmant, but didn't look like him. They all looked sharp and clear, though they had no color. And they were so tiny, but the buildings and everything else were tiny, like the paintings in the cafeteria.

He noticed Joe sitting only a few chairs away staring at the set. The light made his features look starker. When Michael looked at him again, his head had fallen and he was snoring softly. No one else seemed to notice.

He couldn't follow what was happening. The people in this funny mirror were one place and then suddenly they were someplace else. It was like his dreams that way. He walked to the door and turned to look at the others still sitting with their backs toward him. He looked at Joe whose head bobbed slowly up and down as he breathed. The sound from the television became louder for a minute and there were a few moments of music and voices again. Joe's head snapped up.

At supper Joe pushed his food away. "Shit. You have to be more hungrier than me to eat this shit. Turd food. Bear-turd food." He looked over at Michael and then away.

"What was that thing? That box?" Michael asked. No one looked up from their plates.

Joe turned slightly towards Michael. "Shit, you don't know what a television is? It's a machine. You didn't know it was a machine?" He and a few others chuckled.

"How does it work?" Michael asked.

"Technology, I think," said Gus. "Everything works on technology. Soon the whole world is going to be technology."

"How's your job?" Gus seemed to be more interested in playing with his mashed potatoes than with getting an answer.

"I like it," Michael said.

"What you do?" Peter didn't look up from his plate.

"I'm a baker," Michael said.

"What do bakers do? What do you do?" Peter raised his head waiting for the answer. Michael didn't like Peter asking him questions. It meant that Peter was on the inside and he was on the outside.

"I sweep floors," Michael said and everyone chuckled except for Peter.

"I'm Roxanne and Maureen's legs, too."

Some of the men were shaking with laughter. Michael heard them and didn't look up. He felt as if he had left the county farm for only a few days and it had changed. He was no longer a part of it. Someone or something had taken whatever space he had filled while he was gone.

"How much of their legs are you?" Gus could hardly control his laughing.

Michael looked up to answer. "Well, today Maureen said. . ."

Before he could finish Gus shouted over him, "Up to their pussies, too. Bet their husband like that. Trade in two old dames for a nice fresh ass like yours."

A few of the men doubled over. Walter had tried to glare around the table, but finally dropped his head into his hands to laugh. Peter slammed his knife against the table and hacked out a deafening false guffaw. Lester and several of the attendants appeared near the table.

What's so funny?" Lester demanded.

"It's that Dwindie says he's these old dame's. . ."Gus was unable to finish. He pushed his plate away and folded his arms on the table and lay his head down. Lester's presence made several of the older men try to control their laughing. Joe had gotten the hiccoughs.

Michael suddenly realized that no one was sitting next to him. Peter, who had been at his table, had left.

In the hallway he ran into Joe. "Do you need someone in the barn? I can still sweep." Michael tried to look Joe in the eye. "I can do everything I did before."

"Barn's good. I been sick. Gus's been there. I'm going back tomorrow."

Michael finally caught Joe's eyes. "It won't hurt anymore. I know it."

Joe nodded as if he were considering this and walked away.

In the day room he leafed through magazines. There was a *Life* cover with Queen Elizabeth's trip to India and he studied the jeweled elephant and the clothing.

Joshua shuffled up behind him and leaned over the back of

the chair. "Those are Indians. Real ones. Not Americans. Hindu. Joe's not real, you know."

"He's not?" Michael turned the page.

"No," Joshua snapped. "Nothing in this place is real. The television is as close as we get and they turn it off when the news is on. The world is spinning away from us. We are being left on this island. I am going to leave here a complete idiot. Like you or Peter. We have been abandoned on this farm that is spinning into the Van Allen Belt."

"We have?" Michael couldn't concentrate on Joshua's words. He stood up slowly and walked away from him. He looked for Joe in the hall. A new night attendant, was accompanying Harold and some others to the day room. Harold winked at Michael and then shot off to the back stairway.

"Harold, I'm warning you, come back here or you'll be in the locked ward." The attendant sounded more weary than angry. By the time he turned around to look where Harold had gone, he had disappeared.

Michael waited until the attendant had led the rest of the inmates into the day room and then went after Harold. He thought he heard more than one pair of footsteps and when he reached the upper floor where the fire escape began, he heard the floor creaking in several corners. He stopped to listen. The creaking ceased as if it were watching him.

"Harold," he whispered.

Harold panted loudly. Michael inched towards him, not really able to see much until he turned the corner to the small hall leading to the fire escape, where light came in a porthole window next to the double doors. Harold was naked, his body arched on the balls of his feet and his shoulders.

"Baby, baby, baby," he said in a strange excited voice, then laughed. "Do me, bitch. Fucking do me." His voice was angry. "He don't mean nothing." He said changing voices again and grunting in staccato. Harold seemed unaware that Michael was there.

Michael heard footsteps behind him and when he turned around, he saw Joe's stub arm disappearing into the darkness, but without the body. He was close enough to Harold so Harold's leg rubbed up against him. Michael kneeled next to him and placed his hand on Harold's thigh, which momentarily froze.

"Kansas City, there's some pretty little women there and I'm going to get me one." Harold twisted his head back and forth and thrust his pelvis in and out as he sang.

Joe was sitting on the floor at the other end of the hall to the fire escape door. He was naked, but it was hard to see anything since his image was being pulled in and out of darkness, like it did in the laundry room when the sheet was over the blinds.

"Joe," Michael called and Joe melted into the floor.

"He don't mean nothing," Harold said and lay perfectly still. For a second he saw Joe lying in front of him. Then it was Harold again. Michael undressed. He moved his hands over Harold who was warm and slick from sweat. Joe was there somewhere watching them. When he stood up, Joe's legs would swing out and he would fall. It would be just like the last time. The floor would vanish and they would fall to the cellar. He would be pinned to the floor, become part of Joe that only moved when Joe wanted it to. His dreams would stop. The world would not change. He would not have to always be the whole, to be everything. He could be a part of something.

Harold maneuvered under him and now Michael was inside him. His mind shut off. As soon as he came, it seemed like electricity shot through his penis and he tried to pull himself out of Harold, but Harold held him tight. Michael whimpered, then became aware of the creaking and banging as Harold thrust and relaxed. Michael pushed him away.

At the top of the stairs he stopped to listen, then hurried down the first flight of stairs. There was a long winding passage that would take him to the semi-independent men's bedroom. He heard Harold cry out as he ejaculated. He stopped and looked up and down the hall. The walls pulsed with swirling red light. The phosphorescent tubes raced back and forth across the ceiling. He knew Joe was in the small alcove. He could smell him and hear him breathing. He turned his head to the wall when he passed the alcove so he wouldn't look at him.

The red light stopped as soon as he entered the bedroom. No one was there. He smelled Joe's pillow and sensed that Joe was somewhere, in a dream or a mirror. He walked down to the day room. Joe was sleeping in front of the television.

"Harold's going to end up on the locked ward," The new attendant said to Michael and Michael blushed.

"Lord knows what he could be doing. Burn the place down. This old building is no place to play hide and seek. If anyone else acted the way he did, they would be in the locked ward a long time ago." The attendant thought that Michael was not paying attention to him, so began to mumble.

"Hey, Dwindie." Ernesto had come out of no where. "Don't let them get to you. Them guys laugh at nothing. Remember, easy, easy." Ernesto had new black framed glasses that made his head look smaller. His eyes became wavy shifting brown blobs behind the lenses. He took them off and closed his eyes as if he were resting. He opened his eyes and his face relaxed.

"I worked with Joe once in the barn for a long time. The longest of anyone. I know everything. Peter's in the barn now.

You knew that. He replaced you. Gus replaced me. A kid named Darwin replaced him. No one stays long in the barn anymore. Not after me."

"Duende, duende," Joshua shouted from the far corner where it seemed that he had just awakened. Ernesto put his glasses on and walked away.

"I talked to Bernice. My friend Bernice who is doing the article about you. She's doing a transformation angle. Rebirth. What love and care can do, how it turned you around! I'm to be part of it. Mr. Mandment is all for it since it makes him look good. Oh, to be in the world again." Joshua held a letter up in front of Michael's face. "She might turn it into a book. Magazine articles, a week, maybe a month. Books are forever. The pen is mightier than the sword." Joshua had a Manilla envelope from which he had taken the letter. He pulled out a small notebook and a pencil.

"Now to make an appointment. What's your schedule? When do you work?"

"At the bakery."

"Oh, yes, I know that. But when. What day don't you work? Sundays? Planning is so important for a big project like this." Joshua wrote frantically in the notebook. "Optimize her visit. I know so much about you. So much. Not all fit for print. And probably I do not know all that's not fit. Thank God. But primary sources are a must. Ground breaking journalism." Joshua searched in the envelope for a pencil sharpener, but then gnawed at the end of the pencil, spitting out the small pieces of wood he chewed off.

"Well, I don't know. Ask Thomas. Thomas takes me. He knows when he takes me."

Ernesto was watching them from the other side of the room. The lenses of his glasses glinted insistently.

"Excellent source. Excellent." Joshua shut the notebook, clutched the envelope and the notebook to his chest and trotted off.

"Thomas, Thomas," Michael shouted, and Joshua's trot added a nervous skip.

Harold was in his dream that night but he wore a black suit like the men on television or some of the men in *Life* and he spoke in long never-ending sentences. Michael could not escape him. Joe was behind Michael, but as soon as he turned around, he vanished and all that Michael ever saw was the arm disappearing. Joe would speak when he was invisible.

"You went up them stairs. He don't mean nothing. You don't mean nothing."

Harold chattered in the background and Joe's words were more a rhythm than distinct sound.

"Don't tell no one and don't do this with nobody else. Don't tell no one and don't do this with nobody else."

Part 14

He woke up once during the night and tried not to fall asleep again because he knew he would return to the dream, but eventually he could not stay awake and it was just as he had feared. Harold was wearing the suit and was naked at the same time. He knew that Joe only saw Harold naked. When Michael tried to make Harold shut up, he reached out to put his hand over his mouth, but his hand grabbed Harold's cock. Joe dissolved into darkness and reappeared vibrating like the wings of a wasp.

He lay in bed with his eyes open. The red light of sunrise trembled on the blinds. His body felt as if he had been in a struggle all night. No one else in the room moved for several minutes and then Walter coughed and wheezed at the far end of the room. A few men grunted as they began to wake up. Three beds away, Joe sighed, almost the way he did in the laundry room.

Tape 20 – Entry 2

You like someone so much that when you stop liking them, it makes you empty. You can forget about it. But when you are with someone else, it reminds you that you are empty. Maybe not in the minute that you are doing it. After you do it, then you remember that emptiness. And it seems like that emptiness always has been there.

After Thomas let him off, he stood for a few moments to look at the lot behind the meat locker where he had seen the dogs the day before. When he knocked on the back door to the bakery, Les let him in, and immediately ran out of the door, leaving Michael standing in the dark bakery. The women were not there.

"Shit, I thought I could catch him," Les said to no one. He noticed Michael again.

"Abe died, Maureen's husband. There's no work today. I'll take you back. Do you know where Thomas goes next?" Les looked at him intently, as if he could improve communication that way.

Michael took a deep breath and thought. "No, I don't think so."

Les held the door for Michael until he had walked out of the bakery again.

"Get in the car."

He drove Michael back to the county farm. On the ride Les swore as he pushed buttons to change the radio station. He searched for his cigarettes, reaching in front of Michael to see if they had slid across the dashboard. Michael sat stiffly in the seat. He wasn't sure if this meant he wasn't ever going back to the bakery. At the gate Les exchanged a few words with the attendant and left Michael off without driving in. The attendant nodded to Michael and turned back to the pages of *Valley of the Dolls*.

The day was pleasant enough if a person wasn't walking or standing in the sun. He found a clump of large elms with their fan-like crowns and sat down with his back against one of them. It was just seven-thirty. Thomas came in through the main gate and drove by without noticing him. When he closed his eyes, he saw Joe moving in and out of the darkness in the laundry room.

When he woke up again, it was a lot warmer. He unzipped his jacket. Lester was taking a group of inmates for a morning walk and Michael had to move around the tree to not be seen. Harold was walking at the end of the line.

"Get up here, Harold," Lester yelled. He walked to Harold and whispered confidentially before saying sternly, "Get to the front, Harold, where I can keep an eye on you."

The other inmates turned to the front as Lester passed them. Harold skipped behind a tree, then ran bent over towards Michael, who crawled into the bushes and held his breath.

"Joe's in the barn. I like you. I don't like Lester." Harold winked and disappeared.

"Harold," Lester cried. He jogged around the group, stopping to raise his chin into the air as if he were getting a better view. The young summer volunteer cringed. One of the older men in the group sat down on the ground and several others wandered off the path.

"Here," Harold called, standing up from some bushes a long way from where Michael still crouched. Lester crossed his arms, and then raised a hand in his mouth to straighten his teeth. The old patient stood up and the patients who had begun to wander off came back to the line.

Michael watched them until they reached the path down to the river. Thomas's truck drove down to the front gate. He saw three of the yard workers walking towards the elms and darted from bush to bush until he reached the stone wall that encircled most of the farm. Once behind the row of lilac bushes along the wall, he ambled until he was thirty feet from the barn. He closed his eyes and tried to listen for voices or scraping pitchforks. The barn was as still as a church. The heat of the morning and the silence seemed to work together. He heard the cooing of mating pigeons.

He waded up the creek with his pants rolled up and his shoes and socks in his hands. His feet were sucked down into the soft mud which pulled at them as he lifted his leg for the next step. He stopped at a bend in the creek where the bottom was rocky and cleaned his feet before he got out. Four cows gathered to look at him.

At the door of the laundry room, he heard the screams, short and high with the rhythm of a runner gasping for breath after a race. He could not tell who it was. The sounds were muffled like in his dreams or when people became enveloped in light. He opened the first door. The screams became louder and less rhythmic.

"Shut up. Shut up. Cool it. Relax. I can't get nothing going. You fucking squirm so much." Joe's voice was strained as if he had collected his breath to speak.

The other voice whined and groaned.

"Okay. Okay. Okay. Don't go loco on me. You doing it. Okay. Okay. . ." Joe's voice was breathless and threatening. He began to hiss through his teeth.

Michael flung the door open and it banged against the wall. Peter panicked. He grabbed Joe and wouldn't let him go and Joe struggled to stand up with Peter wrapped around him. The sheets Peter was lying on became entangled with their bodies and Joe fell with a boom onto the wooden floor.

Michael ripped the curtains off the window and dirty yellow light fell like a rectangular spotlight on Peter and Joe. It seemed to blind them and they twisted their faces into the light like newborn kittens. Michael pushed a cart with bedding from the ward for the senile and dumped it onto Joe and Peter. Peter wailed. In his fury Michael picked up Joe's work boots to throw at them, but one hit the window and glass shattered onto the floor. Joe managed to pull himself up, but slipped on a sheet and fell. He let out an earth-shattering scream.

Michael didn't stop running until he reached the creek. He didn't bother to take his shoes off when he waded into the water. He had been crying for a long time, but seemed to just realize it when he stopped in the creek to look around. Everything was peaceful. The cows had moved further off and turned their broad necks to look at him for a second.

It did not seem that he had thought anything for a long time. His boots were full of mud and flies circled his face. He slapped a deer fly as it bit the back of his neck, then slapped his body furiously. He slumped back into the grass.

That night he slept in the barn. The mud on his feet dried, cracked and fell off. The sounds of mice running through the hay, owls hooting, and the wind creaking the old wood came from a huge monster that had swallowed him. The beast swayed through the night, through the sky with all the dirt and plants and people in its belly. Michael was inside it, but blind to everything else in it as everyone else was. But he knew about the monster. No one knew they were in the belly. He was the only one who knew.

When it became cold during the night, he pulled himself

into a ball with his hands in front of his face. They still had the smell of soiled laundry and he would run through the events in the laundry room. It felt like his mind had been over it so many times that it had formed a blister. Spasms passed through his body. He tried to curl up against the cold with his hands at his side.

He woke to Gus and Thomas's voices.

"He'll show up. I'm sure he will." Thomas didn't sound like himself. His voice was tired and thin, without the timber it usually had.

"Maybe there's something about what happened in the laundry room. You know maybe everything is like together." Gus said.

There was a long pause.

"Something to think about," Gus said.

"I can only help you out for an hour. Mr. Mandment wants to avoid a state visit and wants me to help him get things straight."

"Joe. Damn Indian." Gus spit.

When they began to work, Michael slid between two bales of hay. He heard Thomas explaining that he would be back, then Gus came up to the loft. He heard him throw some hay down to the cows and then it was quiet for a long time. Michael waited for a long time. He had the feeling that Gus was sneaking up on him and made his body rigid so he would not make a sound. He kept himself motionless for a long time, became tenser, and then he heard Gus snoring. After he tiptoed past Gus, he jumped from the loft onto a pile of hay without making much noise and ran to the river.

By noon he was hungry. He heard Thomas calling his name. He stood up from the grass where he had been lying, but Thomas had already walked away.

When he reached the porch, Joshua, wearing white pajamas and a brown terry-cloth robe, trotted up to him with the album clutched to his chest. The belt robe was tied below his stomach and the lapels were spread wide. There was no one else around.

"Did you go to the house in town? I told Mr. Mandment that you would go to your roots and then come home. Revert back to a rat, you know. So much excitement. I thought maybe the papers would come, but not a word is getting out. I was supposed to talk to Bernice, but no phone calls." Joshua stepped back from Michael. "Dear me. What an odor!"

Lester came out of the front entrance at the moment when Joshua stepped back. He took Michael by the arm and turned to Joshua. "What are you doing out? Everyone's supposed to be in their rooms." Michael was not prepared for the jerk Lester gave him and he lost his balance, so it seemed that he was trying to get away. Lester opened the door with one hand and flung Michael through the doorway. He dragged him down the hall to the nurse's office. Everyone except for the semi-independent and the independent inmates were locked up. The semi-independent men were out looking for Michael.

The television had been unplugged and the radios turned off. An eerie silence hung over the home.

The nurse threw away his clothes and bathed him in water so hot that his skin turned red. He did not react when she guided him into the bath and gave his shoulder a tug to indicate he was to sit in the tub. The male attendant tried the water with his hand and yanked it out again.

"Not too hot?" he asked and looked curiously at Michael's short lanky body.

"Better red hot than dead cold. Get those germs. From the smell, God knows where he's been." She looked around for the shampoo and squirted some on his head.

"Wash your hair," she commanded.

"Maybe you could wash his hair." she said to the attendant. "He seems pretty out of it. Shave him while you're at it. He looks like he's got whiskers. This one's always given me the willies."

Michael closed his eyes as the attendant began to massage his scalp. He felt as if he had become empty. The monster had taken him in its belly to another world. Only outer skin was still here waiting to connect with his mind in the other world.

The attendant was broad with soft flesh. His hair was greased so that it curved back like the prow of a ship. The scent of the hair oil reminded him of Johan and when the sweat on his face dripped into his eyes, he closed them and saw Johan standing before him. He knew Maron was behind him holding him up. Then the attendant took a cup and poured hot water from the bath over Michael's head. He coughed and twisted.

"Come to life, huh?" the nurse said smoking a cigarette by the window.

Later that afternoon Thomas came to interview Michael, who sat in a corner in the nurse's office. Thomas wore a tie and carried a small brown briefcase with the corners worn to a light tan. He faltered as he spoke. The nurse lit a cigarette as soon as he arrived and retreated again to the window ledge.

"How was Peter?"

"They gave him a shot and sent him to bed. Were you here this morning? The whole place was buzzing. Soon as he got that shot, the whole place seemed to get it. Silence."

"Michael?"

"Always been a little weird. Never said more than a couple words to me. You writing that down?" She snickered.

208

"Michael, did you get lost when Les left you off?" Michael's skin was red and shiny and his face seemed to glow now that he had been shaved.

"I got lost," he said deadpan.

"Then you wandered around for a long time?"

"I wandered around. I wandered around in the creek. I got lost."

"You didn't see Joe or Peter? You didn't, did you?"

"I didn't see them." Michael glanced at Thomas who was taking notes.

"Maureen's husband died. You knew that. Is that why you wandered around?" Thomas voice was strained like it had been in the barn when he talked to Gus.

"I wandered around," Michael said.

"Do you want to go back to the bakery? Work in the bakery?"

"Yes," Michael said, answering to Thomas's nervous pleading.

Mr. Mandment blamed Thomas for moving Peter to the barn. Joe had broken his good arm and fractured a bone in his ankle. Peter had cut his feet on the glass when he finally freed himself from the tangled sheets, running naked to the main building. When they went to look for Joe in the barn, they didn't find him. Lester had offered to search the northeast corner and had heard screams coming from the laundry room. He hadn't gone in himself, but had reported to Thomas who found Joe. It was easy to connect Peter to the laundry room by his smell. Joe had been out of his mind with pain and Peter could not stop babbling. Two attendants had held him down so they could clean his feet and pull bits of glass out of them with a tweezers. Joe was sent to a hospital and never came back to the farm. Walter claimed that he had it on good authority that "Joe had been sent to prison for fuckin' 'em too young."

Gus had corrected him, "Getting caught fuckin' 'em too young."

Part 15

Michael spent a week in the day room. He pulled a chair out from a table and away from everyone else. He was aware that Joshua sat on a sofa in the far corner and watched him, then bowed to write furiously in the notebook he carried with the album. The first days he ran all the scenes from the laundry room through his mind, those with just him and Joe and the one horrible scene with Joe and Peter. At night he couldn't sleep and got up more exhausted than when he went to bed. Dark orange light shot from his eyes like the headlights on a car. It pulled everything down that it fell on and made people and objects squat and ugly.

Joshua seemed to know what he was thinking. He opened the album to the wedding picture from the newspaper. "He's never coming back now." Maron glared from the picture.

The second day the new attendant Erland, who was now working days, took the album away because Joshua was obsessive about it.

"Do you know Burgermeister-Frick?" Joshua's voice reached a shriek. "Or Hoffman-Torballe? Both studied with Freud. Both were fascinated, fascinated with my case. And you are going to tell me when I have obsessive behavior? That's all copyrighted you know. Every word. Even the notations in the margin."

Michael watched the scene from his chair. Ernesto walked up to him. "When we were looking for you, it happened again. My glasses began to change the world. I was afraid to put them on. I saw horrible things when I put them on. Your body with the flesh ripped back, like when a dog catches a cat and shakes and twists it until the skin comes off. You couldn't even hide behind your skin. In a few days I'll be okay. *Un descanso.* A rest. You know, that's what it means."

Joshua calmed down quickly. In an hour he was walking around with a handful of papers and the stub of a pencil. Michael had moved to a couch and Ernesto had followed him. As soon as Joshua approached them, Ernesto stood up and put on his glasses and stared hard at Joshua.

"One can never be too careful about lice in a place like this. You were a secret before. And now you have a new secret. When they give me back my album, I will put a blank page and write "August 28, 1962." For a day you disappeared. Will we ever know? But I know. Another secret. I saw you first. I must tell Bernice before I lose my mind."

Joshua paced in front of the couch scribbling notes. He held the pencil stub between his index finger and thumb, jabbing at an idea. "Harold. Does Harold come into this? No stone unturned." For a moment he was concentrated and calm. "Why is it that my skin crawls, almost right off my flesh, when I meet that Mexican?"

Erland came into the day room and Joshua hid the pencil in his palm and shuffled towards a far table where he sat with several of the schizophrenics. "Being sociable. It's good therapy for the manic depressive," he said to Erland as he passed.

Later that day Thomas came to talk to Michael. His voice had regained its calm assurance. "Things happen here that you would never expect. I thought I knew everything."

"Secrets," Michael said.

"Who told you that, Michael?"

"Joshua." Michael sucked his lips in like he had seen Harold do.

"Are you ready to go back to work?" Thomas came right to the point.

"Yes." Michael nodded as if he were thinking of how sure he was of his decision.

"I've arranged to take everyone earlier. I need to supervise the semi-independents more." Michael was surprised that Thomas was talking to him this way.

"Okay, Dwindie, six o'clock tomorrow."

Tape 5 – Entry 2

I think sometimes that maybe I know more about back then, about Joe and Harold and Lester now than I did back then. The truth of it is that I always knew, but didn't know what I knew. When you learn things, it's like seeing what you know. Ernesto said that some things you know for the first time and some things you see for the first time, but you have known them all your life. We need to be surprised he says and forgetting helps. Our minds decide not to see something for a while and then we see it again and it surprises us. Some famous person said we hide things from ourselves and then we need to talk to people so we can see them. I can't imagine the time that I didn't know Joe or that I didn't know about Joe and Peter or Lester and Harold. And I think I know about Ernesto and Joe, but I don't really know.

He and Roxanne were in the back room together for the first week. Les helped from six to seven-thirty when the bakery opened and then came back to supervise, shuffling to the front on his long skinny legs whenever the bell on the door jangled as it was opened.

Roxanne taught him the measurements, which he learned by eying the amounts in the mixer or in the measuring cups. She checked him, but his memory never failed. When she explained a mixture in numbers, he was lost.

When Maureen came back, Les spent all of his time up front and Maureen and Roxanne would play cards in the corner and get up occasionally to supervise Michael.

"He's a good kid, Les, but he ain't going nowhere. He can't read or count. When Roxanne ain't behind him, I am. You know how we want everything done right." Maureen stood up, setting a dishrag over two threes, a five, a ten and an ace. "If I didn't come back, Roxanne was going to quit. It's too much work for even two."

Roxanne was bored with the card game. She took the pastry icing gun from Michael without saying a word. The bell rang in the front and Les skipped back to the shop.

"Mickey looks like he's squeezing his brains out of the tube the way he concentrates when he does decorating," Maureen said.

Roxanne inspected the cake to see how she could finish it. "You think so?"

"Well he ain't got nothing else in that head." Maureen looked at her watch. "Mickey, take out the rolls."

Maureen and Roxanne took their break outside in two folding lawn chairs. The weather was cool. Les had taken down the picket fence and placed two small picnic tables and four benches in the area next to the bakery. He had begun to sell coffee and fresh bun sandwiches. During the week a few customers who worked at the bank and the insurance agency bought sandwiches and coffee and ate them outside, but Maureen and Roxanne were always alone when they took their last break. Les had complained about them taking their break outside, but relented.

Michael filled the stainless steel sink with hot water and detergent. He collected the trays and bread pans and let them soak in the sink. From a small window that was partly covered by the refrigerator, he could see Maureen and Roxanne. He had not finished the border of flowers on the cake and Roxanne had made a large ribbon in a darker shade of red around the rest of the border. Michael knew it was wrong and wanted to do the cake over. Maureen had changed since she returned. He looked out the window again. Both women had the same rusty colored light that Lester had. It was the first time he had noticed that their light had changed.

When Maureen took a few days off, things ran better than usual, but Les was oblivious. He threatened to fire her if she was out anymore before Christmas.

One crisp October morning Les sent for the barber at the end of the block. He was the same man who came out to the County Home to cut the hair of the men and women about once a month. Michael had just seen him the week before but the barber didn't seem to recognize him.

"Give him a good shave and a decent haircut, Dick. When Maureen is sick, I need someone to carry the trays into the shop. I can't have him coming up front looking like that. What the hell do they do? Cut their hair with a lawnmower?"

"Well, at the county home all they want is that they can tell the difference between the men and the women. Two cuts, short and shorter," the barber said defending himself without admitting he had cut Michael's hair. He put his hand on Michael's back and guided him out the back door. Maureen and Roxanne looked up and then lowered their heads again.

The barber led Michael in through the back door to the shop. An old radiator clanked in the corner. Michael climbed up into the chair. His feet didn't reach the foot rest so the barber adjusted it. The barber hummed to himself, only becoming silent when he shaved Michael face with a straight razor.

Michael gazed at himself in the mirror that ran the length of the wall. At the home the inmates sat in a chair in a room next to the nurse's office with an attendant who was there to make the barber feel more secure. The chair had straps in case an inmate became too fidgety.

The barber circled him with the scissors, snipping at the silence. The light blue robe he wore covered everything but his head. He twisted his feet under the cloth. He was floating in the mirror. He had the sensation that he was about to turn into a tree and pulled one of his hands from under the sheet to look at it.

The barber switched on the electric clipper. Michael watched the hair fall from the side of his head. He remembered the chain saw that Thomas had used the day of the storm. He waited for the pain, to watch his own head fall off. Instead his black hair dropped in clumps and he turned his head to inspect the patterns it made on the floor. The barber grabbed his head and put it in the position he wanted.

"Keep still." The barber sprinkled hair pomade on his hand and rubbed it through Michael's hair, then carefully wiped his hands on a towel. He held a mirror up behind Michael's head and he could see the back of his own head. It was like a revelation.

"I guess Les is paying so it don't matter if you see it or not." He spoke to himself.

The barber drew the sheet away and Michael saw his own body again. He was no longer floating. His hands were covered in a blue glow that lagged behind as he moved.

"Done. You can get down." The barber busied himself arranging the scissors and combs for the next customer.

"Thank you," Michael said and the barber stared at him.

"You talk kid? Les said you was almost mute."

"But I don't mean nothing," Michael said and followed the

barber out the back door again.

"Well, I guess you don't."

Maureen and Roxanne made a big deal about the haircut. "You going to get lots of lady friends looking like that," Maureen said, jabbing the air with her cigarette. "If you stop sniffing no one will know you're a rat. Stallion boy. Stud boy."

"I always said he wasn't bad for a small guy. You didn't have imagination. You're not too swell to work now, are you?" Roxanne asked.

"I don't think so," Michael said. He jerked his hand a few times to see if the blue glow would shake off.

"Get them dishes done over there," Maureen said.

Les came and got a tray of donuts. "Wow," he said. "You look like a normal kid. Almost too young to work." He disappeared up front.

"You got the hair cut so Les won't even come back for the trays. He won't even do that." Maureen went into a coughing fit and as soon as it was over, she took the last drag on her cigarette and put it out.

"He got to check on us anyway," Maureen said.

In the back of the truck that afternoon it was cold and Thomas had rolled down the oiled canvas so that the wind didn't come in the sides of the truck. Michael watched Herman's white breath as he snored. He took a deep breath himself and watched the white plumes flutter from his mouth.

"Stop watching me, rat boy," Peterson yelled and raised his fist to Michael, who immediately put his head down. Hank's and William's heads bumped together. Herman groaned.

"Get over on your side." Peterson punched Michael in the arm and Michael swung his arm out and caught Peterson on the nose.

"Fucking weirdo hit me!" Peterson roared.

"Shut up, or I'll hit you, too," Herman said. "You could trip and fall out the back while we're going sixty down the dirt road. We wouldn't know until we got to the home."

The truck was silent again.

"I didn't mean to," Michael said. "It happened before I knew it."

Peterson snorted.

"Look at that faggot haircut he got," Peterson said after a long silence. He farted loudly and no one paid any attention.

He thought Thomas was looking at him strangely when he got out of the truck, but Michael hurried into the entrance and past the watchmen at the desk. No one had been on the porch. It was already dark and a chill grabbed the county hospital as soon as the sun went down.

He checked to see if anyone was in the semi-independent men's bathroom before he went in. He moved his hand in front of the mirror to see if it was really himself, turned quickly around to see if the image moved or if he could fool it. Peter opened the door and looked in and Michael rushed out past him.

There was a blue light which emanated from his body, not bright, but he could see how the walls next to him reflected the light.

Part 16

In the day room the television was off and chairs had been lined up in front of a podium. Joshua was talking to Erland near the door.

"It's not fair. Have you heard of the separation of church and state? I have a right to watch television and not be subjected to this religious hogwash. For God's sake I am an Episcopalian. Do you know what that means?"

Erland exaggerated his underbite by covering his upper lip with his lower incisors. "Don't make a federal case out of this. You can miss a night of television."

"I have missed so much of it already. What does another day matter? I am rushing to catch up." Joshua stumbled past Erland, but before he could reach the television, Erland had placed himself again in front of Joshua.

"How do you expect me to get better?" Joshua whined, then turned and walked away with his chin high in the air to show his indignation.

"They are taking us back to the age of myth. I wish I had never read Comte. I could be like the rest of you, wallowing in the age of myth." A strange muffled cry shook in Joshua's throat and then he disappeared into the far corner.

The home had changed since Joe left. Patients like Joshua who had been allowed some freedom of movement were now assigned to specific areas each hour of the day. Mr. Mandment had hired a man to walk the grounds with a set of keys and he was to check all the buildings. Even the independent and semi-independent men were not allowed on the grounds unless they had signed out at the front desk. These rules affected Michael only slightly since he was gone most of the day and weekends when there were visitors, the rules were more relaxed.

Some of the churches sent cars to pick up inmates on Sunday mornings, and on Wednesday nights a retired clergyman Pastor Magshore preached in the waiting room next to the front desk. The couches were moved to face a small podium and mostly older women, and one or two older men attended. Michael had gone once after he had begun to work in the barn. The minister's head would fall onto his chest and he would seem to be asleep for a second, and then his head would snap up and he would speak of Jesus and salvation. The senile women (Joshua had trained and then tested him on the types of inmates) set their faces into hard smiles. Others (too old and poor to take care of themselves) dropped their heads with the minister's, but did not bring them up when he snapped his into the light of revelation. The mentals, as Joshua called them, moved around the room changing seats.

The night Michael went, an inmate shot out a stream of obscenities in front of the podium. "Fuck. Shit. Cunt. Asshole. Prick. Piss." He stuttered and jerked his way through the list.

"Jesus, Jesus, cast out the demons. Dear Lord, cure this man." Pastor Magshore's head dropped for longer than usual. "And Christ said, 'It is done.'"

The man now seemed to be stuck on one word, "Fuck." Fuck. Fuck. Fuck."

The senile men and women smiled nervously and rocked in their chairs. One of them stood up, then several others. Two old women in wheel chairs hung their heads on their bony chests and wept softly.

Erland and the man at the front desk took the inmate by the elbows and led him away. He immediately became silent and serious. The minister continued as if nothing had happened.

That was the first and last time that Michael went to the regular Wednesday services.

He couldn't imagine that they would cancel television for an evening of Pastor Magshore, whom Joshua claimed was the great uncle of Mrs. Mandment.

From his corner, Joshua waved his hand frantically. He stopped when Erland glanced at him.

"Go calm Joshua down, Michael. You seem to have a good

influence on him." Erland left to block another inmate on her way to the television.

"They are trying to brainwash us." Joshua sniffled. He clamped his arms around his body. "I've had a great setback, Michael. They won't give me back the album. They don't want me to be part of the big world. The big picture. Thomas is behind this."

"I don't mind about the album. It doesn't mean anything." Michael had a sinking feeling that if he talked too much to Joshua, no one else would talk to him. Before he had begun to work at the bakery, he had felt like a part of the group of semi-independent men. Then Joe had left and everyone had become quieter.

"Bernice has canceled. She wants to do a book now on Starkweather. Bad career move. You're what she should do. Some kid and his girlfriend terrorizing the plains, who's interested in that?" Joshua lifted his yellowish eyes up at Michael, who turned away in embarrassment. "God, why am I talking to you? You are only a tape recorder. Oh Christ." Joshua twisted over so he was face down on the couch.

Michael stood awkwardly for a minute before he went to join the people standing in front of the podium. Ernesto moved several chairs out of his way as he walked towards Michael.

"I think I know where Joe is, Dwindie," Ernesto said. "They locked him in the laundry room. They caught him there with someone and locked him in the laundry room. It's always locked now. I hear him when I walk by. He says, 'Ernesto, remember the barn.' I don't answer."

"Why don't you answer?" Michael looked at Ernesto's bleary brown eyes. He wanted Ernesto to take off his glasses.

"Well. . ." Ernesto paused for a long time. "I guess it's because I know he's not really there. Gus says they sent him to prison. I would rather have him in the laundry room." Ernesto sat in a crooked metal folding chair and began to rock. He was unaware of the people around him.

"Ernesto, what is this?" Michael opened his arms the way he had seen Thomas do when he asked questions.

Ernesto turned slowly towards him, then looked as if he were trying to determine where the words were coming from, then looked ahead again.

A man carrying a large Bible in one hand moved through the haphazard arrangement of chairs. His smile seemed to bounce from face to face. Ernesto slumped in his chair and stared at the floor. In the front, the new minister surveyed the room as if he were looking into the far bleachers of a stadium from center field. He grabbed Michael by both shoulders and pressured him down into a chair.

"You, son, are going to be saved tonight!" He looked away

from Michael to the few inmates scattered in front of the podium. Many others sat along the wall or, like Joshua, lay on the couches. "You all are going to come to Jesus tonight. He can cure and make you whole. Ask and Jesus will provide."

Erland shepherded three of the senile women who attended Pastor Magshore's services towards the chairs before the podium. One of the women stopped. "I forgot to feed mother. I have to go home and feed her. How could I have forgotten?"

"You fed your mother," Erland said. "You fed her until she died."

The woman looked suspiciously at him. "I don't know you. Mother doesn't know you either." Her face relaxed and she shuffled on, and the others who had stopped with her, followed.

The preacher darted over to Erland and the three women. His tall skinny body craned over Erland's short stout figure, as Erland gently positioned each of the women in front of a chair and pushed her back so she seemed to fold into the chair. As he turned around the minister was like a horse fidgeting before coming out of the gate.

"God bless you, Erland. Our mission is everywhere."

"Pastor Ray, I'm so glad you came." Erland's underbite became more pronounced and he looked like a kindly ogre next to the tense willowy Pastor Ray, who shook Erland's hand like he was pumping water from a well.

Michael looked over at the woman whose mother had not been fed and wondered if there really was a woman like Maron waiting some place. Perhaps in another world or a dream she was waiting. He closed his eyes to stop the confusion of lights. He could hear a high pitched buzz coming from Ernesto, but when he opened his eyes, Ernesto still sat slumped over.

Pastor Ray walked to the front, held the Bible at arm's length in the air, turned his face to the ceiling with his eyes closed and began to pray in a loud bellowing voice. Ernesto began to fidget and made several moves to stand up, but each time sat back down as if he had been pushed into his seat.

"Tonight the Lord moves us. Bring souls to Jesus tonight as bright and shining as the sun, as cool and clear as rain. Turn us to little children."

"Mother? Mother?" the old woman shouted.

Pastor Ray raised his voice, "Jesus is working in this room with the Holy Spirit. Open your hearts to him. Come naked to your Lord. Hide nothing. He will make you free. Lord, open these hearts and minds. Bring light where you can't see any. Your light, Jesus. Not the light from the fire of hell. Cool the fires of hell in these souls. Pure light. Make souls whole. We thank you, Lord, for moving us tonight. Praise Jesus. Amen."

The minister's arm dropped. His eyes opened on Michael who had been staring at the minister's hips as they had gyrated while he prayed. Now he looked away, then at the minister's piercing green eyes.

"Don't fight it. I can see the Lord has begun to move you. Come to the Lord."

Erland had moved from his seat and was standing next to the podium. He fell to his knees as Pastor Ray thrust out his pelvis and arched back with his hands towards the fluorescent lights of the day room, which pulsated more frenetically. Michael felt a jolt, like an electric shock. Ernesto was shaking. Michael sprung up out of his chair when the second bolt hit him. He was almost flung to the front, his small head landing on Pastor Ray's chest. Pastor Ray grabbed Michael's arms and his body was stretched out against Pastor Ray's. Two men sitting near the back stood up and moved first a few feet to the left and then turned and walked back, as if they were trapped in a circle and were looking for a way out.

"Kneel to the Lord," Pastor Ray intoned and pushed Michael shoulders down. On the way to his knees Michael's face rubbed into Pastor Ray's crotch. When he was on his knees, his forehead rested against the minister's bony shins for a second and then Pastor Ray darted in front of Ernesto's chair.

"Heal this man, Lord." Pastor Ray's voice became fuller and

lower.

"Charlatan. False prophet. Leave us alone," Joshua screamed, lifting himself up on an elbow and then flinging himself dramatically upon the couch again.

Ernesto took his glasses off to wipe his eyes. He glared back at the minister, but when Pastor Ray turned his eyes to heaven, Ernesto slid off his chair and scurried on all fours towards the corner where Joshua lay.

"Jesus can wait. Let us pray for divine inspiration, for holy tongues of fire."

A woman in the back began to babble loudly. Another, who had fallen to the floor, gagged until a clear stream of vomit flowed from her mouth.

"Jesus, thank you for bringing the devil out of this woman." Pastor Ray was on his knees over her.

"Mother, mother," called the old woman.

Pastor Ray jumped to the podium and held the Bible up towards the ceiling. He put his hand on Erland's head and Erland rose up.

"You, brother, are born again. Praise the Lord. Hallelujah."

Michael began to stand, but Pastor Ray stretched his arm out and held him down. He dropped the Bible on the podium, then yanked Michael up.

"You brother are born again. Praise the Lord. Hallelujah."

The light in the room was sparkling yellow and it shimmered like sunlight off the creek on the first day he had walked with Joe to the laundry room. He felt Joe in the room, but couldn't see him. Pastor Ray's fingers pressed hard into his scalp and when he yanked his hand away, it was as if he razed the walls of a dam. Michael felt warmth rush down through his body. His legs buckled under him and he fell again to his knees.

"Close your eyes to pray. Thank you, Lord, for being with us tonight and opening up these souls to your words and your love. May they follow on your path, Lord, and become bearers of your word. Thank you, Jesus. Thank you, Jesus.".

Michael closed his eyes. Joe stood before him with Johan and Maron. Maron and Joe repeated the words "Lord Jesus" as a chant and Johan wore a long flowing black gown with a white surplice, his hands spread out in a blessing. He hadn't noticed it at first when he closed his eyes and it came as a shock to him that Joe was naked. Maron hadn't noticed either.

"Amen."

Michael opened his eyes and Erland helped him up. The light was gone from the room. He closed his eyes again, but saw nothing.

"What now? What do I do now?" Michael asked.

Pastor Ray was blowing his nose into a large white handkerchief. He folded it up and put it back into his pants pocket.

"Follow Jesus," Erland said.

"How do I do that? I don't know." Michael blushed.

"You are already following him. You started tonight when you were born again and Jesus saved you," Pastor Ray said.

"I was born again?" Michael asked. He wasn't clear what it meant to be born.

Pastor Ray nodded with the same smile that he wore as he entered the room. Michael stared at his sparkling green eyes. He thought of them like Joe's arm, something that made Pastor Ray different from others.

Erland whispered to one of the attendants before following Pastor Ray to his car.

One of the men who had been caught within the imaginary circle stopped suddenly. "I was once the archangel Raphael. Then I came to earth and I have been stuck in the molasses of sin. Stuck in the molasses of sin like a greedy fly whose wings no longer do it any good." He once again shuffled hectically within his circle, stopped and shuffled in the other direction. A few minutes after Pastor Ray left the room, both men sat down facing opposite directions.

Joshua was lying on the couch resting his head on his hand.

"I am living in a world of tape recorders. Chomsky is wrong. Tabla rasa. Men are parrots." It was obvious that he meant his speech for Michael, but he looked away as if he were talking to no one.

"Joshua, what does it mean to be born? I thought it meant how old you were, how long you had been some place."

Joshua groaned and moved his gelatinous body to sit up. The pink of his stomach showed through his sweaty white gown.

"It means, it means that some woman spread her legs like two willow trunks and a very small person popped out. We have all been popped from the spreading willow trunks, almost breaking the tree. From now on I will only speak in willows, I mean riddles, because no one understands me anyway. The god Gestapo is upon us. The god Gestapo."

"Can I be born again?"

Joshua looked slowly over at Michael. "Rubbish. It's rubbish." He began to cry and Michael walked away.

In the hall he met a group of inmates accompanied by a nurse.

"Pastor Ray was here," Harold whispered to Michael.

"I didn't see you," Michael said.

"I love those green eyes," Harold said and panted with his tongue like a dog. "He's a big man. You see him?"

Michael noticed the nurse watching them out of the corner of her eye.

"I've been born again," Michael said. Harold dropped his jaw in exaggerated shock.

"Big man. Really big man." Harold squealed and when the nurse glared back at him, he swung his head to the side as if he were throwing back a long mane of hair.

"Disgusting," the nurse said.

"I like you," Harold whispered and moved off with the other inmates.

When the television had been turned on again, the walls of the day room came alive and Joshua was at the front of the group that moved for position in front of the television. Michael stood on his tiptoes to watch them from the small window in the door. He divided them into groups using the wire diamonds in the glass and changed the configurations by moving his head slightly. Each diamond was a little television without sound. The events of the evening came and went in his mind. Perhaps the only way you could change the world was by the way you looked at it. He put his eye close up to the window and used the wire in the glass to divide the back of Joshua's head into two parts. He was startled when Erland placed his hand on his shoulder.

"I was born again," he said to Erland and ran to the semi-independent bedroom before Erland could reply.

Dearest Joshua,

I was quite startled to hear that you are not allowed visitors because of the actions of some rather devious and unsavory residents of the home. None of this has reached the press and I am sure that most people do not want to know the details. I must know all and, unlike the New York Times, both fit and unfit. I still hope that some day you will be well enough to leave, though returning to the classroom probably will never be an option. Have you even considered it? You always had so many difficulties with the athletes. Tom Flinner, do you remember? The last day of class he grabbed you and threw you onto that massive back of his and ran with you piggy-back through the whole school. I can still see the look of terror on your face and his look of savage liberation. We eventually laughed about that.

I have made a marvelous discovery. At the back of the sheriff's office in a satchel, I came across hundreds of photographs stuck together. I whisked them surreptitiously into my purse and walked boldly past the secretary who peered at me over the fat folds of her cheeks and through glasses with lenses like the bottom of soda bottles. I thought instantly of your comments about the

dull utilitarianism of my purses, and left the office with the glow of
vindication. Many of the photographs were ripped. There are jigsaw
puzzles for a lifetime. The stacks were interlaced with sewing and
hemming needles. Of course, I did not make this discovery without
pain. The man who wrote the report stated in his own bucolic dialect
that "there was papers, photographs, needles and old women's dresses
on the floor. It looked like the boy had been sleeping in a mess of
papers and photographs. I don't think the old lady could get up there
and he was alone by himself up there." I hope they protect us better
than they write.

If I thought this project would help you get well, I would
dedicate all my time to it. It is fascinating from an anthropological
point of view, but a smidge too Dickensian. It would have to be
written at the beginning from the distanced perspective of an
investigator and then move into the more lurid aspects. Without the
ever present social concern and the story of the downtrodden soul
who overcomes all obstacles, it would never find a publisher. I ran it
by my agent, and he agrees.

You sound disgusted by the tawdry revival tent Christianity
into which Parrot Boy has fallen, but as far as market, anything with
the lost soul born again sells. I might have to dumb down the prose.
That might be the angle from the start. Think of me competing with
Norman Vincent Peale and Katherine Marshall?

I had a few Hollywood people interested in the Starkweather story, but the Sharon Tate murders have made them leery about serial killers. Word has it that Capote is working on a big crime novel. Imagine? What can a minor luminary, such as I, do?

Michael wasn't much help filling in the gaps. He has these very queer expressions when he seems unable to respond. I'm sure you have noticed. You are usually so perspicacious. For example, when I inquired if he remembered Maron, he replied, "I don't mean anything. They're only words." He also performed several speeches, which obviously were yours. Imagine having a human tape recorder following you around all day. And he seems to have as much insight into what you say, your bon mots and your punditry, as a tape recorder itself.

When I showed him the picture of her which appears in the album, he said, "Yes, I know her. That is Maron." Then he did a rather eerie imitation of a bow-legged old woman. He stopped almost as soon as he began. Of course, I had to suppress both a gasp and my laughter. I left him with the picture and he seemed to converse with it. Really extraordinary behavior. He opened a book and acted like he was reading it but was reciting the Lord's Prayer.

He does look rather impish. I understand perfectly why they have dubbed him Duende, or the bastardized version, Dwindie. His skin is so white that it is almost transparent, the murky blue veins showing in his arms, and his locks are as black as coal. Looking at his hair I thought of Dryden's Absalom, though it is doubtful that his short hair could get caught in the branches of a tree. And he is never quite there. Have you noticed or does he manifest this behavior only with strangers?

He informed me that he had been born again. I inquired if his rebirth had transformed his life. Actually, he seems to have a rather limited lexicon so I asked if it had changed him. His reply was priceless, but not serviceable for the religious market. He said, "I don't know yet. I'm waiting to see."

Which brings us to another matter. The book I am writing is not the book I would write. I considered doing a book on feral children, the great cases, Viktor or the Indian girls in the jungle raised by wolves or ostrich, to do a real study and interview psychologists and social workers, but I would need funding. It is also perhaps a strained analogy to refer to Michael as a feral child. His forest was old photographs, an upstairs jungle of three rooms, and ribbon and laced gingham dresses off the rack from backwater towns on the plains. Looking through old newspapers for the Starkweather book, I have seen these general stores that sell dresses and cloth and gifts, the original department stores. And then almost miraculously seen their like in the photographs, as if style had not changed in thirty years. These stores still exist, though the people who work in *them, as well as the stores themselves are artifacts slipped into the middle of the twentieth century. And his wolf mother was a religious fanatic. It was not that he wasn't exposed to information, but he was hindered from assembling it to any conventional meaning. And without that, whatever meaning he did give it, is lost to us.*

I told you in the last letter that I was suffering from excruciating headaches. I wonder if the worry of freelance is what is causing them. Writing the history of churches, towns, and clubs with all their dates and members and shakers and movers is tedium to the nth. My counterfeit of exuberance and amazement saps real joy for other topics. I admit to feeling preposterous speaking to you about my petty disappointments and setbacks. I have even thought of going back to small town newspaper work. Imagine that after my liberation.

The last time I visited you, I managed to ask around and found out that a woman named Maureen, a co-worker of Michael's at the bakery, played bingo every Wednesday at the basement of Holy Family. By chance I sat next to her and was able to ask her a few questions about her job and the fellow employees. She was most intent on complaining about her employer and said little about Michael. Once the game started it was virtually impossible to talk to her, or at least for her to respond. She had eight cards going at once and I had my meager two, which I could barely handle. My mind was not on the cards, but on the women with their curlers in their hair or head scarves or head bands holding back straight greasy hair. Their clothes seemed to exaggerate the defects of their bodies, and though my clothes were no better than theirs, I felt that at least I knew that I had fallen on hard times. This was their chance, even for just a moment, to feel as if God or fate cared about them. I was startled when Maureen grabbed one of my bingo cards and stared at me with contempt. "You won," she screamed. If she had said, "stupid," it would have been superfluous.

Maureen did mention that the retarded boy they sent from the county home had memorized all the measurements, though he could not count or read, and that they had convinced the owner that he needed constant supervision. The idiot savant. I tried to acquire more information, but she turned all my questions into attacks on the owner.

Are you sure this boy Harold is a good source? It adds more depth to Michael's character, but is unprintable. I suppose these seedy elements can be worked as attachments, father figures, his engendering concern and love on the part of even the most questionable of characters.

I realize that I have included questions and discussions here that the authorities at the home will not allow to slip through their scrutiny, so I will not post this until around Christmas and then in the guise of a Christmas card. Surely they do not look at all the Christmas cards. Onion skin will prevent them from suspecting a letter. I am aware that your fits of depression are always worse midwinter, but perhaps this will cheer you up.

Affectionately,

Bernice

PART 17

Erland asked Mr. Mandment if he could bring Michael to Bible study on his night off, which was Tuesday. Mr. Mandment was against it at first because Pastor Magshore had learned of the revival and was pressuring his niece to make sure he was the only minister allowed at the County Hospital. The pressure was mostly comments about how he was planning on changing his will. Taking Michael to the meetings was not the same as Pastor Ray coming to the county home and Mr. Mandment was afraid of losing Erland, who was a good employee. Michael wasn't asked about it until a lot of negotiating had taken place. Mr. Mandment would set a stipulation, for example that no more than three inmates could go at a time and Erland would agree, and then Mr. Mandment would come up with another stipulation after speaking with his wife. The last stipulation was that a patient's family or guardian had to give written permission, but when it was discovered that Michael had no family or appeared to have no guardian other than the state, Mr. Mandment gave permission for Michael to go.

Michael announced his rebirth at work. He told them about the woman who had vomited the demons. Maureen had been chewing gum that morning and had worked it with a slow rolling motion that showed indulgence and doubt. But Roxanne was interested, had heard Pastor Ray preach, been reborn herself several times.

"Every time Sam hears Pastor Ray preach, he stops drinking. What the word can do!" Roxanne took a deep belabored breath.

"He's drinking now," Maureen said.

"And he won't go to no more revival meetings," Roxanne said forming her mouth into a pout.

Michael went to the Bible study on Tuesday nights. It was already dark when they left, but if there was a clear moon, he could see the lines of stubble on the fields which disappeared at the horizon. The headlights of the car bore a tunnel into the darkness, which the car then followed. He felt empty and worried. The night sky threatened to swallow him and he kept close enough to Erland when they got out of the car at the small wooden church so that if he were suddenly yanked to the sky or blown towards the fields, where he knew that he would be lost, he could grab onto Erland's coat.

His place in the car was always in the back right side. He could see Erland's face clearly when they passed a yard light that was close to the road or when the lights of an oncoming car flooded the old black Buick, which Erland had nicknamed Judas. When Michael entered the car just inside the front gate of the county home, Erland had already picked up several women. The conversation would die until Michael was seated in the back right side and Erland had eased the car into the road again. As Michael pulled his coat tightly around himself and stared out his window, the conversations would begin again where they left off.

The first time he saw snow on the dark fields with the moonlight glinting off it, he felt his smallness like a pang and remembered the dream of being eaten by the monster. In the winter Thomas covered the back of the truck with a heavy canvas tarp that smelled of oil and they road in dim light both morning and afternoon for five months out of the year. Once the truck had a flat tire and they all climbed out and hopped from foot to foot to stay warm as they watched Thomas change the tire, and Peterson help. "Four hands are plenty," Peterson threatened when he felt that anyone was too close to him and Thomas. The light off the field was blinding. The cold wind brought tears to Michael's eyes which ran down his red cheeks. That day the snow-covered fields had not seemed vast. Instead he had felt as if the light and wind were pushing in on him and he had retracted into his hard body.

Tonight the same fields frightened and fascinated him. They offered to remove all distinction and borders between himself and the world. When he sat in the pews made of rough two by fours and closed his eyes as Pastor Ray's voice swung into its first crescendo, he saw the white fields, white like silence, darkness flowing over them, but not penetrating, and he opened his eyes when he sensed his own body flatten against the milky snow and spread out to the horizon in all directions. The sight of the walls of the church gave him a tenuous sense of wholeness, but the tingling of his skin made him feel that it was only temporary.

"Find yourself in Jesus. Lose your old self and find yourself in Jesus."

He was never the first to stand up. One of the older women, Lanana Lorton, who was a habitually recovering alcoholic, threw herself into the aisle at the first command for sinners to come forward. The nights she was absent Pastor Ray had more time to work the room into a frenzy before the first person walked to the front. He usually ignored Lanana until a few others had come forward with their heads bowed and then he rushed towards them, grabbing their shoulders, his eyes closed, his head turned toward the ceiling. The sparkling yellow light shot up and then gathered on the floor in pools. When Erland walked to the front, his thick legs made waves of light that lapped against the wainscoting of the walls. Pastor Ray emanated the light, his head glistening with sweat. Michael watched his green eyes and saw that when he stared at someone, his eyes bore small holes through the person's body, and something was released, like air, and they eventually would slump before him.

At the little Bible groups after the service, voices were drained and calm. Erland lead the group of beginners, which included a few teenagers brought by their parents and some of the big sinners. Erland read from the Bible, halting and stumbling and losing himself in phrases he didn't understand. After the reading, he turned even the smallest phrase into a story. The Pharaoh became the leader of the Soviet Union or Hitler. Michael was especially interested in Saul and David. He asked Erland to explain the story. He could see Joe as Saul, but he couldn't see himself as David. Erland explained that it was like Thomas and Mr. Mandment. He had a Bible with pictures and David played a harp and Saul listened with his eyes set on David's white skin.

Joshua saw Michael's Bible study as cultural literacy. He took out the collection of *Life* magazines, *National Geographic's* and the romanticized Bible images in the papers that Michael brought with him and embellished the Old and New Testaments. Michael was afraid to tell Erland's stories to Joshua. But Joshua had a sense that Michael did not know what a harp was, how it sounded, or what a king and shepherd were. "The word will make you free," Joshua shouted triumphantly when Erland would enter the day room while Joshua was giving Michael the Bible from a "socio-cultural perspective." In Joshua's version of the story, it was true what he had suspected about David and Saul. They had been like him and Joe.

"Imagine if Mr. Mandment wasn't doing his job well and he was jealous of Thomas because he thought he wanted his job," Erland answered when Michael continued to look confused about David and Saul.

Each week they had a verse to memorize and Michael always said it perfectly the next week, but didn't always know where the verse ended and like a tape would repeat it until Erland nodded.

One week Michael saw Winston, the supervisor from the bean field, at the church with a woman with large strutting breasts and hair piled in curls. They sat behind Michael and he turned to look at Winston, unable to imagine that Winston was among the chosen.

"I don't know about this revival shit, baby Rhonda honey, I told you. Look, that guy's an idiot. One of the county homos. Who knows how many other faggots are here?"

"Shut up, Winston. He can hear you," the woman said.

"He don't even know his name." Winston seemed to be

angry at Rhonda.

Michael's head angled sideways and he turned to look at them. He smiled. He could see that there were black marks on them which on their throats went deeper into the skin.

"There are sinners here tonight," Pastor Ray screamed, without any preamble. Michael was used to the sudden explosion of Pastor Ray's voice, but he giggled at the way Winston and the woman jumped. They both looked down as if they hadn't noticed him staring at them.

"I want the sinners to come forward."

A gust of wind shook the church. Michael looked away from Winston and cocked his head to listen. It was what Ernesto called the open wind. It shot across the flat land and it made the trees whip back and forth like they were gagging.

"God is in here. Outside there is nothing. The world is a worthless bauble." He didn't know what a bauble was so he thought Pastor Ray said "wordless babble." He thought that Pastor Ray had heard the nothingness in the wind that he had.

Michael moved past the two women sitting to his right to get into the aisle. He looked back again at Winston's girlfriend. Winston stared at his feet. Michael stood with his back to the Pastor Ray and looked at the woman until she turned white as a sheet and the black spots disappeared, and then he walked calmly to the altar and fell on his knees before Pastor Ray.

After the service he waited silently with the others who had come with Erland. Two of the women sniffled nervously into tiny lace handkerchiefs. Marie Eloise, the woman who had sat in the front seat with Erland, read Psalms, her lips moving silently. Michael stared at the long brown hair on her arms. She stopped reading and looked at him and the two women, as if to count them.

"You all heard?" Marie-Elouise asked.

Michael listened carefully to everything she said because it sounded different from other people.

The sniffling women turned their heads simultaneously to Marie Eloise and Michael wondered if Bonnie and Lois were somehow part of each other like Hank and William. They shook their heads.

"Baptism. Pastor Ray is having a baptismal tank put in under the altar floor. Take at least a month if he does it right. I was baptized in a river. My head went back in the water and when I came up, I was a different woman. I was in the family of the Lord, a child of God. I saw Jesus in front of me and he touched me. I have never felt a touch so warm and real in my life."

The women smiled admiration.

"I have visions," Marie Eloise said. "Pastor Ray should use

me more. In my vision I seen Michael there baptized and he was brighter than everyone. God had taken the dirt and made it gold. It was all God."

Lois glanced towards Marie Eloise, seemingly a bit annoyed that she had not been chosen for the miracle. All three women looked at Michael.

"It will be a greater miracle," Marie Eloise said, closed her eyes for a few dramatic seconds and then opened them with the hymnal in front of her face.

They were alone on the road for a long time before they met an on-coming car. Then a large truck followed them and they were blinded by the light reflected in the whirling snow. When they left Marie Eloise at the farm house a few miles out of town, the only light around was from the yard light mounted on a tall wooden pole. Michael felt as if they had moved from the bouncing light of the truck which had cut their bodies into irregular chunks of light to this light that made them whole again. He watched Marie Eloise lumber out of the car. Waves of light bathed her, falling off her in fluid mirrors. A man was waiting for her by the door. In the warm damp light from the house, another light showed, a dark purple one that fell off her like pieces of cloth.

"Dirt to gold. Filthy dirt. Filthy earth. He's in a better place," Michael mumbled to himself in the back corner of the car.

It was cold and his teeth chattered.

The man who thought he was Raphael the Archangel was waiting in the hall when Michael came in. "I saw something. Do you understand? It's very important that you understand. Understanding without understanding, that's what is important. Let it go. Let what you understand go. Keep the rest. It's very important. I saw something."

"The light?" Michael asked.

"This is the annunciation. I am the archangel. This is the annunciation. I told your mother. But now I have to tell you. Your mother is gone. Gone in fire."

"I'm getting baptized. In a tank. They'll dip me in and then I'll be brighter than everyone. I'll be in the family of God."

"A sister. Maybe you will be someone's sister in the family." The man chuckled and suddenly seemed like Gus. "The less you understand, the better it is. A sister is good." He suddenly reflected seriously on what had seemed a joke.

He moved a few feet away from Michael. "It's too much of a burden. I won't fly. I can't be an angel if they can't make me fly. But I saw something and I had to tell you. But I won't. I won't fly. Joe without Mary. Joe without Mary. Mary without her lamb."

An attendant appeared in the hall and the angel began to pace as if he were looking for an escape.

"I won't fly. You can't make me," he said to the attendant who sighed wearily and took Ralph's arm. Ralph twisted loose for a second, then seemed to shrink and the attendant took his arm again and led him down the hall.

That night in a dream he saw the archangel again; he had grown enormous wings like the men in the picture in Erland's Bible who sat by the grave with the stone rolled away. "Brighter than everyone. Brighter than everyone," he said with each flap of his wings and Michael saw that everyone was blinded by his light, except for Joe who walked towards him as if he were in the light of the laundry room. "A greater miracle," the archangel said before his wings fell off. "I like you," a voice said behind him and he realized that the light was only shining from his front and behind him stood Harold and Ernesto and that Joe had really come from behind him and that was why he wasn't blinded by the light. Joshua was blinded. Somehow he knew that the light was really words. He looked up to see clouds parting and he heard a voice, "Those in front are blinded. Those behind you are part of you already. Don't tell anyone and don't do this with anyone else. Be silent for two days. Then you will be ready."

When he woke up, it was still dark. He could see the moon almost level with the window just above the trees. Peter was still fast asleep and he could tell that some of the other men were awake, but lay motionless in their beds.

He spoke to no one for two days. When Joshua asked him to repeat his Bible verse, he walked away from him.

"God got you down?" Joshua taunted, furious at being ignored.

The archangel rushed up to him and circled him, "Only what you don't understand is worth understanding. I understand everything and only what you don't understand is worth understanding. Wings tell you nothing."

At work Roxanne and Maureen were too busy discussing a hunting accident where a local boy was killed to notice Michael's silence.

"His face was gone. What's his mother going to look at?" Maureen absentmindedly inspected the mixers that Michael had prepared.

"Closed casket," Roxanne said peeking into the front to see what Les was doing.

"His nose was fifty feet away. Bob Donner said his eyeball was sticking to a tree." Maureen sat down again and shook a cigarette out of the pack.

"All the king's horses," Roxanne said.

Until the end of the second day, he had kept his vow of silence. Les had been watching him and Michael concentrated on his work with an intensity that Les admired. He had been gone the afternoon of the first day since his wife was a cousin to the mother of the boy and they had gone to sit at the home of the victim. But the second day Les had ordered him to pack up the old rolls and so he could take them to the home. He repeated the order twice, his voice rising.

"Yes, sir." Michael finally moved his lips without making a sound.

Les grabbed Michael by the head and pulled his jaw open. "Your throat looks red. Does it hurt?" Someone came to the door of the shop and Les left him to rush to the door. He unlocked it and opened it a crack to talk to the customer. He shut the door again and turned the sign that hung from the door around so "CLOSED" replaced "OPEN".

"I don't want you coming to work if you are real sick. Them girls are getting lazy."

Michael lipped "yes, sir" again.

Tape 6 – Entry 6

Ernesto says that he is sure that Jesus exists, but it's impossible to know. He says that the world is made from walls that aren't really walls. They are like layers of gauze. You can see through them, but everything looks dull, like a station too far away. Sometimes for a second, you get stuck in a wall and then you know they are there, but usually we pass through them and don't know it. We look back and it's fuzzy. We look the other way and it's fuzzy. Jesus is the only one who isn't in the walls. But we are in the walls. When you get stuck between the walls, you see the walls and if you let yourself be stuck for a while, you see Jesus. "You can see Jesus," I asked him. He said maybe. Then a long time later he came up to me and said, "You can't see but you can feel. When you are empty, you can feel." I think Ernesto had been stuck in a wall all that time he had been quiet. I said that I didn't feel Jesus. He said that the only way to know him was to feel where he was missing. "I don't understand you" I said. "That's good," he said, "because I'm crazy." He said all of that to me and I will remember it, even if I don't have this tape anymore.

Part 18

"Lost the word. Clammed. Mouth dammed. Man the silent animal mammal. Thomas Merton of the born again." Joshua seemed like he would never stop talking. "I have thought of you all day. Words are fearful things. Little devils. In the beginning was the word. In the beginning of all of our troubles. Sisyphus remembering his stones. Memory stones. Dig them from your self-conscious, remember and toss them out. Not possible without words. Not malleable. Ha! What foolishness!" He doubled over at first in fake laughter, but then he really began to laugh until he ended in a choking fit. The buttons of his shirt had come undone and his belly stuck out, a rosy pink under the worn thin cloth of his t-shirt.

"Tomorrow you will talk," he shouted at Michael, who turned to look at him. He wondered how Joshua knew that tomorrow he could talk again.

"Whatever spell it is, Golden Bough wow boy, tomorrow it is over." Joshua snapped his fingers triumphantly.

Ernesto seemed to come out of nowhere. "I have been thinking about you, Dwindie. I see everything now in twos. Everything has an opposite and can't exist without it. You can't have cold without hot. Hell had to be invented for heaven. Water for fire. Pain for pleasure."

Michael walked away.

"Nearness and distance. Nearness and invisibility. Yesterday, the day before yesterday, the day before that and tomorrow. Joe and Michael. Michael and Dwindie. Ernesto and Ernie. Madness and silence." Ernesto was gone when Michael turned around again. He saw the top of his head sticking above a stuffed chair that had been turned to the wall.

He was not sure that he was awake. His dreams were full of words that did not make sense, but that made him see the shadows of people. His own silence seemed part of the dream. He wondered if words would really come out of his mouth if he tried to talk now. Was the message in the dream that he would not be able to talk for two days or that he must not talk for two days?

That night he was in a lake and a hand rested on his head and brought his head under the water. When he came up again, he realized that the hand was from Joe's missing arm and that the water that dripped from him was really melted lightning that made the lake snow white with sun gleaming off it. The snow was pages without words. A voice from the sun said, "You are now only one name and that name is holy and no one will know it. You are the snow without the words. You will be happy until they know your name. Then you will be all names. In the universe there are many worlds. Now that you are baptized, I will give you a world to rule. Only a person with one name can rule. A person with many names is ruled."

He woke up and looked at the bed where Joe had slept and saw a light shoot up from the bed in the shape of an arm. It frightened him because it moved so quickly and he felt a rush through his body similar to when the truck shot up over a steep hill. He listened for the voice, but only heard the whispering of the wind and a voice far off screaming, "God, you must hate me. God, you must hate me." He thought he recognized it as the archangel's voice. Someone rushed by in the hall. A few minutes later the door opened slowly and he saw Harold peer in. Michael put his head down into his pillow and turned over, as if he were rolling in his sleep. He opened one eye slightly so he could see Harold. Harold pointed at Peter's bed and then moved his fingers as if he were poking out someone's eyes. Then he licked his fingertips and snapped his hand in Peter's direction. He pointed at Michael who held his breath and closed his open eye. When he opened it, Harold was still standing in the doorway mouthing, "I like you." Harold left the door open and scurried off. A moment later the same feet shuffled by even more frenetically, breaking into a run. "I won't," Harold groaned angrily. Several of the men rolled over in bed and others grabbed their pillows and pulled them into them. Then it was silent.

When Michael got up to go to work, Peter was sitting up in bed with his hands on his knees. "Feel okay?" Michael asked.

"My eyes hurt," Peter said.

"Feel wet?" Michael asked.

"Maybe sweaty," Peter said.

Gus pulled himself up so he rested on an elbow. "Same fucking fever I had. Burning eyes and the sweats. Three days in bed." Gus sat up in bed and let his head hang almost to his legs. "Same fucking fever."

Tape 2 – Entry 5

"You need a work history," Ernesto said. "Like where you worked." After the fire I never went back to the bakery. All those measurements stayed in my head. I have a dream where I see it the way it was the first day. I couldn't see any holes, but I knew the walls weren't there when I wasn't looking. Everything was floating. I set my whole mind on what I was doing. I was afraid to close my eyes. I would wake up in the bean field. All that morning Joe talked to me. "He don't mean nothing. Don't tell nobody." It was like the fairytales. I had things to do and if I did them everything would be okay. But after a while the walls got hard. I saw everything together.

It surprised me when Roxanne visited me in the hospital. I couldn't imagine her anywhere else. She was from the bakery. I told Ernesto all of this. He said my work history is that I worked in a bakery. That is all it is.

The week went fast. The topic at work was still the hunting accident. A suicide note had been found. The boy had confessed that the year before he had been with some friends at a hunting lodge. They had driven around one afternoon with their rifles shooting out of the car window and on a dare the boy had shot and killed a man walking along the road. The murder had not been solved.

"It still could be an accident. You know how you plan on doing something and then when you decide not to do it, by mistake you do it anyway," Maureen said biting on her lip.

"It's a shame anyway," Roxanne said. "If he had been closer to God, none of this would have happened."

"A second's urge and hell's eternity. Like these damn cigarettes," Maureen said. "Now you hear they're bad for you."

"There's a lot of truth there," Roxanne said leaning against the counter to take some weight off her legs. Silence fell on the room. Michael stopped to listen to it. He hadn't seen the lights since that morning and now the white light of the bakery hummed softly. The bell on the door in the front chimed.

"I get the urge," Roxanne said and a long time passed again, "and it only seems like an eternity until Sam finishes, usually drunk as a skunk." The two women chuckled softly.

Michael laughed, too, mostly because the silence in the bakery made him nervous.

"What so funny, Mickie?" Roxanne asked. "You don't know what were talking about."

"I know," Michael said in his own defense. "You're talking about doing it."

The two women now squealed with laughter. "Doing what?" Maureen asked.

"Fucking," Michael said in a low embarrassed voice.

"And what is that?" Maureen asked.

"I don't know," Michael said, then made a circle with thumb and index finger and pushed his other index finger in and out.

Maureen collected herself enough to look through the small window in the swinging door to see if Les was busy. Roxanne straightened up and twisted her shoulders to get a kink out of her back.

"You been around them foul mouthed men at the home too long. You need a girlfriend. Ain't there a girlfriend out there for you?" Roxanne winked at Maureen. "A Mrs. Dwindie?"

"I'm getting baptized," Michael blurted out.

"All this religion and you never been baptized?" Roxanne asked. "If some idiot would shoot you walking along the road, you'd go straight to hell."

"It's going to be in a tank," Michael said.

"You better get a girlfriend so you have something to repent," Maureen said.

"I'm going to be in God's family. I'll be something in the family." Michael looked at the women to see their reaction.

"You know what repent is?" Roxanne asked.

Michael walked away and began to measure for the bread.

"It's when you do something you wish you hadn't done. But in the church, it's when you do something you want to do, but you shouldn't do and then you have to be sorry for it. Even if you're not." Roxanne spoke slowly and took short breaths between the phrases.

"He turned off," Maureen said. "Mister Mickie Dwindie flipped his switch. He's gone. He ain't listening."

"Burt said that his mother didn't want to close the coffin until they had everything. He was hot under the collar towards the end. Said that she even wanted his snot in the coffin. God knows what went into that coffin. Burt said it looked like some kind of massacre scene with all the scrapings and pieces. Made him puke to think of it. People can't think straight when a thing like that happens."

"He's on the other side," Maureen said in a voice that imposed silence again.

"God will make him whole," Roxanne bleated.

"He's on the other side," Maureen repeated and turned her back to Roxanne. She was clipping coupons out of a magazine under a towel and keeping an eye out for Les.

"He's in a brighter place," Michael said and the two women turned together to look at him.

The next Tuesday the work on the baptismal tank had already begun and Pastor Ray preached in front of the altar, which was covered by three large white sheets. Winston's girlfriend was there again, but came in late and sat as far away from Michael as was possible. Instead of the tight gray sweater she had worn the Tuesday before, this night she wore a loose dress that seemed to hang from her breasts. Lanana went up first and Winston's girlfriend Rhonda right after her, almost beating her to the altar.

"I am weak. I am weak. Something comes over me and I sin. One second I am fine and the next, I am doing what I shouldn't. In a second." Rhonda was crying and throwing her breasts from side to side. Lanana tried to compete with her in volume, but then flung herself on the floor as if she had passed out.

"I just get to that point and waver there until I tip and then I rush into it." Rhonda shook her body more violently and Pastor Ray gave up trying to put his hands on her shoulders.

"Lord, make your word fortify the flesh. Sinner. Sinner. Let Jesus pull you back. Let Jesus pull you back." Pastor Ray's voice thundered and people stood up from their seats. Bonnie and Lois turned their tear streaked faces to the ceiling. Marie Eloise began to shake and made strange clucking sounds. Pastor Ray reached down and put his hands on Rhonda's shoulders. She crumpled like paper. Michael saw the dark holes in her neck again. He tried to concentrate so she would become white, but he saw her in a coffin with tree bark and branches and then a wave of red light swept across the church and knocked him on the floor.

He looked up and saw the hideous face of Marie Eloise, her jowls fluttering. "You will be the greatest light," she hissed.

Michael's body went stiff. Then the light receded as fast as it had come.

Erland waited for them outside. He had not gone forward as he usually did. Rhonda was now embracing everyone in the church. She gingerly touched Michael and then threw herself into the arms of Marie Eloise.

"You'll have powers some day," Marie Eloise told her. "Powers and great light." She stood back as if to get a better look at Rhonda's future. "It's so clear."

"I'm so weak," Rhonda said and her breasts rose slightly and her lips protruded to show her vulnerability.

"The greatest sinners are the greatest saints." Marie Eloise was annoyed by Rhonda's lack of enthusiasm for her predictions.

"Mickie here is going to have a great light," she said trying to hold the attention of the others.

Erland knocked on the church door to let the others know he was ready to leave. He shifted from foot to foot trying to stay warm and his head bobbed up and down in the narrow rectangular window. Michael and the two women turned toward the door to leave. Marie Eloise came out when the rest of them were already in the car. Erland took one of the women home first because she had a headache. She lived just off the main highway, but from town Erland took a back road so his car tunneled into the darkness, passing occasional farm houses where the light filtered through a heavy mesh of trees. The house was back from the road and dark.

"Say hello to your mother," Erland said and Lois nodded with her small pointed chin. Michael saw that her wings were backwards. They were on her chest and when she became nervous as she walked the graveled path to the house, they began to flutter and she had to strain to move forward. He noticed that Marie Eloise was breathing in the light from the headlights. When the lights went on in the house, Erland turned around and drove down the long straight driveway to the road.

"Grandstanding. A lot of grandstanding," Marie Eloise said as soon as Bonnie got out of the car. "I don't like to gossip, but tonight there was a lot of show. I didn't want to talk in front of the others."

"You think so?" Erland asked.

Michael mumbled in the backseat. "Easy. Easy. Take it easy. He don't mean nothing. Filthy dirt. Snot in the box. Snot in the box. Eye on the tree. A brighter light. Eternity in a second. Eternity starts in a second. Its waters rush into the second's slot. Sew a moment. It is and not. See the U.S.A."

The car slowed down for a stop sign. Without the rattle from the gravel on the road and the strain of the engine Michael's voice became audible.

"Oh my Lord, I forgot all about that child in the back seat." Marie Eloise gasped and chuckled nervously.

As the car slowed down in front of her house, she turned back to offer her hand to Michael, then she turned her face to Erland. It had become almost as wide as her shoulders. "I have visions. I told Pastor Ray that God uses me as a medium, but he doesn't seem to care about God anymore."

Michael remembered the mirrors that had flowed off her body the week before. When her husband opened the door, her body sucked the light into itself and she puffed out as if she would explode.

When they were back on the main road, Michael said, "I don't like her."

"Who?" Erland asked.

"Marie Eloise," Michael said and began to mumble again.

Part 19

One morning in March Michael woke up early. Walter's head and one of his arms hung out of the bed. Gus heard Michael get up and then noticed Walter and got up to look at him.

"He's dead," Gus said. "By God he's dead. Walter's dead."

When Michael came back from the bathroom, two attendants were loading the body onto a gurney. The others stood silently in the corner with their shoulders sloping and their hands hanging at their sides, except for Peter, who faced the corner and had his hands over his ears.

"We all get released from the home eventually," Gus said.

"That ain't funny," one of the other men said.

"Did I say it was?" Gus asked.

"Walter died," Michael declared to Maureen and Roxanne.

"Who's Walter?" Maureen asked.

"He slept with me. We all sleep in the same room. He slept five beds away. He died this morning. Gus said that we all get released eventually." Michael stood in front of them with his arms at his side.

"So he slept with you?" Maureen smirked.

Roxanne ignored Maureen. "Was he a friend of yours?"

"No, but he slept with me and now his bed is going to be empty. Joe's bed is empty. He slept with me, too."

Maureen lit a cigarette as she opened the newspaper.

"How do you feel about it?" Roxanne asked.

"I feel like things aren't right. Walter won't be in his bed. Will they bury him with everything?" Michael still hadn't moved.

"What do you mean?" Roxanne took out a small handkerchief and dabbed her forehead.

"His false teeth and his glasses. Like that boy. Will they put in all the parts?"

"I'm sure they will," Roxanne said. Maureen snorted.

"He always sat at the same place to eat. He slept in the first bed. He won't be there." Michael followed Roxanne as she went to the steel counter where she worked.

"You should have stayed at the home if your friend died," Roxanne said and Maureen looked up from the paper to glare at her.

"I can see him in my mind," Michael said.

"Your mind and here are two different things," Roxanne said.

All day Michael whispered to himself. "You give me the willies. Keep your fucking eyes to yourself. Faggot. Faggot. Fucking faggot. He's in a brighter place. Filthy dirt. That fucking Indian is sick. Sounds like a fairy to me. Are you a fairy, kid? You're a bunch of faggots. On the third day. Roll away the stone. The quick from the dead. You give me the willies."

Once Maureen came up behind him to listen, but couldn't make out what he was saying. When Roxanne asked her what he said, she shrugged. "A loony. Think I can understand a loony?"

Roxanne became sullen and ignored Maureen's jokes and sarcastic comments. She left early, mumbling goodbye. Maureen sat smoking and looking out into space.

"Did you ever know anyone else who died?" she asked.

He had already begun to clean up since Thomas had told him that he would pick him up early. He didn't talk until he swept the floor under Maureen's chair. The sentences came out as if they weren't connected, fast and separated by an almost mechanical pause. "I thought they left. I didn't know what it was. Johan and Maron died, I think. I knew Johan's name. I knew it a long time ago. I went to Maron's funeral. I still see her sometimes when I close my eyes."

"My husband died," she said. "You will never know what that is. Pain and relief. You can't have the two together without feeling bad about it. It makes me feel sick at heart to say it. But it's true. I never said it. You are a little better than a wall. I wouldn't tell a real person any of this." She coughed out cigarette smoke and

Michael jumped back when he saw that it was really fire coming out of her mouth.

"Will you see him again?" Michael asked, keeping a safe distance.

"Don't know, but I don't hope so," she answered.

"I see them all the time, Johan and Maron and Joe. Pain and relief. Remember and forget."

He stared at her as she sucked the fire back into her mouth. He waited for the fire to come out of her mouth again, but his staring at her made her nervous and she abruptly got up and opened the door to the front. "Les, I had to work extra because Roxanne had to go early. Mickie's almost done so I'm leaving."

Maureen turned back towards him as she opened the back door to leave and he could see two small flames flickering from her nostrils.

Tape 12 – Entry 16

Ernesto said on one of the tapes that you can get used to someone else not existing, but not to yourself not existing. He said that the thought was enough to make you kill yourself. Maybe it was a joke. Today Joshua's friend came. She asked me questions about dead people from the fire. I didn't want her to find me. Joshua said I was 99.99999% story. I think about that when I talk to her and get a

feeling like I can't breathe and I think that I am losing my story and
she is taking it. "Even when you're dead, your story goes on," Ernesto
said. A woman from my first job, her name was Maureen, told me
that I couldn't understand pain and relief. I had to ask Joshua what
relief was. He made me look at an ad for someone with a stomach
that hurt and then later they had a smile. That was relief. When I
burned my hand, I thought I was someone else watching me. That
part of me didn't hurt. It helped to be that other person watching me
in pain. Ernesto said that no one is really here and no one is really
gone and that is a relief.

The baptism had finally taken place. It was the last time
Marie Eloise went to the church. She claimed that the tank and
the church were too artificial for her. "Who knows what the
city puts in the water? Where does the Bible say anything about
fluoridation?" she asked a woman, whom she had corralled into a
corner.

There was no call for sinners to come forward.

Michael stepped into the tank and watched the bottom
of his white robe floating in the water. He thought of wading in
the river with Joe and looked up at Pastor Ray who was waving
a microphone in his hand. His voice boomed through the small
church, crackled and hit a high whine before he adjusted the

sound. Erland took the microphone from Pastor Ray just before he climbed into the water. Pastor Ray held Michael and dropped him back, then brought him forward, the water dripping and shining like icicles do when the sun strikes them. Michael shivered and grabbed out for Pastor Ray. The water was cold and the spasm he felt was like the Holy Spirit moving through him. Pastor Ray held him until he caught his balance. He picked up the microphone again and the blue curved lines of his voice pressed against the walls, then bounced back against him. The voice was pushing at Michael's skin and he could feel it entering and leaving.

Erland had folded Michael's clothes and left them on the chair in the small study next to the altar. Michael removed the long white robe which had clung to his body. A pool of water formed around him. The robe slumped into a pile on the floor, sending small streams in all directions. The robe was alive. What was it that he had lost when he took off the robe? The puddle of water moved out across the linoleum floor.

"You could have killed everyone if that microphone had fallen in the water. Everyone in the water would have died right there and then," he heard Marie Eloise say, but it sounded more like words that he was remembering than hearing.

He concentrated on himself. How did he feel different? He waited to learn who he was to be in the family of God. Outside the study people began to yell. Erland knocked on the door. When he came out, Pastor Ray was packing away the microphone and Marie Eloise was pulling one of the women along against her will and repeating, "He's no more a man of God than I'm the man in the moon."

All the people were getting smaller and Michael tried to stop it. The walls of the church shot up and all the people shrank.

Outside there was a wet late March wind that brought the scent of last year's leaves. If he could turn his body towards the wind at the right angle it would lift him off his feet. He saw the wet robe on the floor of the minister's study throbbing and realized that what he lost was his ability to touch people. A wall now existed between him and everyone around him. He huddled in the corner of the back seat. Marie-Eloise turned her whole body away from Erland and sat twisted with her large flat knees against the car door. The two women gazed straight ahead. Occasionally one of them looked over towards Marie-Eloise and then towards her friend and shook her head. Erland turned on the radio.

"I have a headache. Do you mind?" Marie-Eloise said without turning toward Erland. He turned the volume down.

"How do you feel now that you are baptized?" Erland asked.

"Okay," Michael said. "I don't know what I'm supposed to

feel, so I don't know what it is I should look for. You know what I mean?" Michael pressed his cheek against the cold glass of the window.

Marie-Eloise gave a loud snort and Erland swerved the car to miss a deer that darted across the road. Marie-Eloise hadn't seen the deer and turned her head just enough to so that Erland could see her gaping mouth and flared nostrils. She began to puff up again and she sucked the light into her so the sky suddenly became black. She turned her head back. Michael watched her reflection in the door window. Her breath fogged up the window, transforming her reflection into beads of water.

"I feel like when I took the robe off, I lost something." No one answered.

Marie-Eloise grunted, then shook her head as if she were trying to put some thought out of her mind.

"If he had been a man of God, he would have known how to use me. He don't know that electricity and water don't mix. Dobie Gillis died like that. Men and their microphone. You ever stopped to think what a microphone looks like? Did you ever?"

One of the women gasped. Marie Eloise turned her large body to the back and the car rocked.

"Wait until he starts dangling it from between his legs. He ain't no man of God." Marie Eloise turned back to the window causing the car to rock even more than the first time. Erland took a deep breath to show that his patience was wearing out.

The car floated into a cloud. Marie Eloise puffed up again. The others were like cut out dolls. The car was pulled out of the cloud by the yard light in Marie Eloise's driveway, landing hard on the ground. As soon as she left the car, the others expanded to their normal size. No one came to the door to meet her and when she opened the door, it was dark on the porch.

"I lost something," he said again.

"You can pick it up next week," Erland said and pulled out of the driveway.

Michael pulled his legs up into his chest, making himself small and compact. He licked a salty tear from his cheek.

Tape 9 – Entry 11

Sometimes I still feel Jesus come to me at night. His white robes spread across me and his blood fills the empty parts of my body. I see Joshua and he tells me, "You are not story. Stories are stories because they have empty spaces. Stories need spaces. You are whole." Marie-Eloise sometimes comes and tells me that I could have had a great light. "You did it wrong," she says. I try to feel the robes and Jesus' blood filling in the spaces, but sometimes she wins. Sometimes Jesus looks the way he does in the pictures, sometimes like Johan or Joe. Pastor Ray calls and the white robes move away and I see he's naked. He doesn't want me. He's just naked. I think of the robes and blood until the spaces are filled again. Maron is never there when I have this dream. But I think and think and think that she should be there.

In the bathroom he inspected himself in a mirror that was missing half the silvering. There was no change. If something was new, he couldn't see it. He tried to picture the wet robe on the floor in the church office, but no image came into his mind. Instead he heard Marie Eloise scream, "He is not a man of God" and saw the microphone hanging from Pastor Ray's unzipped pants. Suddenly it stood erect and swelled. He ran from the mirror.

That night he couldn't sleep. He heard a voice say, "I am Daniel," and grew cold when he realized that it was his own voice. "Michael isn't and he never was."

"No!" he said through his clamped teeth. "I do." He looked around to see if anyone had heard him. He expected the arm to shoot out of Joe's bed. Everyone had turned to rock and he was the last person alive. He knew it wasn't true when he said it, but after he said it, he became afraid.

"You are not in God's family," the voice said. He didn't know how to answer, but twisted the covers around his head and breathed in his own stale breath.

He woke up early and stood for several minutes over Walter's bed and then over Joe's, which was occupied by a new inmate. He was afraid someone might wake up and catch him standing between the beds. Gus rolled over and Michael froze, the blood seeming to stop and he let the air out of his lungs in a tiny steady stream. He didn't relax until he was in front of the mirror in the bathroom and took a long look at himself. He was not sure the person in the mirror was really him.

"Are you Daniel?" he asked and peered hard. "Was that Michael that was left in the wet robes?" His own voice seemed false and forced. Someone began to open the bathroom door, but turned around and left. When Michael left the bathroom, he saw Harold looking into the semi-independent men's bedroom.

"If I had known it was you," Harold said. He rubbed his hands against the sides of his body.

"I've been baptized," Michael said seriously, keeping his distance from Harold.

"Pastor Ray get you in the tank. He's a big man," Harold stuck his tongue out.

"He had a microphone." Michael blushed remembering Marie-Eloise's comment.

"I like you," Harold said. "Maybe I'll come down some day

when you're in the bathroom early. I have to leave now or they'll look for me. The archangel cried all night. I couldn't sleep." Just before he disappeared at the end of the hall, Harold turned back and waved.

Michael watched him without responding.

A couple months later when he went to the front hall to wait for Erland, Lester told him that Erland wasn't coming. "He's not going to them meetings. I knew all along the guy was a charla. . . A Lester's dentures slipped before he could finish and he repeated the word "charlatan" completely.

"You did?" Michael asked, hoping that Lester would explain what a charlatan was.

"He should stick to his own business. You can be too holy."

"You can?" Michael asked.

Lester looked at Michael as if for the first time and seemed embarrassed about confiding in him. "He wanted me to tell you," Lester said.

Part 20

The next week when he went into the shop of the bakery, Rhonda was standing in front of the counter choosing pastries. She had pulled the sleeves up on her blue spring coat and the front was open. She looked up at Michael and he nodded to her and hurried into the back.

She was gone when he came back with the next tray.

"You know her?" Les asked.

"From church." Michael said.

Les laughed. "She gets around if she goes to church, too."

When Michael took the garbage out, Rhonda was sitting at the picnic table, carefully eating a glazed donut. She sat hunched into her coat with her face turned to the early April sun. She held the donut with her fingertips.

"Michael," she called and straightened up crossing her legs. "You didn't come to church last Tuesday."

Michael shook his head.

"Erland shouldn't believe everything he hears." She scanned Michael's face.

"Winston told me lots of stories about you. The first night at the church, I felt something weird happened to me. You were part of it. The way you looked at Winston and I, I felt naked. He told me a great deal."

Michael avoided looking directly at her, but bobbed his head as if he were pondering what she said. He rocked the trash can back and forth in the gravel. She licked the icing off her fingers before pulling the lapels of her coat together to face the cool spring wind. "No one has ever made me feel like that," she said. "I almost believe Marie-Eloise. Almost. But men are never as holy as they seem."

"Did you see me get baptized?" Michael mumbled. "Do you think he did it right?"

Rhonda stood for a moment. "What would I know? Sure he did." She looked like she was listening for a sound in the air above her, then stepped onto the sidewalk and continued up the street.

"Michael, Les wants you in the front," Maureen called. He rushed through the back door, wiping his hands on his apron and running his fingers through his hair. Les had dropped a coffee filter on the floor and coffee was splattered around the filter.

"Get the broom and mop and pick this up. Every time that bitch comes in here wagging her ass and teats, something happens. You're lucky you're too dumb for her to come after you. Does she have a big mouth?" Les said.

Michael thought the question was strange. "I never

thought about it."

When Michael returned, Les had already walked through the steaming coffee grounds and was cussing and swearing. He pushed the swinging door open so that it banged against the wall. Michael could hear him screaming at Maureen and Roxanne. Maureen yelled back. Then the back door slammed and there were a few minutes of silence. Roxanne began to chide Les, her voice laden with soft droning rebuke.

The bell on the bakery door rang and Michael waited for Les. He heard Maureen again, then Les. When he straightened up to turn to the door, Marie-Eloise was leaning over the counter, her irregular breasts resting on the glass above the tray of macaroons. He felt that she had been watching him for a while.

"I saw that Rhonda from church was in here. What she tell you?" Marie Eloise craned her head to look down at Michael.

"Nothing." He listened to the voices in the back, but now they were talking softly and he could only hear an occasional word without being able to make it out.

"She tell you nothing outside, too?" She pretended to inspect the slices of pound cake that were several days old. "You were there a while."

"She said you were right. I don't know." Michael took the dustpan, broom and mop into the back. Everyone in the back was silent.

"There's someone in front," Michael said.

"Find out what they want?" Les ordered without making any attempt to get up.

When Michael returned, Marie Eloise was looking out the window. Her face became serious when she saw Michael again.

"You know I stopped going to the church after the baptism. Something happened. No one will tell." She looked impatiently at the door to the kitchen. "Why do you think the devil is a man? Thought about that?"

"What about the baptism?"

"I don't see no new light on you. I would know. I have that power. Not a twinkle." She sniffed and her jaw moved as if she were going to say something else.

"With the right water, natural water, it would have worked. Servants of God are always weak. Water is strong." Michael froze. Marie-Eloise noticed her sudden power over him. "You could have a great light. I told you I saw it. I have the power."

"Okay, okay," Les yelled from the back and the spell was broken.

"I'm supposed to ask you what you want," Michael said, expecting her body to expand, but instead it shrunk back each time she exhaled until she was no bigger than he was.

"What I want? To buy something."

He went in the back to tell Les, who rose slowly from his chair, but when he got to the front no one was there. "Who was it? Whoever it was is gone."

"Some woman. She said she wanted to buy something. Some woman. Her name is Marie-Eloise."

"Maureen and me are taking the rest of the day off. If Les screams at us, he got to pay." Roxanne pulled her apron over her head and hung it from a hook. There were half-moons of sweat under her arms. "We're not doing any more so you can start cleaning up. So Mickie Dwindie, do as much as you like. Finish decorating them two cakes. People are coming for them. Then clean like usual. He just flies off the handle like that."

Les shrugged his shoulders and let the door swing shut. Michael found the two cakes. One of them had a photograph of someone else's birthday cake and he was supposed to copy it. On a piece of paper Roxanne had carefully spelled out the name for the cake. He made a good copy of the cake, but left off some of the flowers and added a ribbon. The light had almost died in the kitchen by the time he finished the second cake. Maureen had made paper hands and taped them onto the clock so Michael would know when Thomas would come. She had explained that the long skinny one went around once for every time the fat one moved from number to number. He only had fifteen minutes to clean up.

Les was outside talking to a customer when Michael swept the front. He could smell the odor of Marie Eloise and it followed him to the back when he rushed out the door with the garbage. He took a deep breath of the cool late afternoon air.

He held his jacket in his hand as he waited for Thomas. Crows were gathered in a scrub oak next to the butcher's back lot. Pastor Ray's smell from the first night he had been saved replaced Marie Eloise's. A cloud blocked the sun and two crows fought over a scrap of meat. Michael put his coat on.

Thomas asked him to sit in the cab of the truck on the way back to the home. The others looked at him suspiciously as he climbed out of the back.

"You like your job?" Thomas asked after they had sat silently in the cab for a few miles.

"I like it," Michael replied.

"I hear good things about you from Les and that big woman told me that you were a good kid," Thomas said.

"Hmm," Michael said and slumped down in the seat so his eyes were just above the window of the car door.

"You stopped going to that church with Erland, right? Why?" Thomas said.

"I don't know." Michael turned away from Thomas. Along the side of the road was a small pond that he had never seen before. Cows stood drinking at the edge. The afternoon light turned the water silver. A breeze ruffled the surface and the water came alive.

"No?"

He didn't hear Thomas. The pond was giving off more than sunlight. It was making its own light. He heard it jingle like quarters, then a sudden gust of wind rattled across the water, followed by an eerie sound like Roxanne humming.

"You don't know why you stopped going to church?" Thomas raised his voice and Michael turned toward him.

"Erland didn't want to go. He stopped going. Lester told me when I went to wait for Erland. But it's okay. I don't care."

"You're not sad about it?" They were almost at the front gate.

"No, I'm not sad about it. It's okay." Michael climbed down from the cab.

Peterson spit on Michael's shoes as he passed him. "What he have to tell you, that you fired at the bakery?"

Joshua was pacing on the porch between the two large cement pots with the brown remnants of last summer's petunia. Other inmates sat on benches and chairs facing the front gate;

several with their eyes closed, their faces reflecting the warm early April sunlight that hit the porch. When the truck pulled up to let the town workers off, Joshua stopped as if he were an awkward actor following stage directions.

Michael dragged his foot in the loose gravel to wipe the spit from his shoe. He noticed Joshua with his manic gaze, his face twitching, so he walked up the stairs as far away from him as possible.

"Lost God or lost your ride? I have ears, you know." He scurried across the porch and bent down to stick his fleshy moon face in front of Michael.

There was so little light. The redness drained from Joshua's face and his skin became gray and powdery.

"I am writing to Bernice. She already thinks your story is too complicated. Too many twists. Perhaps this will be simply a brief hiatus in your journey of faith. The more lurid the sin, the more spectacular the salvation. I see your life as a movie. Perhaps these religious encounters are the commercials. In this institution of higher insanity, all movies have commercials. I have to remember to write that to Bernice." Joshua took a small pad out of his loose khaki pants and scribbled with a pencil stub.

"Is Pastor Ray a charlatan?" Michael asked and Pastor Ray's scent of sweat and cologne, the starched and pressed odor of his suit filled his head. He tried to shake it off and took a deep breath.

"He is a dime-store evangelist reeking of male hormones and lust and Dionysian gyrations. A marvelous gew gaw of mid-twentieth century lower-class popular culture." Joshua had his eyes closed as if he were imagining Pastor Ray standing before him.

"So you don't think when he baptized me it worked. Because he is a charlatan." Pastor Ray's smell had become so strong that he began to cough.

"Marvelous show. I'd give anything to be a fly on the wall. I love wet bodies. Humans should have remained an aquatic species." Joshua took out his notebook again and scribbled for a few seconds. He leafed through it trying to read the day's observations. "Have you learned anything, Parrot Boy?" Joshua asked glancing suddenly up from the notebook.

"He is a dime store evangelist reeking of male hormones and lust and Dionysian gyrations. A marvelous gew gaw."

"Excellent. Excellent. Bernice must see this," Joshua screeched and scampered to a bench to write.

Michael closed his eyes and concentrated on the glistening silver of the pond. He heard the jingling of the wind on the water. First Pastor Ray's scent, then Marie-Eloise's faded.

When he opened his eyes, Joshua was still scribbling.

He saw Ernesto's straight black hair over the top of a chair in the day room.

"I knew it was you. The other times I thought maybe it was you, but this time I was sure. It's spring. I like working outside. I heard Joe today. He said to me, "Tell Michael, hello. He is a good person."" Ernesto took a deep breath, then looked squarely at Michael.

"I was baptized. I lost something. I can't touch people anymore. And people's smells, they stick on me. If you tried to touch me now, you couldn't."

Ernesto grabbed Michael's hand, but there was an invisible barrier, like a holy ghost. Michael could feel the warmth and the pressure from the short calloused fingers.

Ernesto rubbed his thumb across the back of Michael's hand as he spoke. "There are no rules in life. Don't let them make up rules and then think you have to follow them. Even your mind will make up rules. Rules and rulers. Twelve inches and they hit you over the knuckles." Ernesto chuckled.

"I saw this water today. It was a pond. It shined. It shined from the bottom."

Ernesto turned back to the wall. Michael waited next to him. "Oh, you mean magic rules. Those are different." Ernesto turned away.

Recently when he had gone to the day room, he had looked at the pictures in magazines or through travel, home repair and art books that had been donated, but tonight he sat before the television. The three front rows of chairs were taken, so he sat at the far end of a couch along the wall. When the image on the screen began to flip, Joshua would stride up to adjust the controls. Scenes of light from the pond flashed on the screen like a secret message. It was hard to tell if the others had seen them. Their faces had become mirrors for the light of the television. They all shone at the same time, went dark suddenly. They had become a part of a great machine, a monster, and he had been left out. He had not been swallowed into the warm stomach with its flickering light. He was out in the cold by himself, like the night he had spent in the barn after Maureen's husband died. And now he could not touch anyone. He saw the thin spirit that had covered his skin since the day he was baptized. The part of him that was connected to the world was lost when he took off the wet robe. His skin became the color of his shoes and his fingers became stiff. He looked across the room to where Ernesto sat with his black hair sticking up over the back of the chair. He looked at his hand and saw that where Ernesto had touched him the leather skin had fallen off and he could see the marks from the small stubby fingers.

He went upstairs early. Peter was already in bed, but otherwise the room was empty. He closed his eyes and heard the sound of the water before he saw the silver light shooting up from the pond. The cows swayed like trees as the wind chopped the lake into forks of light. As he lay with his eyes closed watching the light billowing out of the lake in silver clouds, he knew what he had to do. He moved naked into the pond so when he left the water, he would not lose anything. No wet clothes would drop from his body. In the darkness and moonlight, the cows had turned into bushes that formed a long narrow alley leading to the water. His feet moved over the mud without sinking in and a hand supported him firmly behind his neck as he was lowered into the water. A light broke out of the dark water like a saber and smote him, so he shone. Marie-Eloise was blinded. Pastor Ray cried and embraced him and suddenly he was warm and shining and Pastor Ray himself was naked.

When he opened his eyes, Peter was staring at him. He heard Joe in the corner, but was afraid to look at him, so instead he glared at Peter, who buried his head in his pillow. He closed his eyes to watch the silver pond shine until finally he fell asleep.

He smelled the odor of the laundry room, woke up from his dream and the odor was still there. He had been looking for

Joe, following the scent of the laundry room, burrowing deeper and deeper into the piles of filthy laundry. He could imagine the smell of Joe's breath, his body after a few hours in the barn, but he couldn't smell it. It was gone. Joe had said, "Stay away from Harold. Harold is melting." Then Joe had melted.

Everyone was asleep. He examined each of them to see if they were breathing. The sun was just cracking the edge of the horizon and the trees waved like seaweed in the liquid morning air.

In the bathroom he threw water into his face, cold at first, then hot. His face turned red for a few moments.

"Dwindie. Dwindie."

He looked up first since it seemed like the voice was coming from the ceiling.

"Dwindie." Michael saw Harold peeping from a shower stall. "I've been waiting for you. I have a key." He held the key in the palm of his hand.

"We can't here. I have a key," Harold said.

He arched his pelvis out and rubbed up against Michael. Harold scurried to the door with little steps. After peeking out the door, he strode down the hall on his tip-toes. When he reached a small side hall, he raised his arm to point, and disappeared..

The blood rose to Michael's head. He readjusted the belt

on his robe so it was looser and wouldn't show his erection. At the door of the bedroom, he paused, then shot off for the side hall. There was a door halfway open that he had never noticed before. He looked in and Harold was already naked, lying on thin child's mattress, which was pushed up against the wall. The closet was long and narrow. Michael looked back at the door when he closed it.

"The light," Michael said.

"No one comes here. Lester lost the key. He don't want no one to know he set this up for fucking. So he don't want no one to open it. Not with his key. No way." Harold looked sternly at Michael, "Fast. Fast. Tomorrow bring a towel. Lester brought a towel."

Michael's legs were trembling and his chest tightened as he checked to see if anyone was in the main hall. He heard the archangel scream, "My back is bleeding where they cut off my wings." Someone else screamed, "For Christ's sake would you shut him up." He was at the door to the bathroom when he heard the closet door slam and when he turned around he saw Harold darting down the hall in the opposite direction. Peter was in the bathroom when Michael walked in.

"You weren't in the room." Peter said. He had turned from the sink to Michael. His face and body still sagging from sleep.

"I went to hear what the archangel said." He put his hands in the pockets of the robe to pull robe away from his body.

"You did?" Peter waited for an answer, staring suspiciously.

"Yeah, I guess." He passed Peter on the way to the shower and took his robe off carefully so his back was always to Peter. In the shower he masturbated.

He dressed quickly, glad that the bedroom was still dark. When he reached the truck, Thomas was waiting by himself. Hank and William, who were usually there when Michael arrived, came down five minutes later.

As the truck passed the pond, he peered through a gash in the canvas that covered the back of the truck. The cows were gone. The water was black. He sat up again. He remembered Joe saying, "Harold is melting. Stay away from Harold."

He closed his eyes. Harold lay on the mattress with his long shaggy hair, his tongue flipping in and out of his mouth and his shoulders heaving like waves. Then he lay still, smiled and bit his lower lip. Michael lay down next to him. "Fast. Fast." Harold had said, pulling and jerking at him until they both came. He felt that he had turned inside out. The soft part was now outside and the hard part had sunk below the surface. "Fast. Fast." Harold had repeated after they lay catching their breath for a minute. The hard part shot to the surface. He had gotten up and Harold had pulled him back to kiss him. "That's how they do it in the movies. We can be in a movie," Harold said. He had checked the doorway before leaving. That was all he remembered, but he played it over again in his mind.

Harold waited for him in the shower stall twice a week. When Michael stayed in bed too long one morning, Harold screamed in the high-pitched cracked voice of the archangel, "They took the feathers in your pillows from my wings. They shattered them. They took the feathers in your pillows from my wings. Give them back." Michael remembered hearing those words that last time he and Harold were in the closet. When he stumbled out of the bedroom into the dull softly creaking hallway, Harold was waving to him from the entrance to the side hallway. "They ripped them off me to make pillows. I'm bleeding."

Michael did not follow him at first. He wondered if there was an archangel anymore or only Harold imitating him. He hadn't seen him for several months.

Harold went into his parody of sex, twisting his hips, bobbing his head over an invisible penis, falling against the wall and catching himself with his palms, his legs spread and his buttocks up.

Michael was getting bored by Harold. He felt like it was

a wall that rose until he felt completely alone when he was with Harold. He changed from Joe's voice, to Lester's, to others that he couldn't recognize.

"What movie today? You want to be Troy Donahue? He's hip. Troy, baby. A little dab will do you. Do you. Do you. Do you."

The light bulb clicked and burned out. Harold stopped talking and his body relaxed. His hips sank to the mattress. The only sound was their breathing and the slide and jerk of their bodies. For a minute there was complete silence, then Michael got up and found the door handle. He turned it cautiously. When light came in the closet, he noticed the look of terror and confusion on Harold's face.

"It's okay, Harold. It was just the light." Michael tiptoed to the main hall and then darted for the bathroom. When he left the bathroom he heard the archangel screaming, "My feathers were put on sparrows, not in pillows. On sparrows. Freezing to death. My back is bleeding. My back is bleeding."

It was light now on the way to work. Each morning he looked through the gash in the canvas as they passed the pond. The light had been growing and there had been a few days when it was blood red, like the blood of Christ on Ernesto's holy cards. Then it was dark again because of daylight-saving time, which Joshua claimed was a communist plot. But now it glittered like the first evening he had seen it. In the evening when he came back from work the sun was still high in the sky and the cows swishing their tales to keep the flies off. The farmer had run a fence through the pond so there was a part that the cows could not reach and the edge was grassy. Michael thought that the pond during the day and at night guarded its secret, but as the sun was going down and coming up, it revealed everything.

He knew that the days changed. Soon the pond would be in full light and its secret hidden. Each morning he saw something new, a bird wading in the water, or heard a sound from the water that he hadn't heard before. He had to baptize himself at night when the water had stored the light.

When he reached home that evening, the buildings looked like they had been cut out and placed against the sky. The air was still. Harold waved to him from a bench in the park where he sat with Lester and four other inmates. Joshua paced on the porch and whirled around to face the van as it drove up to the front of the building.

"I cannot take the lunatics. There are medications to silence the insane. How can I get better when these thoughts are inserted in my brain each night by Ralph Roister Doister? Or Ralph Haverham, as he's really called. If he's an angel, I'm an idiot." Joshua spurted out his words, rushing around Michael to lean into first one ear and then the other.

"Bernice hasn't written for a month. You haven't cooperated. I put too much hope on you and you failed me. You think getting out that front gate every day is the world. Don't make me laugh. You have a story. That's all you have. Without your story you are nothing, infinitesimal. 99.999% story and a dust particle of substance." Joshua raised his fist as if he were going to hit Michael, then swung himself around.

He found Ernesto again in the day room.

"I worked in the peony beds. The ants are taking over the world. I saw them. They are more organized than ever and they are taking over the world. *Una hormigacracia.* An . I saw their black bodies pulling in the light. They are very organized. I read a book about it once. A science fiction book. But all that stuff comes true. Later. But it comes true." Ernesto seemed to see Michael for the first time.

"Oh, how was your day?" He took his glasses off and rubbed his eyes.

"Okay," Michael answered.

"Good. I'm glad. Good." Ernesto put his glasses back on. "Something is going to happen. Here something always happens. And nothing changes. I haven't seen Joe. Not for a while. That doesn't bother you, does it?"

Michael stared into the lenses of Ernesto's glasses. His hazel eyes flowed into muddy swirls. As Ernesto turned towards the wall again, the light from a window caught the lenses and shot two arrows of light into Michael's face.

For a moment he was silent. The light turned to water or the water turned to light. After he was really baptized, he would have the brightest light. He would not leave a robe on the floor with stolen light.

"What will happen, Ernesto?" Michael had suddenly become aware of the whole room, the other people, the blare of a commercial from the television.

He was about to walk away when Ernesto said, "Something will happen. Something. *Algo pasará.*"

"*Algo pasará,*" Michael repeated, not sure what it meant.

"Yes, it will," Ernesto said.

Michael walked into the hall. A loud hollow pounding echoed through the halls. When he reached the third floor he saw some workmen taking out a window. The frame was so rotten that it disintegrated as they pulled it out. He stopped to the watch the blue arch and wild shower of sparks from soldering torch one of the men was using to cut the bars of the window away. The man turned towards Michael with the welding mask that made him look like a huge insect. He lifted the mask by pulling it up with his shoulder.

"Hey, bread boy. You live here?"

He recognized a man who came in to buy donuts every morning. He nodded and the man let the mask fall again.

He continued down the hall, but the blue sparks were everywhere he looked. It was different from the colors. It looked like it was between his eyes and the wall and then it would seem to be behind the wall. Instead of flowing or pulsating it hummed, like the water in the pond on still mornings. He went to the bedroom to lie down. The blue light faded as he stared at the ceiling. He closed his eyes and when he opened them, Harold was leaning over him.

"I'm going to go crazy at supper," Harold whispered and smiled like he was telling a big secret. "Lester's after me. I don't want none of that old farmer dick no more. When you come to supper, watch for me. I'll give you the sign. The sign, okay."

He went down late for dinner and only a few stragglers who had been rounded up in the day room were in the line for food. Joshua had not wanted to eat because he had been keeping lists of words on television which he felt were overused. He was still shaken from his confrontation with Erland.

"I was up to ten times for "right-o" when that idiot interrupted. Fifteen times for. . . I can't even remember the word.

"Impossible."

He looked around the room for Harold and saw him at a table with Lester and other inmates, but his back was towards him. There was an empty seat next to Gus. Michael sat down without saying a word.

"Hey, Dwindie, you got to have some money now you're working. Buy Crazy Lorraine a few candy bars and she'll let you in her pants. Ain't that so, Peter? About time you learned about the real stuff," Gus said looking around the table. The other men smiled. Peter blushed.

"Okay," Michael said.

"I can even fix it up for you if you give me a few bucks." Gus winked.

Michael watched as Harold's arms slowly rose above his head. Gus continued to talk. Michael looked across the room. It seemed as if everyone had been waiting for Harold to begin. Lester looked suspiciously around, his hand covering his mouth.

Harold had chewed the threads on the buttons of his shirt so they would pop off when he yanked on his shirt. He dropped his pants and was wearing no underwear. Several of the attendants stood up and walked leisurely towards Harold, who seemed to be gyrating in oblivion until they were a few feet from him, when he darted between them. As soon as he was out of their reach, he skipped around the tables. He was attempting a cartwheel when he lost his balance and fell onto one of the tables, cutting his leg. Several senile patients began to cry. Harold managed to get up and skipped blindly for a few feet, then stopped. The attendants had been getting closer. A few of the inmates began to clap in unison. He stumbled several times. When the attendants made a run for him, he fell onto the floor and squirmed under a table, making his way for the wall, where he spread out with his nose against the floor board. A puddle of blood formed next to his leg.

Several inmates gathered around Harold and the attendants. A nurse brought a blanket to cover him. She pulled a roll of gauze and tape from a large pocket and knelt over Harold to bind his leg. Above the chatter, nervous laughter could be heard like an echo. `

"Calm down. Calm down." Lester mangled the words. He adjusted his dentures. "Quiet."

There was a lull in the talking.

The echo was distinguishable. "I have fallen. But I am ready to go back."

Michael recognized the archangel's voice.

"I trust in the Lord now. I trust in the Lord now. I have my wings."

Lester bent over Harold, who panted in low shallow breaths. His body curled and stiffened. He sobbed, then laughed.

"Don't do this. Don't. They'll have to give you a shot." Lester straightened up to take in the room. It became quiet as he looked around. Michael moved between the tables until he was standing a few feet from Harold. Michael's energy was turning in, winding itself up. Harold grimaced at him, then Lester bent down over Harold again. The nurse came with a large needle and the inmates who were standing around crowded in.

"I trust you, Lord. I trust you," the archangel cried and his voice was suddenly clear. It seemed to flow into Harold's arm through the needle.

Michael heard the same dull pounding that he had heard earlier. Another nurse hurried in the door, pushing her way to Lester. They whispered together, then left. The two attendants waited until Harold unfolded. They helped him up and led him off on wobbly legs.

When Michael turned around, Ernesto was right behind him.

"Did you hear the archangel?" Ernesto droned. "And that noise. Did you hear the noise? It all works together, Harold, Lester, the archangel. What have they wrought?"

Inmates returned to their dinner. One of the fluorescent

tubes flickered and went dark. Outside the summer sun was above the horizon, but behind a pale mist. As soon as the sun was halfway set, the ambulance arrived. Michael thought it was for Harold, but one of the attendants returned and the word buzzed around the room that it was Ralph Haversham who had managed to knock down the wooden barricade the workmen had made for the window they were working on and then jumped.

"Have you noticed how the lights of an ambulance bleat just like a lamb? It is much more comforting than the screeching siren. Who would have to be tied to a ship mast if that were the siren?" Joshua laughed at his own cleverness, but his face was solemn.

Inmates gathered at the windows but they could see only the ambulance since the window from which Ralph had jumped was on the adjoining side of the building and on the opposite side from the day room. An attendant came back, spoke to another one, and they left together. Someone whispered that this time Ralph was dead. He had flung himself head first to the ground.

Even Peterson was quiet on the way to work the next morning. There had been so much talk the night before and several inmates had become hysterical, keeping many of the others up.

Michael looked at the pond just as a breeze rippled across

it, making the reflection of the white farm house and red barn up the hill from the pond flutter as if they were about to lift off the water.

Thomas took a different route into town. He shook their hands as they got out of the truck. Michael was the last to get off.

"Maybe he had too much God. He didn't know how to handle it." Thomas looked at the ground but still held Michael's hand in both of his.

"I want everything to go right. I think if everything works, everything will be okay." Thomas held his breath and closed his eyes. He was covered in a light with the colors of the inside of a shell. The blue light of the welding torch moved across his face.

"Accidents happen in time. I've been thinking about it. If the window hadn't rotted, the men had started later or earlier, if they nailed more boards. One little opening and things go wrong. One opening." Thomas was calm now. He let Michael's hands drop.

"Work hard, Michael."

Michael shooed the flies away before he opened the screen door. When he turned around, Thomas was still standing next to the truck. Michael waved at him. Thomas's light was seeping away.

Les wasn't there and Maureen watched for him by leaving the door to the front slightly open.

"I heard that Rhonda woman wanted Les to go to church with her and tell everything he did to her. Call up Janice. She used to be a friend of mine and I told her I hoped she took less time to divorce Les than it took her to marry him. Call her up and have her go to that Holy Roller church that day," Maureen said as if she were speaking to no one.

"He made Abe stop drinking. As long as he could keep the spirit," Roxanne said without looking over at Maureen.

"One drink is as bad as another."

"I liked Abe a lot better sober," Roxanne said and conversation died.

When Les came back, he closed the door between the shop and the kitchen. The light changed and Michael noticed the thickness of the air.

"You on automatic, Mickie?" Roxanne called out.

"Yes, on automatic," Michael said, but he didn't really know what she meant.

"Good," she said.

Maureen had started a solitaire game and when she took a cigarette break, she would turn over a few cards. "I'm not saying that Les ain't getting his just desserts, but I don't see how you can believe in that kook. Not even Dwindie believes in him anymore. Do you, Dwindie? Dwindie, do you think Pastor Ray can make Les better?"

"Maybe," he said, scurrying away with the trays of rolls that Maureen had just finished forming on the pan. "He has too much God."

"He's on automatic," Roxanne said. "Don't expect no real answer."

Part 21

Ernesto was standing near the front desk when Michael returned that evening.

"I know where he fell. I found some feathers and put them where he fell. I won't forget. If you find feathers, save them for me. There are lots of pigeon feathers in the barn. I want big feathers. I don't want anyone to know. Nothing. *Nada*. Do you understand?"

"*Nada*," Michael said.

"That's right. Nothing."

"Whatever you plan to do, it must be tomorrow. Tomorrow or it won't work."

Ernesto moved on as if his job had been accomplished.

As Michael walked towards the locked ward where Ralph had often lived, he checked the hall to see if it was empty, then looked through the peephole. A man whom Michael had never seen before was tied to a chair. Another man lay naked on the floor. An attendant was washing the man in the chair. The room began to fill with blood. Michael turned away when it was knee deep. The blood seeped under the door. He hurried down the hall, checking his shoes a few times to see if there was blood on them. Red clouds hung in the hallway and he had to dodge them.

When he saw Joshua standing outside the day room, there was a sudden flash and the figure of Joshua shone like hot wax. The clouds of blood disappeared.

"You know it was murder. When they want to murder someone here, all they have to do is leave the right window open. We are so squeezed in here that we will fly from any opening, like air in a balloon when it's pricked. They wanted to get rid of Joe, so they left Peter's legs open." Joshua gave a snort of disgust. "The window opens to nothingness and it bathes us like our mother's milk. Not the horrible nothingness of being, but the wonderful nothingness of not being. Sex and death. Buchner had it all down in *Lenz*. We are fallen angels who want to be Christ."

"We are?" Michael asked.

"Pearls to swine," Joshua lamented. "Speaking of swine, Harold has been sedated. No more floor shows from the Show of Shows."

"There are feathers," Michael interrupted, but Joshua ignored him.

"They are blaming him for diverting the staff so the angel could jump. He is getting the needle as punishment. Imagine unshakeable calm as punishment. If that was. . ."

"There are feathers in the yard." Michael said interrupting Joshua. He added sternly, "Where the archangel fell. Did you see them?"

As Michael ambled away, Joshua called, "That was no archangel. That was a poor tormented soul."

He lay on his bed and thought of the room filling with blood. When he closed his eyes, he saw the naked man on the floor floating face down and the man tied to the chair submerged.

"In the name of the father, the son, and the holy ghost."

The blood turned to water and was sucked into the bodies until the room was dry. The inmates shone with the light from the pond, and the attendants became thin white paper that floated to the floor. Then the attendants tried to take off the clothes of the man who was tied to the chair, but the man on the floor was safe because he was naked.

Whatever you plan to do, it must be tomorrow. Tomorrow or it won't work.

When he closed his eyes he felt the water of the pond on his feet. It was warm as bath water and vibrated like the floor of the bakery when the big mixer was on high. It moved through his body and became stronger as he walked into the water. He felt it around his waist and it lifted him off his feet. His chest parted the water like a wild duck's. The widening wake glittered as if it were hit by brilliant morning sun.

"Harold was your friend. He's gone."

Michael was startled and opened his eyes to see Peter in the hallway.

"I know what you did. I know it. He's gone." Peter shifted from foot to foot as if he were deciding whether to leave.

"I learned my lesson. I told them, I learned my lesson." Peter looked like he was in a window and not a doorway. Behind him Michael could see pure air. He closed his eyes and when he opened them, Peter was gone.

He awoke knowing what he would do that day. During breakfast he could only think of the pond. He nodded to Thomas when he went down to the truck, but didn't answer when asked how he was. At work Roxanne announced that Mickie was on automatic and she repeated this in a motherly voice all morning. The day was a dream from which he was going to wake. He stood off and watched himself work like a machine. It surprised him that he was two people, the one looking and the one being watched and then he began to think of the mirrors and the dreams. The water would enter him and break down the barriers between the face in the mirror and him, between the world of dreams and the waking world. Tears came to his eyes. He wiped them away with the back of his arm and darted more quickly around the kitchen.

"Roxanne, did you give that kid coffee?" Maureen said as

she dug through her purse to find her cigarettes. "Or did someone push the wrong button? Find the button and put him back on medium. He's making me dizzy. Mickie, slow down. Mickie."

He stopped and turned to her. After he looked in her eyes, she lit her cigarette and then waved him away.

He would stop to daydream about the mirrors and dreams melting into one, then scurry around the kitchen oblivious to everything except the routine. When he rushed into the shop with a tray of donuts, he darted back into the kitchen before Les could give him an order.

Les kept luncheon meat and mayonnaise in the cooler for sandwiches. Michael was in charge of making the sandwiches for himself and for Les. The women brought their own food from home. He left the sandwich for Les and sat by himself on a stool next to the mixers. He wasn't hungry so he put the sandwich in the garbage pail and hid it under an empty flour bag.

"Hey, Mickie, what's wrong with you. Are you in love?" Roxanne called from the small table where she and Maureen ate.

"No," he said. Roxanne's voice pulled him away from the pond. It made the bakery too real and the other worlds didn't exist. He concentrated on his plan again. He would wait until he took the garbage out in the afternoon and he would not come back. He knew the road to the pond and could hide in the tall grass if a car passed.

"Something's going on. You've been on automatic all morning, like you had a fire in your pants." Roxanne spoke slowly with her mouth full of tuna salad.

"For men that's what love is, a fire in their pants," Maureen said and rolled her eyes wearily.

"Mickie ain't like that. Are you Mickie?"

"No!" He sounded angry.

Part 22

An older woman on her porch stood up to watch him. He
turned back a few times to look at her. He had to keep the white
pants and shirt from work on when he left, but it wasn't until now
that he realized that it made him stand out more than even the
mismatched clothes from the County Home. White was the color
of the robe at his baptism that had stolen his light. He turned the
corner to walk back to the bakery, but he saw a man whom he
thought was Pastor Magshore walking towards him. At the top
of the hill into town, he stood for several minutes deciding what
he would do. In the distance he saw a tractor coming towards
him and he moved under a barbed wire fence, laying down in the
weeds until it passed. The summer heat made everything droop.
He got up. His white pants and shirt were stained with green
and covered with burrs. The tractor had been pulling a mower
that clipped the weeds in the ditch and the grass so that they lay
in moist angled rows. He moved along the edge of the field. The
smell of the cut weeds cooking in the heat made him sick to his
stomach. It wasn't unpleasant, but it seemed to choke the air.
Walking was easier when he reached a soybean field. He ran bent
over, falling a few times into the dust of the field.

A creek cut along the edge of the next field. He lay down under a willow tree, reaching his arms out to pull at the leaves. The pond was over the next hill. His pants were brown now. He waded into the creek and took off his clothes. He could feel Joe somewhere near, perhaps coming towards him in the creek. The water turned gold. Suddenly it was cold. He carried his clothes in his arms and fell into the dry prickly grass. He put his clothes on wet. The sun beat on his face so that he could feel its pulse. When he looked again, the water was clear and Joe's presence was gone. From a clump of trees far from the road, he watched the truck from the County Farm crawl up the hill, billowing dust behind it. He wondered if somehow he was in the back of the truck and no one knew that his other self was missing. Would he look through the tear in the canvas as the truck passed the pond? Would he see himself lying here?

He slept fitfully. He woke when he heard a man leading some cows across the creek and up the hill. He was nervous until the man's voice and the sound of the cows disappeared, but then he felt abandoned. There was no one else. Perhaps he would never find another person in the world. When he reached the top of the hill, he saw the red truck from the farm again, this time returning to the farm, and thought he could see the look on Thomas's face. He was looking for him.

He could walk back to the farm and sleep in the barn as he had the other time and they would be happy when they found him. He rolled under the fence, cutting his arm on the stub of a cut sapling. For a long time he lay in the ditch thinking of the pain and sucking the blood from his arm. He saw the truck again. He stood up as Thomas drove by, but he didn't see him, so he lay back in the ditch again. It was cloudy, but not dark. He crossed the road hoping someone would see him. The sun came from between the clouds and the pond shimmered cold like metal. The stench of cow manure filled his lungs and his empty stomach. He put his head down into the grass, breathing in the smell of dry dirt and weeds until he began to sneeze. He lifted himself on one arm and looked at the pond again. It had turned to a dark purple. The wind became cold and he took off his clammy tennis shoes and his feet felt warmer for a few minutes.

He crawled between the weeds along the fence until he reached an old bathtub that had been turned into a water trough for the cattle. He was warm until the sun set and the wind came up. In the darkness the ground moved to the groans of the bullfrogs. The crickets' hum made waves of yellow light. He saw the immense sky though the weeds. A small high cloud floated over, veiling but not obscuring the stars. On the midsummer horizon there was still a dull glow from the sun and the moon had not risen yet. He curled up to keep warm. He put his sneakers back on, but without the socks.

He saw the light before he could see the huge moon rise above the barn. The light was pure and unforced and flowed in straight streams. It had been a long time since a car had gone by. He stood up and took off his shirt to look at his arms in the moonlight. A chill ran up his spine. He shivered and fell onto a wet cow pie as he took off his shoes. His empty stomach churned. He shot to his feet heaving.

The ground was dry until he reached the edge of the pond where it became mushy and uneven from the hoof prints in the soft ground. He felt his own feet sink into the mud at the edge. His image glistened in the water, growing stronger as he concentrated. He controlled his shaking so he could lift his hands above his head. The stars around the moon had disappeared and it was surrounded by a luminous blackness. When he stepped into the water, his feet descended in the mud. He came to a drop off where suddenly he was thigh-deep in the muddy water. The water became so cold that his knees ached and he wrapped his arms around himself. He leaned over the water to look at his image, but it was indistinct in the muddy swirls. He could see the moon's reflection in the water several feet away, a huge path trembling in the wake that he had made. He walked towards it, but didn't seem to get any closer.

"Jesus, Jesus, baptize me. Please." His own voice was foreign. A cloud passed in front of the moon and the glimmering path in front of him disappeared.

"Jesus, I promise. I promise, Jesus. I promise I love you." His words sounded hollow and he imagined what Jesus was thinking about them, and then aware that Jesus knew everything he was thinking. If he knew what he was thinking, then he had to come down and baptize him. Or maybe he knew that he said he loved him to make him baptize him.

The moon came out again and he saw his own murky reflection, not so much his image, but a creature floating below the surface. As the moon rose, the white light in the water shrunk and became concentrated. He prayed wild jumbled words.

"Daddie, you're going to eat. Don't excite him. Jesus died. Jesus died for your sins. Praise Jesus. A special light. Jesus is on automatic. Brighter than any light. My feathers were given to the freezing sparrows. Don't tell nobody. Let's pray. Johan, let's pray. This is rat boy. Rat boy, parrot boy, fuck boy. Fast, fast. Fast, fast. Jesus, clean me. Take the shade off my light. This little light of mine. Johan wants to eat.

The words clicked out images that swelled suddenly, pounding at the inside of his head, then disappearing. The flashing images seemed to control his lungs and he began to pant. He tried to shake them off, first by whipping his head from side to side, then by swinging his torso.

Come, Jesus. Come. Fast fast. . . . And on the third day he rose. Mickie. Mickie. Yes, sir. See the U.S.A. The brightest light. Harold is melting. I know what you did.

The words came faster and then he heard a frog hop into the water . He became quiet. The moon was above him. He slipped in the mud and when he lurched forward to keep his balance, his feet slid out from under him. He choked on a mouthful of the muddy water that tasted of algae and dirt. He came up coughing and twisting to get his balance. One of his feet sank into a hole. For a few moments he was afraid that he would not be able to touch the bottom. He spread his arms out in the water to steady himself.

Jesus. Jesus. I am on automatic. The monster. I am not in the monster. 99.999999% story. Jesus, please. The light. Jesus, make me real, not a story. Baptize me. Make me one.

A cloud bank moving east covered the moon. He gagged from the taste of the dirty water. His right leg cramped. He felt dizzy. A car came down the driveway from the farm house and for a second its lights shone on him, blinding him. He hobbled to the shore and lay at the edge of the pond. His head felt empty, like it had been stretched too far. When the words began again, he buried his fingers in the mud.

He edged into the water which was warmer than the cool air until only his arms and head lay on the muddy edge of the pond. Mosquitoes hummed at his ears and he slapped at them, hitting himself. There was a smell that he couldn't recognize, but then he realized it was Joe. He stretched out, pushing his groin into the mud. He could feel Joe almost touch him, but pull back. The car returned. It parked for a few minutes with the lights on and illumined the pond.

He didn't sleep. If he fell asleep, Jesus would come and he would miss him. When he saw the first lights on the horizon, he knew that Jesus wasn't coming. He closed his eyes and was dragged into a nightmare. Pastor Ray, Thomas, Erland and Harold were missing an arm. He felt that he was strange because he had two arms, until he saw Joe who had two arms. Joe was motioning for him to come to him, taking his clothes off, hanging a sheet up over the window. He could see Joe's strong legs and firm dented buttocks. He couldn't take his eyes off the new arm, and behind him stood the others jabbing at the air with their stubs. When Joe turned around, his face was smiling and he was oblivious to the bloody hole where his penis had been. Michael tried to grab for his own penis, but he was paralyzed. He tried to scream to wake himself up. He felt that he was smothering and when he woke up, he was face down in the mud. He rolled on his side to catch his breath. He put his face down into the cool water and when he brought it up again he could see again.

He said, "Jesus," and the word filled the still sky to the dull blue horizon. The word became as fragile as the sides of a bubble. It broke. The pieces fell towards him and he closed his eyes waiting for them to strike him. When he opened his eyes, he was afraid to say anything again.

"Jesus," he said softly and the word came out dead, seemed to slide like spit down the side of his mouth.

He had been shivering sporadically for hours, but when he stopped, he felt that something had left him, something that had been shaking to get out. He was exhausted. His head felt like it would explode. It didn't hurt, but it seemed empty, as if it were filling with air and he had to do something to make it stop swelling. He grabbed his penis viciously and stroked himself. His hands were crusted with mud and sand but the pain focused his mind. When he came, he felt that his guts were coming out and suddenly his whole body hurt and both legs cramped. The pain was excruciating.

"Jesus," he screamed. When he tried to get up, his legs were so sore from the cramps that he had to go to his knees and crawl. He heard cows mooing. Just over a small knoll he saw the heads of two cows. Soon twenty cows were walking down to the pond.

"Come on. Hey, bossy. Come on," a man yelled wearily somewhere behind them.

At first he felt so frightened that he scrambled on his bare knees over the hard stony ground towards the cow tank. He froze after a few feet and lay flat on the ground with his head buried in his arms.

"Jesus holy shit," he heard the man yell. He lifted his head to see the man running off, and the cows moving lazily towards the pond. He lay his head down again. Soon he could feel the breath of one of the cows over him. When he looked up, it jerked its head back, but didn't move. The cows had formed a circle around him.

The ambulance frightened the cows and one kicked him as it ran over him. He took deep heavy breaths to make the pain bearable. He heard a click. He laced his fingers together and held them before his eyes like a veil. The farmer stood dumbly with a camera in his hands.

Thomas was with the ambulance. He kept saying, "Oh my God, Dwindie. Oh my God."

Michael opened his mouth to explain to Thomas, but nothing

came out. His lips and tongue moved, but he couldn't speak.

He thought of when the word had filled the sky and broken.

He explained this to Thomas and Thomas answered like he

understood, but Michael knew that he had not made a sound.

Part 23

One day when the pneumonia was better, Roxanne came to see him in the city hospital. He still had a fever.

"I made them rolls at home, Mickie. You would think that all day in the bakery, I would not let a speck of flour in my house, but it's different, you know. You feeling better?"

She shifted her weight in the small vinyl upholstered armchair.

"Better," he said nodding and noticed that there was a little girl just under Roxanne's skin.

"Someone sent your picture to one of them grocery magazines. "Baker's helper lives like a pig," they said. "Les got GI about it but I told him you was the best. If he didn't take you back, me and Maureen would quit. But I was nice compared to Maureen."

"Oh," Michael said as if he had just understood something important.

"You know that Rhonda woman who came in one day and made all the trouble. They found her body in the woods out by Bernard Peterson on Fox Lake. Some people say she was mixed up with marijuana. Well, that's what Maureen says. But you probably don't know about none of that stuff."

He was seeing Roxanne for the first time. He suddenly caught a glimpse of the young girl's arm flashing out from Roxanne's short stubby upper arm with its swaying flesh.

"Mickie, you talk about as much as a stump." There was silence. "I guess you're sick, though. I knew something was wrong. Remember. I said you was on automatic. Remember." Roxanne became animated and talked faster. He could see the little girl twisting out of her flesh.

"Sometimes you are pretty, Roxanne," he said, and she laughed.

"I have to remember to tell that to Abe. Make him jealous."

When she left, the room became dark. His head felt like it was sinking farther and farther into the pillow and if he stood up, he would be bent over because he would not be able to lift his head.

Thomas was the first person to visit him when he was moved to the County Home infirmary. Michael felt that he was slipping down a hill and when he thought he was about to tumble over the edge of a hole, he felt Thomas's hand.

"What happened to you?" Thomas asked.

"The light. . ." he said and stopped because he thought he

would cry.

"What?" Thomas asked.

Michael took a deep breath and squeezed Thomas's hand.

"My head, I think it's . . ."

"Ernesto wanted me to give you this. I think it has the rosary in Spanish. He said you needed it. Don't ask me because I don't understand a word." Thomas handed him a worn laminated book marker with the Blessed Virgin Mary. Her features were dull pink with a wax-like shine. "I told him I would give it to you."

"It wasn't the right day. It wasn't that day," Michael said.

"Everyone asks about you," Thomas said, nervously ignoring Michael's comment. He slowly pulled his hand away.

When Thomas left, he gasped for air but nothing came into his lungs until darkness filled the room again and he breathed it in.

Maron stood beside Johan. When Joe appeared next to them, Maron pushed him forward. She tilted her head to one side, posing for a few moments with a stiff smile, expecting him to be happy. Then she tilted her head to the other side without changing her expression.

"I feed him, too. Him and Johan. They come from mirrors and dreams and I feed them." Maron looked like herself in one of the old pictures when she was young and her skin was clear.

"Joe wants to do something to you, so I'll leave you alone. Don't tell anyone."

But he knew that she was watching from a picture on the wall. All of his life she had been watching. "It is all in your head." Ernesto's voice came out of nowhere. "Part of your mind throws you one way and another part another way and then there is a part that tries to keep us from tearing apart. But it is the same mind. Father, Son, Holy Ghost and Virgin Mary. You can't get anything out of your mind without losing good things, too."

There was a long silence while Joe shrunk. His chin fell to his chest and his big shoulders slumped. Then fire sprung up all around him, but Joe didn't seem to feel it or see it. Flames burned everything away, except for Joe. Michael wanted to warn himself about the flames which he could see making a circle around where he slept, but he couldn't wake himself up. He struggled for several minutes until he saw that the flames had not come any nearer to him. A small patch of ground was left around his body. He could not walk to Joe. He heard the voice of Ernesto again. "The mind needs less and less. When it needs nothing, it destroys everything and itself."

He woke up and stared at the plastic pitcher on the night stand. Water condensation coursed down it, leaving smooth lines and a ring of water under the pitcher. He didn't want to think anymore. He waited for the next bead to form.

The fever was better. He walked to the window without getting dizzy. He looked across the road that circled the main building of the County Hospital. The building was dark except for a dull sickly yellow glow that came from the windows at the ends of the hallways. Rain began to splatter against the window. He passed his hand over the metal mesh.

He couldn't sleep. He worried that the night at the pond had put a barrier between his life before and now. Yesterday when Thomas was visiting for the last time at the city hospital, he had asked him, "What will you do now?" His life had been closed. He had been on a slow spiral up, and now he was at the bottom again.

"We'll have to see," Thomas had said when he finally understood what Michael was asking.

The rain stopped and the moon shone into the room, casting a shadow on the floor. He studied the dark mesh on the wooden floors. The windows of the main building reflected the moonlight. His mind felt vacant.

The windows began to glow with a stronger yellowish light, inconstant and wavering. Indistinct voices pulsed from the building. Another dream, he thought. Staff and patients were running or walking briskly out of all the doors, filling up the wet lawn. The night attendant in the infirmary ran down the hall pounding on the doors.

"Get out. There's a fire. Get out. It could spread over here. Get out."

Fire and smoke suddenly burst from one of the windows of the main building and licked up the side. He turned away and saw the shadow from the wire mesh vibrating on the floor.

Some of the inmates tried to run back into the building and Erland raced back and forth to block them and lead them into the crowd on the lawn. Michael saw faces at windows, but he couldn't recognize anyone. A thin old man had squeezed his head between the bars of a window on the top floor. The screams seemed to echo between the building and the crowd on the lawn.

He walked outside and approached the human pond. It reflected the light from the burning building, moved in waves forward and backwards. He saw Ernesto. The other semi-independents were leading patients away from the building. Gus was pulling Harold along, but he broke loose and ran back toward the flames. Erland yelled to Gus to let him go.

"Joshua is not coming out," Ernesto said. "He will never be found."

"He will never be found?" Michael asked.

"He is released. The prison and the prisoner are

destroyed." Ernesto kneeled on the damp ground. "God doesn't want me released yet. I am in his hands. I will be in prison for a while yet. On and off. On and off."

"How do you know about Joshua?" Ernesto had turned away and Michael had to walk a maze between people to face him again.

"I saw him sit down on the floor with his head swaddled in his arms. Like this," Ernesto said lowering his head and clasping his hands behind his head. "I wouldn't listen to him. I wouldn't. He said they were turning us from rats to pigs and pigs to rats and if by some miracle we got stuck in between, they would let us go."

Michael wandered through the crowd looking for Joshua. The fire turned faces and clothes orange. The crowd was hypnotized by the fire. They stood so equidistant from each other that they could have been dots on cloth. He touched no one and no one seemed to notice him. He came out the front of the crowd and looked back at them. Erland began to walk towards him, but took off suddenly in the other direction to help restrain one of the inmates from the locked ward.

The crowd looked like they were in the day room watching television; the same anxious glare, their faces flickering with light. A row of wheelchair patients sat with their mouths open and their heads hanging.

A part of the building collapsed behind him, sending a fountain of sparks into the air. The crowd flowed back. In the distance he could hear the fire trucks and ambulance. Then the archangel appeared in the place where he had died. His body was covered with motley feathers and his wings beat to the pulse of the distant sirens. A line of men and women were forming behind him and Michael recognized Joshua, who turned and waved to him. He had never seen his face so calm and content. For as long as he had known him, Joshua had never let himself expand into his own body, but kept himself hidden and wound up within it. Now he relaxed until he filled his skin.

He scurried through the crowd to Ernesto. "Did you see the archangel and all the people?"

Ernesto didn't reply for a long time. "Yes, over the building. I saw him."

Michael shaded his eyes with his hand and tried to concentrate on the sky above the building, but he saw nothing. Then he looked over where he had at first seen Raphael. He floated up with his wings spread but not moving. He drifted towards the horizon with a line people behind him.

"I am split by everyone who leaves," Michael whispered to Ernesto. "They split me. When they leave, part of me is always someplace else." As soon as he said this, he realized that they were lines from one of Joshua's poems. Above the horizon where Raphael had led the others, he saw a few dark lines like scratches that he recognized as words.

Ernesto took his glasses off to rub his eyes. "There are buildings and you see the outside. There are people and you see the outside. Now we see flames and the pain is inside. We don't see it. I keep thinking of the pain. I can't help it. But after the fire it is always quieter than before the fire. It was not an easy way to leave. *Desmasiado doloroso. Desmasiado doloroso.*"

Tears ran down Ernesto's cheeks. He put his glasses on and covered his face with his hands, shaking with steady monotonous weeping. "*Desmasiado doloroso. Desmasiado doloroso.*"

Michael rested his hand on Ernesto's shoulder for a few minutes, before he walked away. Ernesto seemed unaware that he had left. Now Michael felt that he was burning up. He wobbled for a few feet before he fell to the ground. Everyone was still looking up at the flames and didn't notice. The crowd was changing. A man had begun to scream, then a woman, then several others. Michael felt the heat of the fever and mistook it for the flames of fire. More and more voices joined the wailing. He walked through the halls of the home. Most of the bodies were charred, but a few were bright red. The red rose up through their heads, darker and cooler than the flames, and found the trail through the sky that Raphael had left. The flames became hotter, but they didn't touch him and he knew they wouldn't touch him. When the red had left the bodies, they slumped into black sacks.

Fire trucks from several small towns arrived at the same time and Erland scampered to the front gate to organize the entrance. He led a group of volunteer firemen back to the crowd and they began to herd the inmates down to the fence along the creek. No one bothered to pick Michael up until Thomas arrived ten minutes after the fire trucks had parked on the lawn in front of the home and the volunteer firemen began to shoot water into the building. As Thomas was lifting him, Michael saw Mr. Mandment's black Lincoln Continental pull up twenty feet away.

To Michael it was a messenger. The dark windows reflected the flames. He knew it was a car, but it looked so heavy and bleak that it might sink into the ground, which was melting from the fire.

"You're burning up," Thomas said when they reached the fence.

"No, I've been saved. It didn't get to me. I was protected." He couldn't take his eyes off the car. The door opened and blood gushed out. Then it began to pull everything in. Michael turned away.

Thomas took his coat off and put it around Michael. Then he looked over the crowd.

"Lie down and keep covered," he said and then ran back towards the firemen. Michael fell asleep and when he woke up, Mr. Mandment's car was still parked in the middle of the lawn, but the crowd along the fence was smaller. With the help of Erland and other employees, the firemen were leading the inmates to the infirmary and the barn. The fire no longer leapt from the building, but worked steadily. The water from the hoses, the same color as the moon, which had regained its prominence, arched up into the dark sky, spreading out as it fell. Everything except for the water seemed unbelievably still. The collapse of one of the walls sent sparks up into the air again. But sitting far away, Michael heard no crash, but only a long sigh.

He noticed Ernesto with a group that was being led away by Lester and five firemen. He could hear Ernesto thinking, "Fire returns us to the unexplainable." That was a line from one of Joshua's poems, but it was Ernesto who was thinking it.

He heard someone else thinking, couldn't recognize the voice at first, the whisper. Then he saw Harold lying on his stomach behind the lilac bushes. He wasn't sure if he was real. His face was dirty and puffy and he looked heavier.

"I escaped. No one knows that I am here. No one.

There are about ten of us who came down the fire escape. We're all hiding. I'm unaccounted for. After all these years I'm unaccounted for." Harold's voice was childish. He motioned for Michael to join him. Maron stood next to the bush by herself. She nodded approvingly. He crawled into the bushes during the clamor of an arriving police car. He watched people pass, seeing only their legs through the mesh of the thin black lilac stems. Harold kissed him on the back of his neck, then put his lips next to Michael's ear and whispered incessantly until Michael fell asleep. He could feel the warmth of Harold's body, even through the blanket.

When he woke up, he was thirsty. His clothes were wet from sweat and he had kicked the blanket off his feet. He crawled out of the bushes and stumbled towards the infirmary. The hallway was covered with sleeping women. He went to the laundry room and saw that it was lit up and he could see the heads of people in the windows.

On the way to the barn he met Thomas, who mumbled something to him, and took his hand. He led him to the truck where some of the semi-independent men were waiting. A woman whom he had never seen before handed him a glass of water and a white mushy bread and butter sandwich. He drank the water and chewed wearily on the sandwich until it had formed a dry ball in his mouth. He took another glass of water and swallowed the bread.

He fell asleep as soon as he was in the back of the truck and didn't wake up until they were outside the church where they were to sleep.

Dear Harold Osterhammer,

You probably do not remember me. I talked to you briefly at your sister's house in Lincoln some years ago. At the time I was working on a freelance article about the Starkweather killings. I think I mentioned to you this other project on which I was working, the story of a feral child who also has qualities of an idiot savant. The man's name is Michael Durbin. I use the present tense having no idea whether he is living or not.

The material I am sending you (I refrain from referring to it as a book) has been collected over thirty years. You will see that it includes transcribed tapes; an anonymous narrative which might have been written in part by a friend of mine Joshua Brent, a brilliant poet and wonderful human being who was committed to a mental institution in his late thirties and died there in a fire; letters I wrote to Joshua Brent; and entries from my diary.

Joshua was the first to see Michael's case as worthy of

recording. The narrative cannot be completely Joshua's because it records the circumstances of his own death and events following it. Having known Joshua for so many years, I also find the text too full of what I would call popular imagination.

I received the tapes from Michael Durbin himself, or to put it more precisely, he left them when he moved or disappeared, and my name and phone number were attached to the box which contained them. There were one hundred and forty-four. About half of them were severely damaged, but I listened to and transcribed the ones I could. Most are repetitive or mundane, the verbal shopping lists and diary of a man unable to write or read, but with a phenomenal memory for words. I have speculated whether some of the reflections on the tapes were not Joshua Brent's burned into the memory of Michael Durbin.

If you decide to use this material in any way, I must insist that you not use my name. The letters reveal my feelings for a man whom I loved, who could not really love me in the same way. I must also request that Joshua's real name not be used. The same is true with all other names.

There is no gothic tale here, though it may appear that there are bits of Jane Eyre. The modern novel must have a hero. To me Joshua Brent was a hero since he had the courage to live a life of deep depression and shattering disappointment. The text, however, reveals him as silly and obsessed, qualities which he may have acquired after his mental breakdown, but which never dominated. And Joshua is not the main character.

Joshua's last request was that this story be told. He felt that if it were told, it would bring him into the world again, free him intellectually from his prison, from the institution. Now that he is dead, perhaps it can make part of him live again. But I cannot pull it together.

I have followed your career as a publisher and editor. Your sister sends me little notes to tell me what wonderful things you are doing. I trust that I have chosen the right person.

Sincerely

Bernice Ylvesaker

Part 24

Bernice's Diary

June 22

 I feel like I have abandoned Michael Durbin. First his natural mother and now his narrative mother. On the anniversary of the fire, there always seems to be someone who wants to write an article and I must appear on some document or in an article as a witness. I wasn't. They ask me what I saw and then I explain what the farm was like, who the characters were. "Why don't you write the story?" one asked me last year, the tenth anniversary. "I am working on something else," I told him.

 But I become weighted with sadness each year. Someone wanted to call it a depression, but that isn't right. There is not indentation. I am weighted with sadness and the word sad originally meant heavy, and that is how I feel, as if I had a burden I had to carry. Like the mule with the sugar that crosses the stream to lighten its load, I wade through time until it melts. When I tell them I am working on a related story, then I feel guilty that I have abandoned Joshua's story, his discovery, Rat Boy. But when I look back on my life and see that I cannot put the pieces together, that they don't fit, and I will never get Michael's story right, I see that my life is disintegrating, and that much in my life that I would like to change is now in the past.

I met a younger man at my present employment. He looked like Joshua when he was younger; a bit heavy, intelligent, charming. I suppose he found me interesting. What is one to expect in a small print shop that does wedding announcements and business cards and flyers? Any housewife with a year of secretarial could do my job, proofreading copy before it is etched into matrimonial twenty-five pound linen stock and inventing business flyers to litter the streets. And I took his interest as some light flavor of desire. I always know they are homosexual. Hope and disappointment thrust at one another until there is no telling the difference between these bloodied figures of speech. Other men do not pay attention to women like me. I invited him home for dinner and made a fool of myself. As Joshua would have done, he acted as if he didn't notice, but I don't have the energy to have another friendship like the one I had with Joshua. And the path from despair is so well etched that it took little time for me to encounter the path back to equilibrium. But each time the drop is more breathtaking, the bottom deeper. My fear remains what I might be capable of doing to myself in those moments of despair.

I found a lead on Michael. I was sent on special assignment as a stringer to look at the state mental hospital. Ernesto Pereda, much older looking, his hair white, his eyes lifeless, was waiting at the front desk. I think he might have noticed me, too. He claimed to be expecting a visitor, Michael Durbin. I asked the nurse about him. She said that there was no visitor, but that once a year a man with a strange voice called and that this was Michael Durbin. Ernesto never talked himself until the receiver was hung up. She explained that patients were not often allowed phone calls, but that since Ernesto seemed to have no other connection to the outside world, they allowed it. The woman who had spoken to me was just going off her shift and when she left, I introduced myself as a friend of Michael Durbin.

"Do you know Joe, too?" he asked.

"Joe Pinhook?" I responded and Ernesto smiled, but it was as if I had connected and lost him with the same question. He shuffled off.

"And Joshua Brent," I called to him.

He turned and looked at me as if your name, as if the name had burned him. I saw anger and fear in his face and am not sure why. It was perhaps jealousy. I know you meant a lot to Michael and then Ernesto lived with him. But minds are not logical. I almost said the twisted mind, but perhaps mine is not normal either.

I told the nurse that I was an old acquaintance of Ernesto and was worried about him. I asked if I could get in touch with his nearest kin. She told me that the information was private and I smiled apologetically for asking. It worked and she slipped a piece of paper to me later that afternoon. The address was a working class neighborhood of Grand Heron. It was on Polk Street and had a little note, "over garage", as if that were part of the mailing address. I have put a note to look it up the next time I have to go to Grand Heron.

One of Joshua's dictums was, "The value of anything you say is dependent on the value of the opposite. If the opposite is meaningless, the statement is worthless. People are good and people are bad. Always think positive and always think negative."

I have been trying to decide to whom I am writing this journal, certainly not to posterity. I am writing it to Joshua, even though he has passed to the other side. Perhaps he was not one of those people who could make the jump all at once. Instead, he moved from the world first. I have imagined a thousand times the pain of fire. I wake up thinking of it. At times I think of the phoenix recreating itself in the fire. Afterlife? There is something, but it is not life. That is only a metaphor for what comes later, since we can only think of our existence in terms of biology.

It was with trepidation that I finally met Michael. I found an old picture of myself to determine whether he would recognize

me. My hair was longer, my glasses dark and serious as if I were
mourning for Adlai Stevenson by trying to look like him. That was
more or less the face that Michael had seen twenty years before.
And what had the damages been. The face in the picture that I used
in a byline was not looking sincerely into a camera. It had the look
of seriousness from a different era when youth looked dreamily
askance at the future. The lapels were felt and already a bit old-
fashioned when the picture was taken, but I was giving household
advice, of which I knew nothing, but I began to read women's
magazines and old household remedy books, and invent experts
or friends who were mothers of six. The lapels were Joshua's idea.
No one trusted a pretty woman's advice, unless it was on beauty.
I was flattered that he felt I should do something to make myself
appear unattractive, wear the old-fashioned dress, don the black
framed spectacles, lift my chin and gaze at the source of all wisdom.
I believed that I was already unattractive. But perhaps he felt I
should create a bit of mystery as to whether my appearance was due
to nature or to fashion. I mentioned this hoping that he would make
his compliment more outright, but he merely ignored me.

So I hope the face that Michael saw on those few visits to the
home, that Joshua remembered and thought of occasionally, was
a bit more feminine, perhaps less serious, and more intelligent. If a
picture captures only a billionth of our lives, and is made with light

343

and posing, then our unsculptured selves must reveal more hideous and more perfect creations, each second perhaps a contradiction of the last and the mind is free to remember us at our perfect angle.

I seem to be unable to do anything anymore without turning it into a journalistic reflection, to end every encounter with the annoyingly trite ironies that news magazines use to summarize tragedy and trivia. My manuscript about Michael is full of them. "Perhaps to compensate for his early world of silence, he peopled his later life with real and imagined characters." "If memories are truly the building blocks of life, Michael would be a mansion. His memory was phenomenal. But he appeared to have lacked all glue and the blocks covered a large dry plain without ever forming a wall or even a fence."

I seem to be writing Joshua's more than Michael's. It is not mine. That is told more simply and powerfully in the photograph. The slow crawl to the grave. I am capable of great self-pity, but in print it becomes too obvious. Some of my letters to Joshua, at least when I thought of us as equals, were often lengthy complaints. After he was committed, I could become light and chatty, always aware of what my words might do. Words seemed so powerful and edged. I worked at pointing the edges in the right direction.

When I interviewed Michael, Maron and Johan's neighbors, I always thought of Joshua. His life had been so expansive, all *borders broken by his passion for reading and his intellect. When he had his first breakdown, he became another person: petty like the neighbors, focused on the trivia of the famous. His constructions were not like Michael's; his were fabulous twisting towers, but made of celluloid and vacuum tubes. Even when I speculate like this, I know that it is Joshua's legacy.*

But I began to describe my visit to Michael Dwindie Durbin. What most struck me was how normal he seemed. But I wondered how he had ever been called Dwindie. He was still small, I am almost tempted to say petite because when you looked at him, you couldn't help but think that he could still buy boy's clothes. There was no desire on my part to mother him. He seemed leery of me, and instead of being ethereal, he was almost sodden. When I asked him about Joshua, Harold, Ralph, all he said was, "Yes, I knew them. Yes." He had a funny way of talking, as if he had a personal foreign accent. I don't remember this when I spoke with him at the home. The story does not have a fabulous ending. He has reached the edge of humanity. They tolerate him for some of his talents, but they never feel that he is a part of them. In a sense he is Joshua's son. When I asked him if he remembered Joshua, he recited lines of poems, some of which I had read but had never received a copy. He seemed glad to recite them. These are the strange powers of the person that drew Joshua to him in the first place. Everything

makes its impression, but nothing makes connections to meaning.
Some of the lines were uncannily appropriate and others irrelevant.
He is the monkey with the typewriter who occasionally writes a
line of Shakespeare, or in this case, remembers a line. Perhaps his
survival is a great feat.

I mentioned the abundance of mirrors in his room. There
was a pause that I came to recognize later on the tapes. That silence
made me feel as if someone were listening and spying on me. I
thought of how in the long pauses in the tapes, I often felt that
he was listening to me. I noticed the matted brocade on the front
of my dress, the worn lapels, the whimsical satin rose on my hat
which had faded in the hours I had stood waiting for busses. I had
missed the white mark on the back of my coat where I had leaned
up against the chalky paint of the wooden balustrade in front of his
door. At certain angles the mirrors would reflect into each other and
my image would be mixed with his in a dizzying infinity. I looked
only straight ahead at the mirror behind him and then into his face.
I had cleared my throat and with a deep breath brought my face
into the attitude of intense interest and pleasure, the brave face of
the interviewer when I noticed his mouth opening in a mirror.

"I like to see all of me. All of me at once."

And why not? I mused. Why not?

I wrote a short article about the home and much to my surprise, I received a letter from a man who told me that he had adopted Harold after the fire and that they still lived together, though Harold had suffered a stroke and did not want to talk to strangers. He was not dead after all. The man said that Harold wanted to know where Michael was. I wrote back to say that I had lost contact with him. Can you imagine years of remaking the image of Michael, importing significance to their encounters, and then to meet Michael as he is? Is there anyone who harbors the fantasy of seeing me again? I fear those people are all gone if they ever existed.

I do not really know Michael. I am afraid that he will be so different from my creation, Joshua's, even the tapes. Have I made him too much the feral child, too much the idiot savant, too much the victim of neglect and morbid religious fantasy? Have I made him at all?

Part 23

Tape 6 - Entry 11

I told Ernesto stories. I told him about the revival meetings. I said, "Ernesto, I saw Pastor Ray look at people with his eyes and make small holes and the pain would come out of them." Ernesto put his glasses on to look at me. I couldn't tell what he was thinking. The next day he said, "Dwindie, it wasn't the pain that came out. It was the part of them that was struggling. They became nothing. Nothing cannot have pain. A person can't be like that for long. Who you are comes back." After Ernesto became too sick to live on the outside, I told Thomas, who was looking for someone else to live with me, that Ernesto gave me a lot of advice. Thomas said, "Look at Ernesto. Can he make sense of his life? Don't think too much about what he says."

Tape 6 – Entry 14

When Ernesto left, I promised myself to never like anyone that much again.

Tape 30 – Entry 1

When you are young, your body and who you are at that

moment seem like they are the same. I watch children shine, catch light, glisten into other people's skin. Old people's skin wrinkles like brown paper and sags, and the inner sag is what you feel most. It is a package. According to Joshua's notebook, I am forty-five today.

Tape 8 – Entry 16

There are days when I ask myself, "Who are you? What name will they call you today?" I remember a fever I had when Ernesto and I were living together after the fire. For three days I could not sleep and the sweat woke me up when I tried. On the third day my mind was filled with thoughts. They were like those deer flies that bite you. I couldn't shake them. Finally a person named Daniel took over my body and I had to fight to give myself the name Michael again. Some days when I wake up thinking of that fever, I say, "I will fight to be Michael." It makes sense when I say it, but I don't know what it means. I think this Daniel came once before, but everything gets blurred. I remember but not always what happened when.

Tape 17 –Entry 9

Ernesto found the album. He said it was hidden in the barn, but Ernesto sometimes makes up stories that he thinks you want to hear. Or maybe they are stories that he wants to hear. I have looked at it now hundreds of times and have tried to invent myself from

it. Joshua's friend had made trips to the towns where Johan and

Maron lived. She put a note for Joshua, "Amazing, every town they

lived in was twenty miles from Starkweather's killing spree." When

Ernesto read it to me, I asked him who Starkweather was, but he

didn't know. Later I saw a movie about it. But that is much later,

when I hadn't seen Ernesto for many years. I made Ernesto read the

album to me. Then he read it into a tape recorder so I wouldn't ask

him anymore. It was the same one I am using right now to record

this. But I don't think Ernesto ever read the album the same way

twice. Someone once explained to me that when a word is written

a thousand people can read the same word the same way, like the

tape recorder. A person told me though, a waiter in a restaurant

where I worked as a dishwasher, that music notes were different,

that everyone played them differently. He told me, too, that he

wasn't really a waiter, but really was a musician. I was really a

dishwasher then. The date on that note from the woman Bernice

was the year before the fire. I don't remember much of Bernice, but

there were long letters before and about the time. She typed up her

notes on carbon paper and sent Joshua a copy. Ernesto told me that

the smudges are all from Joshua's fingers. He kept her letters in the

album. I don't know how Gus's playing cards, the ones with the fat

women and ten different men, got into the album. I thought maybe

Ernesto had put them there, but I don't know how he got them. I used to sort them according to the men, so I am sure there were ten different men. There were more women on the cards than men, I think, but it made sense to me to sort them according to the men. A lot of what makes sense to me I cannot explain.

Tape 28 – Entry 1

The last of Ernesto's tapes broke today. It twisted like the others into the machine and came out creased. I had already started to invent my own Ernesto tapes, the ones where he made lists of advice and the ones where he read the album. At work Frankie said I should get a new tape recorder. They don't last forever. When I visited Ernesto in the hospital, I would listen to his tapes afterwards, making Ernesto. When he got really sick and they sent him to the state hospital, I stopped listening to them so much and began to imagine what he would say. We are like tapes, he would have said. We wear out. What is left of us is still there, twisted and creased and it doesn't make any sense. But it is still there.

Tape 3 – Entry 4

I have asked others if they saw the colors, the green light Maureen's hair gave off when she took a long drag on her cigarette, or the throbbing yellow light when I knew or thought Joe was near.

And they say no, but some say nothing special ever happened to them, so it could be true. Ernesto told me the third time I asked him that he had seen the lights, too, but the first times he told me he hadn't seen them. But now I wonder if it is from a dream. Do we even exist by ourselves? I have asked that and I have answered it a hundred ways. The spider is alone waiting for the fly. It thinks of the fly, makes its web, and waits. But does it think of itself or just the fly? I haven't seen colors since the fire. The fire itself was so many colors and the screams made them brighter.

Tape 12 – Entry 7

Bad things come in three Ernesto said. The angel fell, I got pneumonia in the pond, and the home burned. After I got pneumonia, he knew the home would burn. Cold to hot. He didn't say anything to anyone. After it happened, he told me he saw it coming. I asked him why he didn't count Joe's accident as one of the bad things. He said that was a different group of three, maybe three all together. That woman at the bakery, her husband died. I got lost. And Joe and Peter. The last one is always the worst, he said, at least for someone. My three maybe isn't your three.

Pause

Maybe it's true. Maybe I have had only part of a life.

Ernesto said that the stranger the pieces the more important they are when they are going to make the whole thing. I asked him who they were. He just said think about it. I have thought about it for a long time now.

Pause

Hello. This is Michael Durbin, Dwindie. Hello. Can you hear me? Hello.

www.ingramcontent.com/pod-product-compliance
Lightning Source LLC
Chambersburg PA
CBHW021527250626
47154CB00006BA/2001